Viji
Krishnamoorthy

912

BATU

ROAD

clarity

912 Batu Road

Clarity Publishing Sdn. Bhd.,
51-21-A Menara BHL Bank,
Jalan Sultan Ahmad Shah,
10500 Penang, Malaysia.

www.clarity8.com

4 6 8 10 9 7 5 3

Published by Clarity Publishing 2021
Copyright © 2021 Viji Krishnamoorthy

The extract on page 245 is from the play "Sybil" written by U-En Ng which was produced by The Actors Studio Sdn. Bhd. "Sybil" was directed by Faridah Merican and the Artistic Director was Joe Hasham.

ISBN 978-967-17657-4-6

CIP data is available from the National Library of Malaysia

Printed in Malaysia by Phoenix Printers Sdn. Bhd.

ABOUT THE AUTHOR

Viji Krishnamoorthy was born in Ipoh, Perak to a Tamil father and Hokkien Chinese mother. She spent her early school years in Kuala Lumpur and then in Madras (as it was then known). She completed her tertiary education in the UK.

She previously worked as a freelance writer for several magazines and this is her debut novel.

The author is happily married with two children and lives in Kuala Lumpur; but enjoys spending time in London.

In memory of
Daddy, Appa & Amma
My triumvirate

For:
Mummy & Kala
Ranjit, Nikhil & Maya

A NOTE TO THE READER

This book is a tapestry of fiction and historical fact. Many of the characters existed and some of the events did in fact unfold. The address 912 Batu Road was the house my father was born in and which I am told by my elders, is the site of the current Mara building.

I would like to make particular mention of and recognise two rather forgotten war heroes. One is Gurchan Singh and the other is Sybil Kathigasu. I have drawn from both their books – *Singa The Lion of Malaya*, published by Quality Press Limited, London and *No Dram of Mercy*, which was republished by Media Masters Private Limited Singapore as a collection of books carrying the title *Faces of Courage*.

The scene from Chapter 30 of my book was drawn extensively from Chapter 5 of *Singa The Lion of Malaya*. Ho Thean Fook, who you will meet as Moru in Chapter 13 has also authored his own memoirs; *Tainted Glory*, published by the University of Malaya Press.

For other reading material, please refer to the bibliography at the end of this book.

MAIN CHARACTERS

The Past

Rangaswamy Iyer	Arrives in Penang in 1922, and begins his career as a teacher in Penang before moving to Kuala Lumpur. Friend of Tan Chin Nam and father of Ramesh. Geeta is his granddaughter.
Tan Chin Nam	A successful businessman and a life-long friend of Rangaswamy. Husband of Elaine Tan and father of Tan Kah Hoe. Ken is his grandson.
Elaine Tan	Chin Nam's wife and mother of Kah Hoe.
Tan Kah Hoe	The eldest son of Chin Nam; enlisted with the 5th Malayan People's Anti-Japanese Army.

Bob Nakamura	Bob is a Japanese photographer living in Kuala Lumpur and a close friend of Chin Nam and Rangaswamy.
Terlochan Singh (Tochi)	A dresser at a government hospital in Penang. Father of Satnam.

The Present

Ramesh Iyer	Rangaswamy's eldest son and Geeta's father. He is against Geeta's relationship with Ken and believes in keeping the Brahmin traditions alive. Also referred to as Anna (older brother) by Krishna.
Geeta	Daughter of Ramesh Iyer, she is torn between her duty to her conservative parents and her love for Ken.
Krishna Iyer	Ramesh's brother and Geeta's favourite Chitappa (uncle), he tries to protect his niece without hurting his brother and he finds himself revisiting old wounds.
Tan Kah Sing	Chin Nam's youngest son and Ken's father. His hatred for the Japanese has informed most of his business decisions.
Ken Tan	Chin Nam's grandson, he works as an architect in London and is in love with his childhood friend, Geeta.

Historical Characters

Gurchan Singh

A policeman who went undercover and kept the Malayan people abreast of the true events that were unfolding during the Second World War; also known as 'Singa of Malaya.'

Sybil Kathigasu

Sybil was a nurse who supported and treated members of the resistance, together with her husband during the Japanese occupation.

Chin Peng

The head of the Malayan Communist Party.

1
GETTING TO THE MANDAPAM
KUALA LUMPUR, 2008

Geeta stood at the edge of reason, bathed in saffron. The colour of silence. Day was breaking, the sun gently stretching its orange-gold tendrils across her face. Still half asleep, she rubbed the cold out of her arms, cradling her misgivings in the rise and fall of her breath.

The rest of her family was up before the first crow and the smell of her mother's decoction coffee permeated the house. *If you are going to wake up early, then this is the way it has to be,* she thought, pleading with her eyelids to crack open the crust of sleep. Her only immediate thought was coffee, and plenty of it. So she allowed her keen sense of smell to guide her to the source, Amma's first edition, ever silver coffee filter sitting where it always did, on the kitchen counter right next to a tumbler of steaming fresh milk, frothing at the rim. Pure instinct led Geeta to pour out a third of the muddy brown liquid into her tumbler followed by the pristine white of the milk. No sugar, no condensed milk, just a 100% kick-start to a long, long day.

"Geeta, can you please come here and help me with the sari. It's been a while since I last tied a madasar," asked her mother tentatively, sensing her daughter's annoyance. Parvathi could almost feel the resentment building inside of Geeta and she put on a brave smile as Geeta approached her, gingerly holding the piping hot lip of her tumbler of coffee.

Parvathi stood hesitantly in her petticoat and sari blouse, the hook and eye in a silent game of tug of war across her chest. Through years of bathing with turmeric, Parvathi's ample midriff had turned the colour of pale yellow, almost the shade of wheat halva. It quivered at the slightest touch and glistened in the heat. More annoyingly, it kept getting in the way. The layers of fat permanently secured on Parvathi's waist made it difficult for Geeta to look round her mother at the mirror.

The grey Usha fan, a relic from the past, groaned at the task at hand and was not spared the wrath of the younger woman standing below it. "What is the point of Appa working so hard if we can't make life a little more bearable by fixing an air con downstairs," grumbled Geeta. "This wretched fan should have been thrown into the Gombak River after Tata died."

The sweat that was dripping down Geeta's back had turned a patch of her light green pyjama blouse moss green. With her mouth contorted, she snapped at her mother, "Why couldn't you wear a normal sari? You know how much I hate fighting with nine yards of material and for what? Only to make you look like a man!"

Parvathi's wine red and mustard sari seemed to have a mind of its own. Geeta tried to tie it again and again, yet the sari stubbornly refused to succumb to folding and pleating. It was as if it had taken Parvathi's side against Geeta. The air was thick with the rustling-tussling of the silk being pulled and tugged. With a big heave of her shoulders, Geeta let the balance seven yards slither to the floor.

"I can't for the life of me tie this damn thing," she announced and stomped out of the room. Parvathi stood silently in front of the narrow, speckled mirror part of an almari left behind by her late mother-in-law. Clad in a silk sari blouse with a fast spreading damp patch, Parvathi contemplated her daughter. She dreaded the times when she had to ask for her help. *How did she get this way?* she wondered. *Haven't I always reminded her that a lady should be soft spoken and mild mannered and not hot tempered and cantankerous? She has picked the right profession to match her fiery temperament.* She imagined her daughter in court, fiercely arguing her points. With just the slightest hint of exasperation creeping into Parvathi's otherwise calm face, she set about tying the rest of her sari in her usual quiet way.

Parvathi never used make up. Her room was sparse. Her dressing table was nothing more than a plank mounted on the wall just below a square mirror. On it, a large black comb with wide teeth on one end and narrower, pointed mean-looking teeth that scraped the scalp on the other, a small tin of Mysore sandalwood powder, Impulse spray and a little red vial of kumkumam.

Whining has always come naturally to Geeta, she thought. She wore it so comfortably, like a second skin. Blaming others for anything untoward that happened in her life seemed to be a favourite pastime of hers. At 27, she had already earned herself a reputation for being a spoilt brat within the close knit Brahmin community. Gatherings at the Brahmin association were not her scene. Parvathi would always have to prepare her words with care before asking her to attend important prayer dates. *How could I even start to broach the subject of an arranged marriage with her?* she wondered. *She is so different from her cousins.*

"I despise the lot of them," would be Geeta's typical immediate response when asked to go to the Samajam. "They are no more than a bunch of hypocrites who go there to poke their nosy noses into everyone's private lives. 'Aisay Geeta, how are you finding legal practice?' or 'Aiyoh Geeta, some weight put on!'" she mimicked some of the Brahmin Mamis.

However, this time round, Geeta didn't have much choice as it was her cousin's wedding. Sowmya's impending kalyanam had been the talk of the Rangaswamy family ever since Lakshmi Mami (the renowned matchmaker) had suggested they match her horoscope with engineer Vishnu's eldest boy, Vivek.

The astrologer had come to the Raman residence early one Sunday morning. Dressed in a short-sleeved blue and white checked shirt that was starting to fray at the collar and a veshti, he read the horoscopes and delightedly prophesied a perfect match. Sowmya had been dragged out of bed earlier that morning, looking prim and bewildered in equal measure. She listened as the rotund man speculated about her future. Her eyes took on a glaze as if it were someone else's life under scrutiny. "She will bring the boy's family luck and good fortune. There will be three children – two boys and a girl. Her husband will rise to great heights in his career," droned the astrologer.

The announcement of Sowmya's wedding arrived the way all bad news does, when you least expect it and without warning. This time it was served along side dinner. In Geeta's home, dinner was a traditional south Indian affair of rice, sambar, rasam, two vegetables and yogurt. Standard fare on the Ramesh dining table was a little round ever silver container that held lime pickle and an old Nutella bottle full of ghee.

Geeta was about to put a handful of rice and sambar into her mouth when her mother casually mentioned how perfectly Sowmya's and Vivek's horoscope matched. *Excuse me, hello, did someone say perfect match? And who on earth is this Vivek fellow? How come I am always the last to know? How could you be so casual about a horoscope as if discussing a cricket match? It sounds more like a horror-scope,"* thought Geeta. She couldn't help but let out a low, black laugh from the depths of her stomach, tickled by her own joke.

"Sowmya's getting married?" she asked. Umpteen questions swirling in Geeta's mind – *why, how, when, what for?* Her questions fought with her recently swallowed food, causing a tidal wave of anger that rose to the top in a loud, angry burp. *How could Sowmya agree to this without a fight?* Geeta couldn't fathom the workings of Sowmya's mind. Granted, they weren't the closest of cousins but they had shared secrets when they were younger and she didn't expect her to agree so easily to the first proposal that came along. After all, Sowmya was a professional, a Chartered Accountant and an attractive girl with a reasonably good sense of humour. *You stupid, stupid girl,* she thought.

Sowmya had always given her the impression that she wanted to flit if not fly on the wings of freedom just for a couple of years more. Her parents on the other hand were more traditional and they had always made it clear to Sowmya that there was no other way but the Brahmin way. Even then, she had circumvented the issue by hiding behind the safe veil of her studies. But now that was not possible any more. She was a working woman and more importantly, of marriageable age; a stain she bore on her sleeve for all the community to see.

Geeta felt her goose bumps rising and spreading down her arms and legs when she contemplated what Sowmya was about to do. *Wasn't she afraid of what the future might have in store for her? Hadn't she dreamed secret dreams for herself? Didn't she want to taste it teasingly on the tip of her tongue? Their parents had drummed on about love being a journey of discovery. But what kind of a journey would it turn out to be? What if he had perverse habits like passing wind at the dining table? Or worse, what if he tried to kiss her with bad breath! Could they share jokes? Would he realise that when she started to chew her lower lip it was a sign that she wanted to be alone? How many more 'ifs' and 'whys' had Sowmya contemplated and how had she come to this insane decision to take a leap into the unknown?* wondered Geeta.

Geeta knew that it was only a matter of time before her parents would start lacing their conversations with lashings of marriage. She swore to fight it. *How can I possibly agree to a system so archaic? I could never be like Amma, the silent woman in the house.* She knew she was being unreasonable when she snapped at her mother, but Amma could be tiring at times. She could go on and on about the same point and flog it to death.

Geeta had picked a turquoise blue and lime green sari. This was one of her favourites. The lime green pallu with trails of little silver flowers danced in the sunshine when she moved. Geeta looked graceful in her sari. Her long jet black hair that had been nurtured and tended over the years, loosely braided into a single plait with a string of white jasmines tucked into it. Thoughts of Sowmya and arranged marriages were running through her mind when she heard Amma's soft knock on her door.

It was at that point that she decided to be a little more tolerant and possibly even nice to her mother. So, instead of barking at her mother on the other side of the door, she took a deep breath and in the calmest of voices said, "I'm ready Amma, just give me a minute."

"Aisay, you look like the Goddess Lakshmi herself!" proclaimed her father beaming proudly at his beautiful daughter. Geeta found it hard to resist her father's attempt at light humour as she succumbed and allowed a smile to temporarily fix itself on her lips. She knew that she would have to physically remove many a Mami's nose out of the folds of her sari with an explanation as to why she wasn't in any hurry to settle down.

Now, with Sowmya out of the way, Geeta knew there would be no respite and little reprieve from her family and by extension the community. As she started her father's car, she realised that she was humming Gloria Gaynor's *I Will Survive* just as M.S. Subbalakshmi's distinctive voice flooded the car. *Chalk and cheese,* she thought wryly as the deafening reverse sensor fought with M.S. for attention.

2

THE MANDAPAM
KUALA LUMPUR, 2008

The mandapam was beginning to fill and Geeta quickly made her way to the dressing room assigned to the Queen of the Day. The heady smell of fresh jasmine greeted her as soon as she opened the door. She inhaled deeply, loving the scent that spoke to the depths of her Indian core. She could vaguely make out Sowmya's reflection in the mirror as it jostled for space with the reflections of 'Pudu Mami' and 'Puchong Mami'.

Sowmya's natural hair was down to her shoulders and insufficiently long enough to braid into the traditional plait that was required of all Hindu brides. As such, Pudu Mami, (because she lived in Pudu of course) was busy weaving in a length of waxy false hair. Thin and wiry Puchong Mami (because she lived in Puchong of course) stood rather impatiently, waiting to work a long strand of jasmine flowers into her plait and then the customary head accessories.

Sowmya acknowledged Geeta with a wink and a grimace as Pudu Mami tugged away at her hair. Geeta shrank back to a corner and found a stool to sit on. At least she was away from all those prying eyes in the main hall and it was a lot cooler here in her Kanchipuram sari.

Sowmya was wearing the sari her parents had given her. Of course, black and white were not acceptable wedding colours so she picked her next favourite colours, baby blue with a navy border with the requisite gold work on the body and pallu. Some of the jewellery she wore belonged to her maternal grandmother; four gold bangles on either hand along with glass bangles that match her sari. The rest of the jewellery had been carefully selected and bought throughout Sowmya's adolescent years, as every self-respecting Brahmin bride had to have her own stash.

The checklist was extensive:

Gold necklaces of varying lengths and thickness	✓
Gold bangles (thin, medium and thick)	✓
Diamond earrings with traditional seven stone setting	✓
Gold navaratna set (inclusive of earrings, necklace and bangles)	✓

And the list went on depending on how wealthy the parents were or how parsimonious they were with their own lifestyle; careful not to break the chain of saving-buying-saving-buying.

The Mamis were finally done with Sowmya. They had wrestled with and cajoled her hair and body into a traditional bride, one whom Geeta could scarcely recognise. Sowmya turned to face Geeta, her bangles jingling-jangling with her.

"You look lovely," said Geeta with a tinge of sadness. Sowmya looked at her with her dark kohl-lined eyes and shook her head, "Please let's not go there," she pleaded, "Or I'll cry and you will have to re-apply this awful makeup for me." They hugged and were quickly pried apart by Pudu Mami who grumbled about crushing the bride's sari. Sowmya squeezed Geeta's hand and instinctively they both drew in their breath as the dressing room door opened and the two cousins stepped out, Geeta walking right beside Sowmya.

Sowmya was escorted to her waiting groom. As was custom, Sowmya's father placed his daughter's hand in Vivek's and asked him to marry his daughter. Still holding hands, they were led to the swing to begin the oonjal ceremony.

Geeta never left Sowmya's side. She stood beside her ready with a tissue to dab at the sweat before it carried her make up down her face.

When it was time for her to change into the nine yard sari given by her in-laws, it was Vivek's sister who tied it.

As the ceremony built up to a crescendo, so did the double reed, as its music picked up speed and shrillness in its race against the chanting of the head priest and his eager assistant. Sowmya, trying hard not to appear ungainly, sat on her father's lap as her husband-to-be tied the first knot of the yellow thread that held the mangalasutra around her neck. Vivek's sister who was erudite in Brahmin customs, tied the other two customary knots.

That's it, she's now married to the whole blinking lot of them, thought Geeta. *Doomed forever. Tied like a dog on a leash for life.* Finally the wedding was over and as far as she was concerned, Sowmya's life too.

As she was shaking bits of yellow rice off herself, Geeta made a face and looked up only to be met by Krishna Chitappa's bright smile. "My favourite niece," he declared, "Where's your smile on a happy occasion like this!" Geeta felt relief and sadness overcome her at the same time. She hooked her hand in his and they discreetly made their way in search of her other cousins as the priest droned on.

3
KUALA LUMPUR
8TH DECEMBER 1940

It was not yet dawn in the Rangaswamy Iyer household and yet the birds were in competition with the sounds coming from the kitchen below. Vairavar, the cook was busy bossing the servants around; in one corner Malathi was working hard grinding a potent combination of fresh coconut, roasted coriander seeds, dhall, green chillies and fresh coriander leaves which would soon lose their individuality to become a pale green coconut chutney. Right next to her sat Revathi, battling with the hefty stone grinder that she worked manually to grind rice and black gram dhall.

Vairavar stood at the stove stirring the sambar while humming a Tamil movie tune. Coffee was unhurriedly drip-dripping into a stainless steel container and as the kitchen sounds were building up to a climax, a different tempo was beating upstairs in the private quarters of the household.

A devotional was playing in the background and Swamy, as he was fondly known, was standing at the altar, giving thanks for another day and indeed another year. He couldn't believe how quickly he had reached forty. It was certainly a time for reflection and introspection given the drama that was currently being played out on the world stage.

His three children were growing up so quickly. Ramesh was a gangly twelve year old, Lavanya outspoken at six with always something to say and Raman a sprightly three year old. He loved them all dearly but it was Lavanya who held his heart. *She is a reflection of Appa,* he thought fondly.

Her ability to speak her mind invariably gets her into trouble, but it's her quick wit that saves her from any harsh punishment. Ramesh is what every twelve year old is; confused and complicated. Raman has such a curious nature and already a love for books, he thought. I must remind Saraswathi to take him to the library," he said aloud.

"What was it you want to remind me about?" asked Saraswathi as she strode up to the altar. "Happy birthday and may Ambal shower her blessings on all of us," she said as she lit the lamp.

Saraswathi was dressed in a sky blue cotton sari and her long wet hair that was usually plaited into a thick braid was wrapped in a thin cotton towel. She was eighteen when she got married. Her father had answered an advertisement in the matrimonial section of 'The Hindu', horoscopes had been exchanged and the respective astrologers had smiled at the match "made in heaven". That was how Saraswathi had married a teacher from Malaya and sailed to a new land and a new people.

There was still much to be done for the party that evening. Saraswathi was working out the details as she made her way down to the kitchen to start her day. There was lime rasam to be made, tamarind rice, yogurt rice and of course the milk payasam, which she made herself for special occasions like birthdays and festivals.

She was fortunate to have Vairavar in the household, as he had learnt from her all the family favourites and was competent in the kitchen. Of course with that came a certain degree of arrogance and truculent attitude.

"Kalai Vanakam Vairavar," she greeted him with a slightly upbeat tone, as he was prone to mood swings especially on a day when there was a feast to prepare and he rankled at the unwelcome presence of strangers in his kitchen. But nothing could begin without her first tumbler of freshly brewed coffee.

The guests started trickling in at seven that evening. The first to arrive was Swamy's closest friend, Tan Chin Nam.

"So where is the big birthday boy? I had the hardest time picking out a present for your husband, but I finally settled on *The Complete Works of Shakespeare*. It was a choice between this book or one on Theorems, but I figured dear old William was a far better fit for our Swamy."

"Come in and have a drink, Chin Nam. Would you like an F&N orange or sarsi?"

Soon, 912 Batu Road was swelling with laughter and noise. The loudest voice belonged to the robust and portly man by the name of Gates. Mr. Gates was the headmaster of Victoria Institution, the prominent government English school in Kuala Lumpur and Swamy's boss.

In no time, the living room resembled the Victoria Institution staff room. The conversations swung from pupils and their antics to parents and their idiosyncrasies and finally to world politics. One thing was obvious; the teachers at Victoria Institution were passionate about the subjects they taught and held great respect for each other. The only outsiders at the 40th birthday celebration of English and Mathematics teacher, Rangaswamy Iyer, were really insiders - Tan Chin Nam and Reiko 'Bob' Nakamura.

Amidst the loud chatter and hearty conversations, there was a feeble attempt made by Bob to gather everyone around for the ubiquitous group photo. After many rounds of shuffling and re-shuffling of short people, not so tall people and tall people, heads stopped bobbing and to the count of three, Bob Nakamura's Asahi winked before a blinding flash recorded for posterity the lively gathering on the verandah of 912 Batu Road.

"Speech! Speech!" shouted Lim, the Geography teacher.

"Hear! Hear!" echoed Bob in agreement.

Swamy knew there was no way out for him as he cleared his throat.

"It's amazing how quickly time flies. It feels like only yesterday when I first landed in Penang after the war. It is incredible for me to think that I have lived almost as long in Malaya as I had in the country of my birth. I am grateful to have been able to raise my young family here and of course to have made such wonderful friends and colleagues," he began, to encouraging cheers. Swamy's jovial face took on a more serious turn as he continued.

"We live in precarious times. Europe is at war and Japan is poised to strike our part of the world. Already, they have taken China and have parked themselves in Indo-China. I am told that they are building air bases. This can only mean that we need to be steadfast and strong in the wake of any possible attack. I know this may seem morbid, to talk about heavy issues like an impending war, but I know that it weighs heavily on all our minds. It is truly my wish and hope for all our families to face whatever comes our way with unity and a brave heart."

"I also want to thank all my friends here, European and Asian for their encouragement of Bob. We all know how Bob is just as disturbed as we are over the recent Japanese aggression. I want to say this, Bob Nakamura, come what may; you will always have a friend in me. Finally, Saraswathi and I want to thank all of you here for taking the time to be with us tonight. It means a lot to us."

The guests were silent and some shifted uncomfortably from foot to foot as their minds contemplated the prospect of war.

"Dinner is served," announced Saraswathi, sensing the growing unease of the waiting yet polite crowd and breaking the sombre mood.

The sound of forks and spoons clinked in time with the appreciative sounds of approval coming from the guests. Dinner plates were soon cleared making way for dessert and coffee. It was nearly midnight when the first set of heavy and contented stomachs belched their good nights and made their way to their cars.

4
KUALA LUMPUR
9TH DECEMBER 1940

It was time for the annual trip to Bob's studio and Chin Nam's family was getting ready to leave the house. Tempers were flaring and little quarrels were erupting over who had taken the tin of Cuticura powder. The children in the Chin Nam household were rambunctious and often referred to as 'a handful' by some quarters. Their screams and loud footsteps could be heard nearly all the way down Parry Road. "Your screaming will chase our neighbours away! Can't you children learn to talk instead of scream and walk instead of run?" grumbled Elaine.

The houses on Parry Road were chaste and proper. Gardens were well kept and neat hedges of ixora lined most of the driveways. Walls were painted a crisp blinding white and the verandahs were hidden from the glaring sun by black and white bamboo chicks. The inside of Chin Nam's house was furnished in the traditional Chinese fashion. The living room was predominantly furnished with mother of pearl inlay rosewood furniture. Elaine had always wanted to change some of the chairs for modern furniture but Chin Nam would never hear of it.

"These chairs lived in my grandfather's house and I'm not giving these away. It's like asking me to throw my parents out of the house," he told her melodramatically. It was always the same

26

argument but Elaine never tired of asking.

"One day I will make you choose between those wretched chairs and me," she fought back.

The squabbling threatened to jeopardise the family outing and cast serious doubts as to whether the family photo would eventually make it to the wall of 53 Parry Road.

"Stop the bloody screaming and let's go!" Chin Nam yelled.

As they drove past Mr. Hillman's house, it was impossible to miss the green van with the yellow print "Chin Nam & Co" neatly painted across its small body. Chin Nam felt proud as he pointed out, "Take a good look children, there is everything I work so hard for, parked in front of Mr. Hillman's house." He had always wanted the words "Purveyors of fine comestibles" painted on the delivery van even if he ran the risk of sounding pompous and being laughed at by his Chinese friends. Chin Nam & Co was one of the few stores in Kuala Lumpur that sold imported foodstuff and it was the preferred choice of the large British community. From potted meat to Lavender soap, the shelves were well stocked with 'fine comestibles' and was also popular with many of the city's elite and discerning locals.

Bob's photo studio stood on busy Rodger Street, right in the heart of Kuala Lumpur. On any given day, the aromas on Rodger Street assaulted the olfactory senses of passers-by. Row upon row of Chinese sundry shops displayed baskets of salted dried fish or prawns, inviting not just the old Chinese ladies looking for condiments but flies looking for a free meal. Bob's studio stood out like a sore thumb.

"It's time you moved out from here," declared Chin Nam.

"I know, traffic is awful and there is always the rickshaws and motorcycles to contend with, but the location is perfect as it is so easy to get to," said Bob, defending his little spot. "And it's a bonus that it's so close to the Club."

The walls of Bob's studio were a gallery of Kuala Lumpur and Selangor's Who's who, adorned with images of Europeans and local elite in Kuala Lumpur and the rest of Selangor.

Bob was tagged "the man with the mean lens" by his friends and clients. Wherever and whenever there was a wedding, official function, dinner or any other happy occasion to record, Bob was there with his tripod and wrinkled black leather camera case, worn from the constant action of opening and shutting its cavernous mouth.

The Tan family flirted with the small mirror hanging on a wall in the studio. Kah Hoe, a vain 19 year old was busy fixing his hair, making sure every strand was combed to the right, just the way he liked it. His younger brother, Kah Heong, a slightly pudgy 15 year old was indifferent to his looks as he figured no matter what hair style he sported, the thick glasses on his face would not make him a candidate for 'Mr. Good Looking'. Seven year old Kah Sing was the book-worm in the family, with his nose buried deep in a book nearly everywhere he went. Today was no different as he was bent over the latest Biggles novel. Then there were the twin girls, Kye Li and Kay Li who were six going on 16. Elaine and Chin Nam had tried hard for a girl after the birth of Kah Sing and they were over the moon when they were blessed with not one but a pair, just over a year later.

The twins were the apple of their father's eye and could do no wrong. Therein lay the root of all the problems and squabbles of this family. The girls were spoilt and threw tantrums when they didn't get what their little hearts desired. Many an amah had come and gone, all citing the terror twins as the reason for their quick departure. But little was done to reprimand the girls and while their reputation grew larger, their popularity shrank. None of the other girls on Parry Road wanted to play with the Terrible Tan Twins (T.T.T).

Stuck in Bob's studio, on a stuffy and muggy Monday morning, things were not going their way. They pulled and tugged at their white broderie anglaise dresses, fussed that the pink bows were not straight and cried that their hair was tied too tight. Poor Elaine struggled to set things right while trying to stop a fight that was brewing between brother no. 2 and the girls.

"All right, gather around and take your places," interjected Bob who was at his wit's end. "Boys in the back, girls seat yourselves on either side of your parents."

It was always at Bob's studio each year that Chin Nam took stock of his stout and portly figure. *I need to lose a few inches around my waist,* he thought to himself, though he liked to believe that at 46 he still struck a dashing figure in his tan suit and dark brown Oxfords. Similar thoughts were going through Elaine's head except she didn't need to lose any weight. She was trying to figure out how to deal with raising her five children without losing her mind. She was always the perfect hostess, her dinner parties were much talked about – her Nyonya food a hit with the British and locals alike. The one thought that kept eating at her psyche was her desperate need to do something for herself. *But what could I possibly do?* she wondered to herself.

"One, two, three, cheese," said Bob, the flash bringing their thoughts back to the studio; plastic smiles fixed for posterity.

Just as Chin Nam and his family were about to leave, Bob pulled Chin Nam aside.

"I want to carry on from what was said last night at Swamy's house. Thank you very much for having faith in me and for seeing me differently from the rest of my countrymen. You know how much I hate what's going on. I am so glad you and Swamy don't think I am one of them. I know your strong dislike of the Japanese especially with what happened in Nanking. Thank you for making me feel like I belong here," Bob said while holding Chin Nam's hands in both of his.

"You don't need to apologise for what the Japanese are up to. You are first and foremost my friend. It is unfortunate that you are Japanese, but heck, I always forget with a name like Bob," laughed Chin Nam.

"Well, my options were rather limited. Didn't I tell you that my parents in their desperation for a baby girl named me Reiko?" said Bob. "I think it was an unfortunate name," he smiled.

5
SUNDAY LUNCH
KUALA LUMPUR, 2008

The cooking always started early on Sunday in Geeta's parent's house. Prema, the trusted cook, bustled about the kitchen getting lunch ready for the whole clan. She loved it. In fact, that would be an understatement. She thrived on it. The tradition of Sunday lunch was very much alive in the Ramesh Iyer household. Ramesh, being the patriarch, always hosted.

As forgetfulness and plain laziness were expected of the younger generation, phone calls were made the day before to make sure that all would grace the dining table at no. 2A. The matriarch, Parvathi made the phone calls herself. She did not trust anyone else to do this and the person at the other end had better have a damn good reason if he or she couldn't make lunch. Flippant reasons and lame excuses were unacceptable and everyone knew that. Geeta's brothers Suresh and Ravi had been missing from this special get-together for years now, as Suresh was working as an ENT surgeon in Manchester, while Ravi was an aeronautical engineer in Houston. The truth was that no one liked missing Sunday lunch, not the in-laws, out-laws or even the by-the-by laws. The Raman household however, were missing as their entire family and their new in-laws, had headed up to Cameron Highlands for a joint holiday, a carry-on of the wedding the week before.

The family started to gather from 12 noon onwards. A good indication of the number of family members in the house was the growing pool of slippers, shoes and high heels strewn outside the front door. Those who arrived a little late were welcomed by jeers of "Oi, why so late lah!" or "Aiyoh, what time do you think lunch is!" But best of all were the shouts of "Hi" and the hugs that followed.

One thing was for certain, between noon and 2.30pm, madness and chaos reigned in Parvathi and Ramesh's house. Adult voices fought to be heard alongside the screams and excited chatter of children, until the little ones were finally fed, watered and sent off to play outside or upstairs to Ramesh Tata's room to watch cartoons. There was a hierarchy at the dining table and the seating arrangements in the living room to cope with three generations of Rangaswamy Iyers under one roof – a potent and combustible combination of personalities and characters. So, this was how it worked; the third generation was allowed on the sofas and chairs but if any second generation family member wanted a seat, the little one(s) climbed on to their parent's lap. If an elder needed a seat, then the second generation was relegated to the floor or the arm of a sofa. That was the law and it was never broken.

Conversations flew across the living room, diagonally and sideways. There was a cocktail of heated and animated dialogue that bubbled away. A measure of medicine mixed with a touch of education and a dash of law. The cocktail stirrer however, was always politics. It never left the glass.

Discussion centred around the recent elections where the opposition coalition caused what was hailed as a "political tsunami." Whilst not winning the elections, they denied the ruling coalition of their usual two-thirds majority in Federal Parliament. Phenomenally, at state level they won five states.

Nearly everyone was present. Lavanya athai, Ramesh's widowed sister, was in her favourite seat, the Captain's chair with its orange cushion pad and fading, fraying gold thread. No one dared take her chair or suggest that she change the cushion. Her two daughters Sandhya and Manjula were there with their husbands, the two Gopals and their children. Sandhya was always late because at 45, she was still throwing warm cash into the freezing fountain of youth. Sundays were her one day of indulgence when she headed to the gym at 8 in the morning before she made her way to Uma, 'the hair lady' she swore by. "Look, no gray hair at my age," was her defence for her extravagance. For one and a half hours, she allowed Uma to apply a thick paste of henna, some dubious mud-like substance and pungent coconut oil to her hair. Her daughter, Aishwarya who was 18, was always a favourite with the little ones.

If you had to describe Manjula, you would have to use two words – strict and no-fuss. Well…and highly-strung too. At 40, she was experiencing a multitude of emotions. There were days when she thought she would never make it to the end of the day. Then there were others when she felt she ought to cut her hair short, abandon the sari and live in a flowing kaftan; in an attempt to live the independence that had been denied to her for so long. She always knew it was her hormones ganging up against her, playing nasty games of hide-and-seek, poking out from behind an invisible curtain and saying "Boo" when she least expected it. She hated feeling so fragile and had often dared herself to leave it all behind to join an ashram in India. Having raised two boys and a girl, her well-worn phrase was, "You came to live with me, not I with you. Therefore, my rules rule!"

As was expected, the conversation snaked its way back to last week at the mandapam. Sowmya's in-laws were dissected, put back together and then ripped apart again.

"Did you notice what her sister-in-law was wearing?" commented Sandhya, screwing up her face with displeasure.

"I know, I thought that she looked awful in that shade of pink and all that make-up made her look like one of those Chinese Opera singers!" remarked Geeta who seemed to appear from nowhere, her hair all wrapped up in a thin Indian cotton towel.

"Hey Geeta, when is your turn ah?" asked Lavanya athai. You're not getting any younger you know." Geeta glared at her.

"Eh, and did you see how much jewellery Lakshmi Mami had on?" piped in Manjula, saving Geeta from having to answer. "It was as if she wanted to show the whole Brahmin community her entire collection all at one go and on one big, thick neck!" Even Ramesh, the normally quiet one who always denounced gossiping had something to say, commenting on the colour of the veshti on Sowmya's father-in-law. New relatives were slowly shredded in the living room until Parvathi announced in Tamil, that lunch was served.

The break in the conversation was deafening. The not-so-little-ones scrambled with the not-so-old-ones in their usual fashion, making a bee-line for the ever silver plates stacked up on the sideboard. In the old days, everyone had their names etched on their plates but with all the additions to the family, that tradition was put out to pasture many years ago. Only three people had their own plates – Ramesh's oval shaped silver plate that was given to him during his poonal ceremony, Parvathi's oval ever silver plate that was larger than the rest and of course Lavanya athai's ever silver plate. You never ate from their plates, ever.

There were always two types of rice served every Sunday, jasmine rice and basmati rice (the preferred choice of Geeta). Potato curry was the family's all-time favourite and this week it was accompanied by murungakai sambar, lime rasam, cabbage with freshly grated coconut, taufu fried with onions and chilli powder, vendakai poriyal, yogurt, two types of pickles and two Jacob biscuit tins filled with crispy, crunchy appalams.

The third generation towered over the elders seated at the table as they attempted to fill their plates. They then made their way to the living room to eat, plates balancing precariously on their knees. Rice and sambar mixed easily with conversations of college and school, the hip-and-happening and the not-so-happening.

"Can you believe on Friday I was stopped by the police for not wearing my seat belt," announced Parvathi. "Before the policeman had a chance to say anything, Appa wound the window down and shouted, 'Don't ask me for money, just give me a summons lah!' The policeman was so offended that he yelled at Appa saying he shouldn't go around accusing the police of taking bribes."

"Well how would I know?" said Ramesh peeved. "Everyone says that the police are corrupt."

"At this point the poor policeman was totally angry with Appa and insisted that it was untrue. I think he was so exasperated that he just waved us to go!"

The laughter that broke out was so loud that no one heard Krishna come in and demand to know what the entire fracas was about. Space was made for him at the table and the entire episode was retold.

"It's not the first time you've put your foot in it, remember how you could never remember that Finnish doctor's name Anna and kept calling him Lakshmanan instead of Latvannen?"

Krishna was the keeper of all secrets in the Rangaswamy family. He was gifted with an impeccable memory and a wicked sense of humour; it was great fun for the younger ones to unravel both. He was the fun uncle in the family and he made it his Sunday ambition to fight the very curse that possessed the rest of his family – the Sunday Siesta. This was a tradition that was sacred and to defy it was sacrilegious. However, defiance was part of Krishna's make up. So, when stomachs had been sated with heaps of rice that were fast expanding and demanding that the bearer lie horizontal, Krishna jumped up (when all fast activity was strictly prohibited past the witching hour of 2.30pm) and gathered the young ones (who were not party to the conversation of corruption and politics) into his car and drove them off to the Hock Seng Mini Market for ice cream and Marvel comics.

It was over the din of "Goodbyes" and "See you laters" that Krishna raised his voice a notch higher for Geeta.

"Geeta, guess what, I may have something interesting for you. Since you're always asking me for stories from the past, I went rummaging through my boxes of correspondence and found some old letters that my Appa had written to his Appa. I promise to bring it next Sunday or if your inquisitive self can't wait, come by my house and I will show them to you."

After the assembled family struggled to match their shoes in a medley of 'snap the shoes' followed by yelps of "aiyoh its so hot", they made their way to their cars with phone calls to their respective maids to turn the air-conditioning on in their rooms, ready to receive their heavy bodies for their siestas.

Geeta waved her favourite uncle off. As exciting as his discovery was, it would just have to hang on. She had a hair dresser's appointment followed by a much-awaited dinner; her lawyer friends had been planning this dinner for weeks and after many messages back and forth, this was the only day available to all.

Geeta had made the reservation for 7.30pm for a table of 10 at Leonardo's. On hindsight, she should have asked for a table in the quietest part of the restaurant, she thought to herself. *Ten loud litigators in one place is going to be a nightmare for other diners. Oh fuck it!* she chided herself as she backed her car out of the driveway. The restaurant was one of her favourites. She loved the ambience – low lighting, rustic red brick wall and exposed rafters. The food was excellent and they had a wide range of vegetarian dishes. She was already working out what she was going to have for starters.

She was heaving and sighing when she finally walked into the restaurant, ready for a stiff gin and tonic.

"I hate parking in Bangsar," she whined to Evelyn. "It's a nightmare, even on a Sunday night." The others slowly started trickling in and soon the chatter of law and the latest TV series dominated the table. But eventually, as with all lawyers and with all dinner conversations where lawyers were present, the conversation morphed into bitching about members of their chosen profession. By the time dessert was finally served, there were even a handful of judges and registrars at the dining table too.

In spite of the flowing conversation, thoughts of her grandfather's letters tested her psyche. By her fourth glass of wine, she was imagining how they must look, tied up with a purple ribbon, tea-stained with age and smelling musty. So at

35

11pm sharp, after an exchange of "Goodnights" and air-kisses, she made the phone call. Krishna Chitappa was not up but his housekeeper answered the phone on the third ring.

She was at his Pantai Hills bungalow exactly seven minutes later. Krishna Chitappa was a successful gynaecologist with his own private practice, as well as the part-owner of a multi-disciplinary medical centre. More importantly, he was the family's personal physician and entertained no shortage of relatives dropping in for advice on subcutaneous foot cysts to sprained ankles and beyond. He lived alone in a big house with his driver and driver's wife who served as cook and housekeeper, a perfect packaged deal.

The interior of his home was continuously evolving. Geeta never knew what sort of "book sculpture' may be rising from the floor or sticking out of window ledges or even poking out of walls. Books were Krishna Chitappa's respite, his escapism and his art.

Shelves were often added to carry the burden of heavy books on nearly every subject, from medicine to self-hypnosis, history to philosophy. His pride, however, was his Churchill collection which included signed copies of Winston Churchill's *History of World War II.*

Krishna had never married and it was one of the family's most taboo subjects. Everyone in the second generation burned with curiosity but no one had the courage to ask, so no one ever knew. Of course there were veiled whispers that spoke of a lost love, a dead love and even so far as a rotten love. But no one dared to validate the rumour or attach a name to the source of the whispers.

Krishna knew Geeta only too well. *She is just like me. If I had a daughter, she would share all of Geeta's genes,* he would often think to himself. Of all his nieces and nephews, he loved her the best and made no effort to hide it. From the day she was born, they had made an immediate connection. As a baby, she would cry and every time he picked her up she would look intently into his eyes and somehow be comforted. And he, who had no patience with children, would hum to her and allow her to sleep on him for hours at a stretch. He could easily relate to her curious and stubborn spirit which is why he left the letters with Hema before he went to bed. He knew she would come that very night or else sleep would elude her.

He was right.

6
KUALA LUMPUR
8ᵀᴴ DECEMBER 1941

The months before the Japanese invasion were tense. The question that hung in the air like a thick choking cloud of dust was not whether the Japanese would invade, but when. The British were confident that due to the year-end monsoon season, the earliest possible window of opportunity would be February 1942. They were of course wrong. The Japanese struck just before midnight on 7th December 1941. Their forces made landings in southern Thailand, on the beaches fronting the South China Sea. Almost simultaneously, the Japanese landed in Kota Bharu in Malaya's north-east.

Months earlier, in July 1941, the Japanese and Vichy France entered into a mutual defense pact allowing the Japanese to occupy Southern Indo-China, thus providing them a launch pad for a Malayan invasion. In retaliation, the Americans imposed an economic blockade leaving the Japanese all the more desperate to occupy South East Asia, an area rich in resources that Japan so desperately wanted. The big question was whether America would enter the war.

Expecting an invasion, the British undertook defence initiatives. Indian and Australian servicemen arrived in Malaya and Singapore. Defensive positions were taken up to protect air bases in north Malaya. The trunk road snaking from the north to the south of Malaya was protected by the all important Jitra Line, poised to defend any advance by the Japanese on their ultimate target, Singapore.

The British however, were both under-prepared and over-confident. Their training was inadequate and their equipment obsolete. Their Buffalo fighter planes would prove to be no match for the superior Japanese Zeroes.

The Japanese invasion was the reason for the birth of the Malayan Peoples Anti-Japanese Army (MPAJA), whose members were predominantly Communist sympathisers. Soon after the start of the invasion, volunteers were trained by the British at the 101 Special Training School in Singapore. The MPAJA became the guerillas that were inserted behind enemy lines to carry out sabotage attacks on the Japanese. The common cause was the cement that bound the Communists with the British colonialists in their goal to defeat the Japanese.

It rained all night with a longing; as if the rain could wash away the fear that had festered and eaten its way into the soul of every Malayan. It was Swamy's 41st birthday and understandably, he didn't feel like celebrating. As usual, he had woken early for prayers. He looked into the mirror and saw strands of gray poking through his sideburns and deep worry lines tattooed across his forehead. The sound of the pounding rain provided background music to his despondent thoughts sloshing around in his head. It took firm knocks on his front door to drag him out of his thoughts.

Chin Nam was standing outside, soaking wet in a fast growing puddle of water. The look on Chin Nam's face confirmed their worst fears. He could physically feel his world crumbling around him like dry caked clay; his small and intimate world crushed under the weight of cumulative fears. Looking at his friend so vulnerable and scared, he realised that life would never be the same again. *What would become of his job, how would his family manage? Would he have enough to see them through and worse still when and how would it end? What would be the scale of human loss?*

A war always brought with it a bleak landscape of carnage that hurt everyone and benefited no one.

Chin Nam tried to form the word "war," but his mouth refused to speak it. He started to shiver and it was then that Swamy noticed Chin Nam's clothes pasted to his body. Chin Nam, who was neither opposed to nor prone to physical signs of affection, allowed Swamy to hold him gently and lead him into the safety of 912, both bereft of words but flushed with pain.

Swamy waited for Chin Nam to dress and offered him a cup of strong, hot coffee. Both nursing their tumblers, they sat silently listening to the BBC news service until Chin Nam whispered hoarsely, "I've hardly slept the last couple of days and I've had the radio on just in case I miss any news developments. On the news broadcast at five this morning I heard it all too clearly. The Japanese have landed in Kota Bharu and bombed Singapore."

"I am worried and terrified, Swamy. You know my loyalties lie with the Anti-Japanese league. I have contributed heavily to the China Relief Fund. If the bloody Japanese ever find out, you're looking at a dead man. It would be easier if they shot me in cold blood. Remember the atrocities in China?"

Swamy tried his best to remain positive.

"The British will defend us, Chin Nam. They have Indian and Australian forces here in full command and my cousin in the 11th Indian Division told me they have set up a strong defence at Jitra, to prevent the Japanese from taking control of the roads. I have tremendous faith in the British and they will put up a strong fight. They will not give in until their last man is down."

"Well, we have no option but to wait and see for now," said Chin Nam ruefully. "If this war finds its way here, I think we should all flee to Singapore. The Japanese will never touch Singapore. Happy Birthday Swamy. How different things were last year"

"Thanks" muttered Swamy, his birthday already a fading distant memory.

"I wonder how many of our friends will remain friends at

40

times like these? Most of my friends and I have very strong anti-Japanese feelings and I am not about to start hiding that fact now," said Chin Nam. "Just as most of our friends also know that you are pro-British. Who can we trust? I hope we can count on our friends."

"We need to tell Bob," said Swamy. "He's rather clueless about current events, I will drive past his studio on my way home tomorrow. I have been trying to see him but his studio has been locked up with a notice on the shutters about him being away on an assignment."

"You know him. Always cocooned in his own world," quipped Chin Nam. "I hope he comes home soon. I think I should be on my way. Elaine will be wondering where I am. I didn't wake her to tell her, I came straight to you."

"I ought to tell Saraswathi too. She's having a lie in and I don't have the heart to wake her. I will be the quintessential harbinger of doom and that too on my birthday."

Chin Nam rose and gave his good friend a hug, a most unusual gesture for Tan Chin Nam but then these were most unusual times.

The British defenses fell like dominoes once the Malayan campaign began. Despite valiant attempts, the ill-preparedness of the British allowed Japan's 25th Army under the command of Lt. General Tomoyuki Yamashita, (later to be nicknamed the Tiger of Malaya) to gain ground over a short space of time.

Apart from landing infantry on the beaches of south Thailand and north-east Malaya, attacks were made by air on various air bases including Kota Bharu, Alor Star and Butterworth. With this strategy, the Japanese were able to decimate a substantial portion of British aircraft, reducing air cover protection for the navy and infantry. The same strategy was adopted by the Japanese at Pearl Harbour, soon after the initial invasion at Kota Bharu. In one swoop, they intended to fatally wound the British and the Americans. Ironically, the only sliver of good news was that America had been dragged into the war. What Churchill had been trying to do for some time, was finally achieved by the Japanese themselves.

Just a day later, on the 9th December, Kota Bharu fell to the invaders. Despite heavy casualties, the Japanese momentum kept on going. By the 10th December, the Japanese approached the Jitra Line. Defended by Punjabi and Gurkha Regiments, British forces were forced to retreat until the final decision was made to withdraw to Gurun, some 30 miles south. The all-important and much talked about Jitra Line had been broken in 48 hours.

7

PENANG
24TH DECEMBER 1941

*"Ik o'mkaar
Sat-naam"*

*"God is One
Truth is His Name"*

The deep voice of Terlochan Singh broke the silence of his home just as the early orange streaks of dawn warmed the crows that nested on the roofs of the terrace houses lining Sri Bahari Road. The brown patchwork of iron in various shades of rust was not a pretty sight even for menaces like crows.

Terlochan was not one to bow his head in prayer but he was desperate. He was built tough but had the gentlest hands and the kindest way with the patients that came to the Government clinic he worked at. He was a dresser and was fondly called Tochi by his patients and friends. This morning, thoughts of work hovered in the periphery of his mind. All he could think about was the fate of his family and his beloved Penang.

A fortnight ago, Japanese fighter planes had conducted air raids on Butterworth, across the channel. Thousands of people had witnessed it from the Esplanade, what they believed was a safe place. The next day they returned for more, hoping to catch a glimpse of the enemy and the Royal Air Force duel it out in the air. It had gone badly wrong. Those who lined the streets of George Town to watch the spectacle soon realised in horror that their city was the target. With nowhere to hide, people fell like bowling pins; the body parts of neighbours, families and friends strewn carelessly along the dusty roads in the aftermath of the Japanese bombing.

On that fateful day, Tochi dressed the same as he did every day, in his starched white cotton shirt and white cotton trousers. The only colour he permitted in his work attire was his turban. He had yards of colourful starched muslin that he deftly wrapped into turbans each morning. Today, he had on a navy blue turban to match his mood. He picked up his big jute marketing bag and made his way on foot to Chowrasta Market to buy fresh fruits and vegetables, like he did everyday.

Tochi's first stop was always at the fruit seller where he picked the same fruits – oranges, pineapple and bananas. He would always remember that very day and that exact moment his world changed while standing at the fruit stall. It happened so fast, one minute he was choosing oranges and the next there were people running, screaming "We've been hit!" "Run, run!" in a gibberish of languages and dialects.

All around him people were running and falling over. Tochi looked on in horror at the body parts that had scattered all over, as if a tempestuous child had dismembered her dolls in a moment of blind and unreasonable rage. People lay dead on the ground, their heads smashed open like burst watermelons; the dying trampled on by hysterical survivors.

Tochi couldn't look at the carnage around him but he forced himself to carefully pick his way out of the market. Out of the corner of his eye, he saw a baby cradled in its dead mother's arms. Without thinking, Tochi pulled the baby out of her grip and ran. Shops along the main road were on fire and he could smell something vile that he only realised much later was the smell of burning flesh. He would throw up for days whenever the memory of that smell corrupted his mind.

His clothes were no longer white and no longer starched. Instead, he resembled a speckled hen that had escaped slaughter. In the ensuing melee, he had also lost his turban. Tochi couldn't have cared less, he held on tightly to the baby and ran all the way home, praying that they wouldn't be hit by a bomb. He didn't know how long he ran and he had no idea that he was still screaming when he reached his front door. His wife's look of shock jolted him back to reality and he suddenly remembered he was carrying someone else's baby.

Dalip quickly took the baby without asking and hushed him as she shut the door on the mayhem outside. For a moment he felt safe. They spoke no words. She carried the crying baby, making calming sounds as she did so, as if patting a baby over her shoulder was part of her daily routine. There was a purpose in her gait. She brought Tochi a towel and pointed him to the bathroom. She carried the baby to the kitchen sink, stripped off his swaddling and washed off the grime and blood. He watched her blankly. *Whose baby have I stolen? What have I done?*

He turned to the bathroom to clean himself knowing full well that all the carnage he had witnessed could never be washed, scrubbed or cleaned away. They would later, after several futile attempts to locate the baby's father or family, name him Satnam, meaning truth.

In the days after Black Thursday (as the 11th December came to be known), Penang witnessed more devastation and human loss. Tochi and his colleagues at the Clinic worked around the clock as the injured and dead were wheeled in; a constant roll call of wounded, dead, barely alive, dead, dead. All the while, Tochi was wary, looking out for familiar faces amongst the dead. Some of the faces were so disfigured that he wondered how their loved ones would recognise them in the after life.

His worst fears came true on the morning after the Police Station on Penang Road received a direct hit. His cousin, Amar Singh who was on duty there the evening before was one of the fatalities. Tochi felt the blood drain from his face when he saw Amar lying on the stretcher with a huge patch of red on the sheet that covered him. He knew he would have to be the one to break the news to his ailing parents, a task he did not relish. He cursed the war. *He was only 25, he didn't deserve to go like this,* he thought as he pulled the sheet over Amar's face.

The doctors and nurses at the Clinic remained stoic even though their hearts warned them otherwise. They needed little reminder that the days or even weeks to come would be grim and gruesome. They tried to maintain a semblance of normality in their day-to-day routine. Once in the operating theatre, conversations resumed but invariably meandered back to the war.

"The British won't let us down" chided Dr Menon, in response to OT nurse, Sister Tan's accusations that the British were not doing enough to protect Penang. "If the Japanese attack us by land, the British will be there in full force. They are determined to keep Penang at all costs. Even if Malaya is overrun, Penang will always be a thorn in the Japanese backside."

At midnight on the 13th December, an orderly walked in with some news.

"I just cycled past the E&O hotel," he declared. "There must have been hundreds of women and children gathering in the lobby and the porch,"

Sister Tan looked up, her mouth set in a grim line, "I told you, those ang mo kows are up to no good. My instinct tells me that they are making plans to run and desert us."

She proved to be a soothsayer. What the orderly had witnessed that night was an evacuation of European children and women. Within days, there was a total evacuation of British troops and European men, leaving Penang to defend herself. On 19th December, Japanese troops set foot on the island. Many would say that they had simply strolled in.

For Penangites who had sworn their allegiance to the Crown, the betrayal was too much to bear. In the Clinic, the sense of despair quickly turned to anger.

"Those fucking white cowards. All their talk of fighting the enemy and protecting our land. They crawled away at night like cockroaches from the gutter!" swore Tochi.

8
A PEEK INTO THE PAST
KUALA LUMPUR, 2008

The letters were on the passenger seat next to her and she could almost feel the palpable rhythm of her grandfather's voice inside. Unlike what she had imagined, they were not tied up with a purple ribbon nor were they musty. The first thing she did when she collected the bundle was to put them straight to her nose. There was a vague hint of a woody, earthy sandalwood scent about the envelopes. Then she ran her hand again and again over the weathered letters as if the words would reach her through her fingers.

By the time she got home it was nearly midnight and only the porch light was on. In the early days of Geeta's career, her father would patiently wait up for her and let her in, wearily asking her how her day had been. Two months later, he gave up and finally handed her, her own set of house keys.

She filled her tumbler with water and slowly made her way upstairs. Her room was cold as the air-conditioner was left on. She put the letters on her bedside table and switched on the reading lamp. She thought about having a shower first and then maybe taking a peek into her past. But the moment was lost and she knew that she ought to save the letters for a day when she could afford them a little more ceremony, so she put them away in her drawer and silenced them for the night.

It was 7.30am when Geeta's alarm screamed obscenities at her. She had to be in the office by 9.30am for a meeting with 35 anxious Hakkas so there was no time to lose. Satnam Singh & Co was a boutique litigation firm that boasted one senior partner (the man himself), one junior partner and seven associates, including Geeta. At 67, Satnam worked out of his sprawling home office in Bukit Tunku. *At least he doesn't have to battle traffic to get to work,* Geeta groaned to herself as her car joined the jam at Jalan Duta.

The office was a beautiful modern annexe on Simpangan Tunku. Satnam of course, had the largest room and the rest had decent-sized rooms carpeted in gun-metal gray. They were lucky to have their own private spaces and not be stuck away in cubicles like most of their colleagues in other law firms. The other perks of the job included the designer kitchen and stand-by cook, ready to cook up breakfast, lunch and sometimes even dinner for the lawyers, staff and their favourite clients.

The Hakkas were already seated in the room, all 35 of them squished around the conference table. They were all in their 50s and 60s and looked at her with wary eyes.

"Mana itu Bangali orang?" asked one of them. She had to explain that 'Mr Satnam' was in court and that he would be back soon to join them. Geeta hated the ignorance of the Chinese when it came to Indians. They ignorantly called all turbaned Punjabis 'Bangali' without the slightest care for accuracy. *Punjabis are Punjabis and Bengalis are Bengalis and never the twain shall meet. And who the hell are 'Bangalis'!* she argued in her head.

They all seemed to take their cue to speak the moment Geeta sat down. The sound of cackling geese. She had to raise her hand and demand that they stop.

"Who here can speak English?" she asked and all of a sudden there was silence. No hands went up for a good five seconds until one hand went up very slowly.

"Er...I can," said a timid voice that belonged to a man who

introduced himself as Chin.

The other 34 Hakka clients cackled their Hakka approval and Chin became the assigned spokesman.

"A long time ago, sometime in the 1930s, there were various small bus companies in KL. These companies used to run various routes and also competed against each other. These people were our forefathers. It was then decided by them that instead of being competitors, they should all come together and form one larger bus company. They pooled their buses and each became a shareholder in this new company. It was like a cooperative.

"They called this company the Nanyang Omnibus Company, for Nanyang meant the Southseas which is what Malaya was called by the Chinese. The Company was run entirely by these people and their families. The drivers, conductors, clerks and administrators were all a part of the group. In fact, it was understood that any immediate family member was entitled to a job at the Company.

"The Company did well and grew in size. More buses and routes were added. The generations that followed included professionals such as lawyers, doctors and accountants. Some of these younger professionals got together and took control of the Company's board. We allowed this to proceed as we wanted the younger generation to modernise the Company. This allowed the Company to prosper.

"About eight months ago, we were approached by a competitor who made us a good offer to buy the business. There were a lot of discussions about this and the general consensus was to accept it. Many of us are old and our children do not want to work as bus drivers and conductors. We thought we might as well cash out and enjoy a good retirement. So at the last shareholders' meeting of the Company, we approved the sale and left it to the directors and the lawyers.

"The sale went through and the Company received RM40 million. Then the problems began. We thought that as the business had been sold, the money would be distributed. We were very disappointed when the directors refused. They now want to use our money to invest in other businesses. We just want our money."

Geeta who had been furiously making notes finally looked up at Chin and the blank faces around the table.

Where is Satnam? It's been 20 minutes… think woman, think.

True to form, Satnam made his typical entrance, just short of being grand.

"Good morning everyone," he boomed. "Thank you for being so patient." He took his place at the head of the conference table as 35 pairs of eyes scanned the new arrival up and down. Breathing as one, the 35 Hakkas sucked in all the oxygen from the room. Everyone had expected a big, burly Punjabi, not a tall, slim Chinese man dressed in a well-cut suit and bright tie (that would no doubt have elicited a comment of "A little too loud, Mr Satnam", from Justice George).

Luckily, there was no mistaking the sardarji in Satnam when he opened his mouth to speak in his distinct Punjabi accent. A true Punjabi at heart, he would regularly have his chef prepare chapattis painted in a layer of ghee, with saag, fresh green chilies and raw onions for lunch at least three times a week.

"So, what's the story," he asked. Geeta introduced the Chinese face as Mr Satnam Singh and the Hakkas looked at each other in total puzzlement and disbelief.

"Mana boleh dia Satnam Singh! Dia muka Cina ma! Kita mau Bangali lawan," exclaimed a concerned, leathery face.

"Saya bukan Cina lah! Muka saja Cina tapi bila buka mulut, saya Bangali lah! Jangan takut," Satnam responded with a laugh.

"Waah, belum you buka mulut ah tuan, saya ingat lu sama Cina woh," added another craggy face softened by a broken grin.

Pleasantries now firmly aside, Geeta related the story to her senior partner. Satnam turned to the group and asked "How many percent of the Company's shareholding do you own?"

"About 68%," responded Chin.

"Hhm, not enough for voluntary liquidation," he thought aloud.

"What about removing the directors?" asked Geeta.

"I did think of that but it would be too slow a process. By

that time, the money will be gone. But I have an alternative," said Satnam confidently. "Loss of substratum. We can present a Petition to wind up the Company on this ground. We will also have the added advantage that any disposition of the property of the Company including the sale proceeds will be void unless the court permits."

"Uhhh, can you please explain what these words mean, especially that sub, sub something?" asked Chin.

"Basically, it means that if a company is formed for a particular purpose and if that purpose or what we call the substratum of that company fails or ends for any reason, then a shareholder can petition to wind up that company," explained Satnam.

"Is there any precedent for this?" asked Geeta.

"Yes, yes, of course. In England, many years ago, a company was formed to mine phosphate but the promoters failed to get the license to do so. The company was then wound up. More recently in India, when Indira Gandhi decided to nationalise banks, many former banking companies were left without their banking business. Numerous other examples," he said.

"Geeta, I want you to take full instructions and get all the documents together. Get Azhar cracking on the drafting. I want both the Petition and an injunction application filed tomorrow morning. We will need an injunction to freeze the money."

With that, Geeta found herself burning the midnight oil, assisting Azhar with the Petition that had to be drafted overnight. She spent the next day parked at the High Court trying to convince the Registrar to fix an immediate date for the hearing of the injunction application. Being his usual obstructive self, the Registrar played hard to get and kept Geeta waiting outside his door for hours. Finally, after much persuasion and grovelling, the Registrar grunted to her that he would try and speak to the judge to see what he could do. *Screw this fucking system,* thought Geeta.

By Thursday afternoon, the injunction had been obtained and it was served on the directors and the bank the next morning.

An air of celebration hung over Satnam Singh & Co. There was very little work done all day and by the time it was 5pm plans had been made to meet at Murphy's for a drink. Geeta was bone tired. Every fibre in her body begged her to say no and to heed common sense and head home. So despite the cajoling and begging, her muscles screamed in victory as she slipped her car into reverse gear.

The bathroom was fogging up with steam. She heaped a handful of her favourite Laura Mercier bath salts into the tub and climbed in. She could feel the strain and the tension slowly leach out of her pores. This was one of the rituals she loved to indulge in, but because of her long working hours, the bathtub had been relegated to a toiletry repository as time always forced her into the shower stall.

The steam was still rising from the bathwater, trying to let itself out through the cracks in the window. Geeta stood by her bedside drawer and tentatively pulled it open, watching the stack of voices of her ancestors waiting to make her acquaintance. *It would be nice to sip some cold Sauvignon Blanc,* she thought as she untied the string.

8th December 1922

Dearest Appa,

I hope this letter finds you in the pink of health and that you and Amma are well by the grace of Ambal. I must apologise for such a long lapse, after my initial telegram. I have been trying to find my feet. I know how my silence must have worried the both of you. I am sure this letter will put your mind at ease when I tell you I am safe and in good health.

It is my birthday today and I can hardly believe that I am 22! I have so much to tell you and I don't know where to start. I have so many visions in my head, I need to gather my thoughts or they will all come tumbling out!

Let me start from my point of disembarkation. The Elephanta docked at Swettenham Pier in Penang on the 28th October 1922. The harbour was dotted with hundreds of boats in different shapes and sizes. Alongside the big ones were the smaller ones called sampans or shoe boats that are used for carrying passengers. I was struck by the number of Tamil coolies all lined up in their 'kailis' waiting to carry our bags. They were mostly young men accustomed to lifting heavy bags with one swift move. The others I saw were distinctly different in feature and colour. The Chinese people are fairer with flat features I have never seen before. The noise was deafening but that is to be expected and it is not unusual for someone from Kuthur!

It was the smells that appalled me. How can I begin to describe them. But I shall try. The air was salty like sea air is but there was a dank stench that hung in the air that infiltrated the pores of my body (which Amma, I tried very hard to wash off!). I later learnt that it was the smell of fish that had been salted and left to dry in the sun. What a dreadful business, that! Traders lined the port area, selling their wares to any willing buyer. I tried not to make eye contact as I kept looking for the representative from the Agency. He had my name Rangaswamy Iyer on a white board held up high above most heads.

Mr. Singham, a Ceylonese Tamil was pleasant and kind. He had made arrangements for me to stay with him and his family for the first two weeks. I am now writing to you from my 'new home' – a room in a shophouse on 30 Love Lane, which is right next to the school I am working at. The name of the school I am at is St. Xavier's Institution. It was named after Saint Francis Xavier, a Jesuit missionary. The school is run by Catholic Brothers who are known as the De La Salle Brothers founded by St John Baptist De La Salle. I am holding the position of a junior clerk and I help with the enrolment of new students. It's a good start and we all live under the watchful eye of the Brother Director, an Irishman called Brother Flannan Paul.

My new home is very centrally located both to work and food. It is the closest I will feel to being at home as there are pathars, astrologers, textile traders, sweets sellers and a small eating place that serves Indian food, I have my fill of sambhar shadam and thosai here on a daily basis. It is my only place of sustenance as finding vegetarian food here is not that easy.

There is also a temple not far from me called the Maha Mariamman kovil. It stands out as it reaches up into the sky, welcoming all devotees to come in and worship. It is a place I come to very often as I find great comfort breathing in the scents of the udubatthi and listening to the prayers being chanted. It gives me a sense of home, a sense of belonging and a sense of peace.

I have to go now so I will end my letter here. Please give my namaskarams to Amma and to you, Appa.

I will write soon with more news from here.

With much love from your loving son,
Rangaswamy

Geeta read the letter eight times and for the first time in her life, she felt a connection with the strict man she knew as her Tata, whom she had never met. She soon fell asleep with his words swirling in her head, leaving behind colourful traces of dreams she would have no recollection of the following morning.

9
KEN
KUALA LUMPUR, 2008

Geeta woke up on Sunday morning with the sun streaming into her room, glaring at her to wake up. In all the excitement of what was impending, she had forgotten to draw her curtains. She had a million thoughts running through her mind. This Sunday was full of secrets (deception even!).

She got dressed, muttered her excuses about not being able to make Sunday lunch and dashed out of the house. She took a slow drive to KLCC with Adele blasting through the speakers. She made a mental note of the shops she wanted to browse in and had promised herself a white handbag from either Tod's or Prada. *I deserve it after all the hard work I've put in,* she told her protesting conscience.

Parking at KLCC on a Sunday wasn't the most pleasurable experience, with hordes of families spilling out onto the parking bays. She followed the crowd up the escalators into the belly of one of the world's tallest buildings. She left the masses behind as she walked into the tan leather walls of Tod's. *There's nothing like making up your mind that you are going to spend money!* thought Geeta with a smile. The staff were attentive to the point of sickly sweet and after checking out a few handbags she made her way to Prada. She finally found a bag she liked and quickly handed over her plastic money before any second thoughts seeped in.

It was nearly 4pm by the time she found herself at CN Towers. The exterior was clad with shimmering steel with contemporary wooden slats on every window, shielding the wealthy from the sharp rays of the strong sun. With two towers twisting up towards the already crowded skyline, every unit promised a majestic view of the Petronas Twin Towers. She passed through the security system and made her way up to the penthouse where her boyfriend Ken Tan lived with his father, Tan Kah Sing. She had been looking forward to seeing Ken and her excitement had grown two legs and was standing beside her. He took her breath away when he opened the door. At 6'2", he struck an imposing figure. He looked gorgeous barefoot in his linen pants and white linen shirt.

He pulled her to him and kissed her long and hard. She could smell his aftershave and she felt his hands in the small of her back. He finally pulled away from her and they stared into each other's eyes. It had been so long since they last met and they both had so much to say. For now, all they could do was hold each other in silence. She felt like jelly and cream left out in the sun to wobble and melt.

Geeta finally pulled herself together and asked to be shown around. Ken and his father had only recently moved in to this vast space. The living areas of the penthouse were completed in an open concept plan, with the walls a pristine white to match the marble flooring. Ken had had to convince his father that a white sofa and ottoman wouldn't look too stark in this set up. With the subtle injection of accents of colour and trophies brought home from their frequent international travels, their home looked far from sterile.

Sitting on the balcony, Ken told her of all the exciting architecture projects he had been working on in London. They chatted for ages and didn't notice Ken's father until he stood there right in front of them. It was nearly seven and neither of them had noticed the passage of time.

"Hi you two, would you like to join me for a drink?" asked

Kah Sing. They both nodded and he left to fix the gin and tonics.

"So, does your father know you are here?" he asked Geeta and she in turn gave him a meek smile.

"No, I told him I was off shopping and ran out the door," she admitted sheepishly.

"You're going to have to tell your parents some time soon, you know?"

Before his father could say anything more, Ken jumped up and announced that he had prepared a vegetarian meal for Geeta. Thanking him silently in her head, she turned to him and gave him a relieved smile.

"How lovely and thoughtful of you," she managed to say without sounding too trite.

"I managed to go out and get stuff for a simple Mediterranean grilled vegetables and couscous," he said proudly. Kah Sing took his cue, grunted something about having to pop out for a while and left the two of them.

"I won't join you for dinner but I shall be back for dessert," he announced as he made for the door. Geeta was sure she felt some tension between father and son a moment ago. Ken hadn't mentioned anything to her and she wasn't about to stir up a hornet's nest. She only had Ken here for two weeks and she didn't want to sour the atmosphere by raising touchy family issues.

Geeta hated calling home to inform her parents that she wouldn't be back for dinner. Even at this age, there would be questions of why, where are you and how late are you going to be? It irritated her no end that she couldn't just tell them the truth without being interrogated. *Like I am still a ten-year-old!*

Ken opened a bottle of her favourite red and stuck Chris Botti in his player, filling the room with his mellow music. It seemed impossible for them not to raise the topic of her parents and while Ken apologised for his father's brusqueness, Geeta hushed him and agreed that perhaps it was time for her to face her demons.

"I know what your father says is true. I can't keep pretending to myself and lying to my parents, it's been three years after all.

I keep rehearsing different speeches in my head, but I never feel brave enough to tell them. Perhaps tonight will be a good time, after all the red wine!"

"G, you must be one hundred percent sure that this is what you want to do. It is very easy for you to lose it all with a single conversation."

This is what she loved about Ken, that he could be so selfless and thoughtful. For a man with his background, with all the luxury that he had been cloistered in, he was neither self-centred nor selfish. There was no doubt in his mind that Geeta loved him very much and that she would eventually muster the courage to face up to her parents.

Geeta set the table while Ken busied himself heating up the food. As they sat down to the simple home-cooked meal, she filled him in on her work and he listened patiently. It was 9.30pm when Kah Sing turned the key and walked through the front door.

"Am I too late for dessert?" he yelled from the door.

"No, we've finished and will be starting on dessert any time now. Your timing is perfect!" Ken called back.

"Pecan ice cream is perfect for me. Just let me have a quick shower and I'll join you both" his voice trailed as he closed his room door.

Am I imagining it, all this supposed family tension or am I superimposing the tensions of my own home? she wondered.

Kah Sing joined them both in the living room and for a short while there was only the sound of spoons making music with the bowls.

"I am sorry for being very intrusive earlier today," said Kah Sing to Geeta. She shook her head in disagreement.

"No, Uncle, I deserve it. I need to find the courage to tell them what I have to say and they are going to have to be adult enough to hear it. It's not like I am undecided. It's just that I know it's going to be so much harder for them, because you and my father are such good friends."

"I find it very hard when I see him, Geeta. I feel as if I'm betraying him. Your father and I go back such a long way that I think he will understand. He will not want to give you up and I would certainly tell him that he would be an arrogant fool if he did," said Kah Sing. "I would much rather the news came from you first and then we can all sit down like mature adults and work things out. You don't need to give up anything. Only, you will have to live on this side of town! Once in a while you will have to listen to this old man rant and rave but you know you are very loved in this house." Geeta couldn't stop the tears from streaming down her cheeks and she gave him a hug.

"I know," she squeaked.

"Dad and I will always be here for you," said Ken and at that moment she knew she couldn't love another man more.

"I promise you both I will speak to them soon," she said with new-found resolve.

It was getting late and Geeta felt tired. As Ken walked her down to the carpark they held hands in silence. The only sound were her shoes clipcloping on the cold concrete floor. Each was lost in their own thoughts, concerns and issues. Geeta broke the silence and asked Ken why his father had initially seemed upset when she arrived.

"He wants me to come home for good, to ease my way into the business and eventually take over."

"That's not such a bad thing," she said. "It would be lovely to have you back for good."

"But the timing sucks. I need to be in London for at least two more years, so I can settle what I have started there. If I quit now, I will have very little credibility. I wish he would give me a little time. I know I have to come back one day and I do want to come home, but not right now."

She knew not to push him too hard.

They got to her car and she startled the night with her electronic remote. She kissed him hard. She watched him shrink in size through her rear view mirror until she followed the ramp up and out into the ink blue night.

Her head was a bumper car track with worries that kept colliding with each other.

Deep down inside, Geeta had no idea how she was going

to approach her parents. Leaving Ken behind, her earlier false sense of bravado soon drained away, leaving behind a weak and procrastinating woman. She was left alone to fight her battle with the Brahmins.

Be rational Geeta and prioritize your worries.
Worry No 1: Telling Appa and Amma
Worry No 2: See Worry No 1!

How can I be so hopeless and be such a coward. For all my talk of feminism and the scathing remarks I made about Sowmya and her arranged marriage! At least she believed in it and she felt it would work for her. What do I believe in? I know I don't believe in arranged marriages and I do love Ken. Then why can't I summon the courage and tell them that. Surely, I can deal with the emotional blackmail that is sure to come my way.

She was so deep in thought, she drove on auto-pilot all the way home. The familiar smells hit her as soon as she walked in - a combination of Sunday lunch smells mingled with the scent of udubathi, lazily drifting its way in from the prayer room.

This is my comfort zone. This is what's familiar to me, gives me a strong sense of belonging.

She could not bid her eyes to stop crying. She opened the fridge door, yanked a green plastic bottle that had in its previous life housed 7Up, grabbed a tumbler and trudged up the stairs.

She lay in bed and pleaded with sleep to lie by her. Sleep had different plans however, and denied her its company. She lay awake waiting for the distant sound of the Azan to announce the arrival of another new day.

10
KUALA LUMPUR
11TH JANUARY 1942

As it was imperative to hold Singapore, British military strategy was to consolidate its forces in Johor, the southern most state of Malaya. Whilst waiting for reinforcements, the strategy was also to prolong the Japanese march south by taking up defensive positions in Kampar and then Slim River, strategic towns that dotted the route to Singapore.

The British forces were annihilated in both towns, leaving Kuala Lumpur just further south of Slim River, defenceless and abandoned. In the days that followed, she looked ugly and stank. The retreating British army had set fire to vast supplies of rubber that made the air taste putrid and sour. Black clouds from the burning rubber pyre choked the sky, a black backdrop against which the Japanese walked in.

The city's once teeming streets were deserted except for the looters who had come out to steal whatever they could. Boxes and cartons were strewn on the roads, emptied of their contents. Not too far from the looting was 912 Batu Road. Feeling old and dispirited, Swamy sat with his friend Chin Nam, deep in conversation.

"I don't know what to do," he mumbled.

"There is only one thing for you to do, Chin Nam, and that is to stay here in my house. There is no way you can return home. The Japanese will reach us in no time and I can guarantee that you will be on their list. Your best bet is to stay here for a couple of days and I will make some arrangements to move you and your family to the home of a trusted friend who works in the Railways. They will never think of looking for you in the Railway quarters. Tell your neighbours that you are going to Singapore. That should buy us some time," said Swamy convincingly.

With that sorted, bedding arrangements were made up for Chin Nam and his family. The two friends stayed up well into the early morning when Vairavar ran in screaming incoherently. Swamy grabbed him and shook him, to calm him down.

"The Japanese are everywhere," he stammered in Tamil. "They are swarming the streets like rats. I saw them do bad things, saar." He was sobbing uncontrollably as he described the atrocities he had just witnessed. "There were still some looters on the roads and they grabbed them and slit their throats, just like this," he gestured his hand slicing across his neck. "They grabbed women and raped them there and then, saar. A few of the soldiers caught a young boy and yelled something to him in Japanese and when he begged and cried, they beheaded him on the spot," he recounted, with tears streaming down his face.

Swamy and Chin Nam listened in horror as they realised that their worst fears had come true. The Japanese were finally here and they were determined to make their presence felt.

"Wake the servants, the children and the women!" Swamy bellowed to his cook. Vairavar scuttled out as fast as he could, screaming for everyone to get out of bed. *Think, Swamy, think,* he willed himself. Chin Nam's face was ashen as he thought of the likely end for him and his family. He slapped his own face hard to break the morbid spell.

"I think the first thing we need to do is get the women and children out of here. They need a disguise," Swamy said.

He strode into his prayer room and grabbed the scissors he always kept in the right hand drawer, to cut the wick of his ghee lamp. He glanced at Ambal's picture and went in search of his

62

wife. He found her in the bedroom.

"Cut her hair short," he instructed Saras pointing to Lavanya. "Just do it!" he yelled before a startled Saras could protest.

Driven by fear and confusion, Saras watched as thick black sheets of hair fell to the ground.

"Now, get her out of her nightdress and borrow some clothes from the servants and get her to change. Dress her up as a boy. Get the boys to change into tattered clothes too."

Saras looked shocked but knew better than to argue with Swamy. She was beginning to understand what her husband was up to. *Disguise them, make them look like the servants and hopefully they will leave us alone. Ambal save us,* she offered her plea in silence.

Well that's fine for my family, thought Swamy. *What about Chin Nam? How are we going to disguise them and what excuse can I offer for their presence here?* he wondered. Without the slightest hesitation, Elaine took the scissors from Saras' hand and began to cut her girls' hair. Soon, the floor resembled a carpet of spent hair and a heavy shroud of hopelessness fell over 912.

Each morning, Vairavar would reach 912 Batu Road with important snippets of news from the market place and the streets. The latest was that all wireless sets had to be surrendered, that there should be no dissemination of anti-Japanese sentiments and that books or magazines with pictures of the King and Queen of England were taboo. Quite simply, to be in possession of anything British was a risk in itself, for the punishment could range from a slap in the face to the most unimaginable torture and even death.

Swamy realised that he only had a few days to sort out the contents of his home. He knew his home would eventually be a target so he needed to take steps to hide the things that meant the most to him. He would never part with his books so he instructed his gardener to dig deep holes in the back garden while he wrapped his books with oil paper. These were then placed in boxes and lowered into the ground, miniature word coffins. He was adamant about keeping his radio, his one connection with the outside world and his only source of the truth. It was Chin Nam who managed to talk sense into surrendering it to the Japanese. "Those bastard Japs had the cheek to give me a receipt for it. The absolute nerve!" he complained to his friend.

All across the country, Malayans terrified of the consequences began burning their English books and magazines. The stories of torture spread as fast as the flames that licked the pages, before breaking into an angry fire. Cars were being confiscated. Swamy's friend's Humber Super Snipe was driven off unceremoniously by a Japanese soldier who was probably too young to even have a license. Swamy and Vairavar drove Swamy's Austin 7 deep into a rubber plantation close to home, leaving it to rest under a canopy of rubber trees. They hoped to retrieve it once the British returned. Who knew how long that would be.

Swamy would never forget the morning of 22nd January 1942. He remembered particularly that the sun had been strong in the sky and that there had been a beautiful breeze blowing. For a split moment, he had forgotten that there was a war going on. He was standing on the verandah of his home waiting patiently for Vairavar to come back from the market with vegetables and his daily news of the Japanese. What he saw approaching in the distance made him stand up a little straighter.

It definitely looks like him, he thought to himself. *Or am I starting to see things?* he chided himself. There was no mistaking who it was and Swamy's face broke into a big smile as he watched his old friend climb up the steps.

"Bob, where have you been?" he said, arms outstretched. Bob Nakamura did not return the same warm smile. His face was worn and it had an icy edge to it. His eyes were cold and the small hairs on Swamy's neck stood on ends.

"Is Chin Nam here?" he demanded without flinching or returning Swamy's smile.

"What's the matter with you, Bob? What's going on?" he pleaded, trying to understand what was unfolding before his very eyes.

"I am here for Chin Nam" he said, his voice taking on a stony edge. "I went to his house but it was locked up and I knew that you would be the one person who would know his whereabouts."

Bob refused to say Swamy's name. Swamy's eyes took on a look of confusion which was soon replaced with a glazed look of realisation when he saw a group of Japanese soldiers marching up to his house.

"Is this who you always were, Bob?" his voice was laced with bitterness. "We accepted you as a friend, we took you in and embraced you and this is how you pay us back?" he spat out.

Bob did not react and he looked past Swamy, his eyes scanning the interior of Swamy's home, a place he was very familiar with.

"What are you thinking? Are you thinking of all the times you shared a meal with my family, of my 40th birthday party when all my friends stood around you and promised you their friendship? You are deceitful and an ingrate."

Bob looked unflinchingly at Swamy and said, "Chin Nam is a traitor. He has been funding the Chinese cause and I am here for him. I'll only ask you once, where is he?" his voice suddenly low and threatening.

Chin Nam, who was upstairs heard the familiar voices and walked down to find Swamy face to face with their old friend. All the oxygen in the room was replaced with animosity and tension. Bob turned around and barked instructions in Japanese to the soldiers standing by. They immediately snapped to attention and pulled Chin Nam out of the house. Kah Sing, hiding behind the pillar at the top of the stairs watched silently with tears streaming down his face, too terrified to offer any protestations. He could only watch on helplessly as Bob and his men dragged his father out of 912 Batu Road.

11
DARK CLOUDS
KUALA LUMPUR, 2008

Dusk was starting to fall. Day was surreptitiously turning into night, discarding her bright colours and donning a dark blue cloak. His office was modern and sparsely furnished with contemporary furniture. He wasn't sure if that was what he wanted it to look like, but Ken had convinced him otherwise. The only piece of furniture that he had insisted upon was his old Moran armchair, arms a little worn but as comfortable as the Pagoda t-shirts he wore to bed. He watched the sky shed her daywear, preparing herself for a night of dark secrets and deceit. Kah Sing swirled his favourite drink, a 16 year old Lagavulin. The only sound was the single ice cube tinkling against the crystal tumbler providing background sound as the street lights flickered to life outside.

He swirled a mouthful of the peaty amber in his mouth, teasing his palate before allowing it to flow down his throat. It was always at this time of day, that the little voices scrambled out of the many compartments in his head to wreak havoc. The voices of Guilt, Remorse, Bitterness and Sadness nudged each other fighting for attention. Sadness was always the loudest.

It was only this golden liquid that was able to quiet the voices, hushing them into a temporary silence. Fate had played her trump card five years ago with the death of his beloved, Mui Leng. Living alone in their home that had her personality stamped across each piece of furniture was physically painful. So he had packed up, given away most of their belongings and moved, leaving all signs of her handiwork behind. The pain was still raw. The longing and the loneliness were so painful that on some days, he still struggled to get out of bed. He had mastered the art of keeping his pain suppressed allowing it to stack up, layer upon layer like kuih lapis.

Now he was frightened of self introspection. He was afraid of peeling back the layers for, like an onion, these would sting his eyes and cause him to cry. He was no longer entirely comfortable in this corporate environment. It hung on him like a badly cut suit. There were days when he thought the seams would give away and expose him for what he really was: a sad, old, lonely man. He had been playing charades with his personality for so long that he had forgotten who was behind the mask.

Chin Nam Berhad had humble beginnings. In its toddler years, it was still Chin Nam & Co. From a ground level shop on Holland Road, Chin Nam & Co had expanded and bought the entire building. Like a bird that had flown the proverbial nest and spread its wings, under Kah Sing, the company had proceeded to invest in a range of businesses, including housing and retail developments, hotels and restaurants. It was still a wonder to Kah Sing, how he had found the energy and stamina to nurture and grow a tiny seedling like his father's business into this giant conglomerate, like a banyan tree stretching its branches far and wide.

Kah Sing's thoughts turned to Ken, his only child and the heir to the family fortune. His hands made sweeping movements through the air. *How much of this does Ken want?* he wondered.

He needed to ask him questions, the answers to which he was afraid to hear. The truth was always more difficult to swallow.

Lies, half-truths and untruths always had a softer, gentler side. His head told him that Ken would have no choice but to come on board soon and join him on this journey. At 75, it was time he took a backseat. His heart though, whispered otherwise. *Don't do it. Don't force him into something he has no interest in. Look at you,* it said mockingly. *Don't crush his dreams.*

The words came tumbling out of Kah Sing's mouth as soon as Ken walked in. Like dirty pebbles falling to the ground. He wanted to pick them up, wash and give them to Ken on a platter. But there they lay in a heap by Ken's feet, waiting to be trampled on. A look of pain spread across Ken's face.

"What are you asking of me, Dad?" he asked incredulously. "How can I stay on now? I am in the midst of the biggest break I will ever get in my career and you are asking me to throw it away? I am due back in London in just over a week and it's going to be hard work for the next year. You know how much I wanted to be on the Limehouse project. Listen Dad, I'm not saying I'm never coming home. I just need a few years, that's all. I need to finish what I have started. Just give me a little time," he softly negotiated with his father. "I will take over from you, but not just yet. I need to resolve several issues Dad, personal and otherwise."

Kah Sing looked sadly at his only son. *What am I doing?* he thought. He opened his mouth to speak when he heard a gentle knock at the door. Rizal had no idea there was a wounded lion licking his wounds behind the closed door. He had with him his ubiquitous black folder tucked under his arm, held tight as he often worried that someone might snatch it and, with it, all his hard work. Kah Sing barked a curt, "Enter!" Rizal eagerly stepped in and was too excited and distracted to notice the dark look on the Chairman's face. Without hesitation, he released the folder from its safe place and pulled out a sheaf of papers.

"I have some good news, boss." he started. "The bio-technology company in Japan that I have been in preliminary discussions with are open to further negotiations with us. Their figures look good and I think we should seriously consider invest…" Rizal was not prepared for the tirade that came hurtling his way.

"ARE YOU MAD!!!" screamed Kah Sing. "Don't you know I have never done and will never do business with the Japanese? Don't you people know that I hate the fucking Japs. Take that proposal and chuck it in the bin, where it belongs!" he yelled.

"What's got into you?" Ken demanded, after Rizal had silently slunk out. "All the man did was come in with a proposal and you bit his head off. The staff are starting to talk about your erratic behaviour and I must agree with them."

Kah Sing swirled around and pointed an accusing finger at Ken.

"Don't you dare ask me to do business with the fucking Japanese. You haven't lived in fear and terror the way I have. When they invaded Malaya, they brought with them nothing but torture, death and rape. All we experienced for years was fear and hardship. Don't you forget that I saw my father - your grandfather - dragged away like a criminal. I saw fear in a proud man's eyes. Those bastards destroyed our family, so don't bloody tell me to do business with those dogs!"

Kah Sing's pain poured out of him and this time even whisky couldn't plug the leak. Grief upon grief, sorrow upon sorrow. Ken knew there was nothing left to be said and he left silently, closing the door on a man hunched over under a gathering of dark, angry clouds.

Geeta knew immediately when she heard his voice that something was wrong.

"Meet me, please. I need to see you. My father and I had kind of a heated exchange."

"I've just got home. I'll leave in 10 minutes. Shall I come to your home?"

"Yes," he replied.

Wrapped up in each other's arms, watching the twinkling city lights from the penthouse's vast balcony, Ken spoke to Geeta of the evening's earlier events and his father's immense hurt. She could feel the rapid beating of his heart against her shoulder blade and made no attempt to speak until she was sure he was done.

Silence finally settled over the pensive couple, a spell Geeta was reluctant to break.

"Ken, your father has obviously been through a very difficult time. It wasn't that long ago that your mother passed away either," Geeta gently spoke. "I think deep down, he just wants you to be happy but has trouble expressing his feelings."

"I don't want to think of him anymore, G. I'll be back in London in a week's time, let's just enjoy this time together." He hugged her closer to him. Now more than ever he needed the balm of her soothing words.

Leaving a disconsolate Ken was difficult for Geeta and for a brief moment, she entertained the idea of not returning home that night. *What a pair we are,* she thought on the quiet drive home. *At least Ken has the guts to tell his father what his heart desires, unlike me. Destined to play the role of a faux Brahmin daughter for an eternity.*

Padding quietly up the stairs to her bedroom, she softly 'clicked' the door shut and looked for her favourite salve for a sad heart, her grandfather's letters.

8th March 1924

Dearest Appa,

I am so very sorry to have read about Sita athai's untimely demise. It tore at my heart to read about it. She was my favourite athai and I still remember all her lovely ways. The way she used to put me on her feet and lift me. The song she used to sing to me while she held my little hands keep playing on my mind.

"Tenna marathalai yeradhai
Thengaiye pirikhadhai
Mamarathelai yeradhai
Manggayei pirikhadai

70

Aathele virzharaiya
Shethalai virzharaiya
Amman aathe kutaile virzharaiya"

Don't climb up the coconut tree
Don't pick the coconuts
Don't climb the mango tree
Don't pluck the mangoes
Do you want to fall in a pond?
Do you want to fall in a mudpit?
Or do you want to fall in your uncle's pond?

I remember how she used to worry about my poor eating habits, feeding me from her hand, mouthful after mouthful. She was a woman with nothing but love for us. It breaks my heart to think that I won't see her anymore. All I have of her are the letters she wrote to me and the memorable times I had with her which will forever be etched in my memory.

My work here is going well, by the grace of Ambal. In fact, you will be happy to note that I have been recently given a junior teaching position! It is only temporary but the headmaster of the school noticed that I had made some corrections to a letter he had written and was duly impressed. All your insistence on my learning English well has paid off! I will tell you this, Appa, I really enjoy the little bit of teaching that I do. It is a wonderful feeling to teach young eager minds, to fill their heads with words that can grow to become big ideas. What a gift it is to be a teacher!

I have made a new friend in my workplace, a Sikh gentleman named Devar Singh. He is a clerk and we have found that we have quite a bit in common. He has very kindly taken me under his wing (as he is a little older than I) and has taken me on his Sunday visits to the Gurdwara on Brick Kiln Road. We both enjoy the vegetarian food. I have never eaten so many chapattis! He has taken me to his home, I have met his wife, a gentle, soft spoken woman who comes from a village near Chandigarh. They have three lovely children. The one I connect well with is their 7 year old son, a precocious and handsome boy named Terlochan.

I need to go now, Appa, as I have some English papers to correct.

My namaskarams to Amma.

Your loving son,
Rangaswamy

12
LONDON
2008

Ken had been away for only two weeks now and Geeta was already missing him terribly. She was also very worried for his safety. After 9/11 and 7/7, London was always an attractive target for terrorists. She was going to visit him in December, over Christmas and as an added treat, celebrate his birthday on Boxing Day. She could hardly wait. She had made all her travel plans already – booked and paid for the ticket and had crossed out the three weeks she was going to be away in her legal diary.

The only thing she had failed to do to date was to inform her parents of her year-end plans. At least Ken had worked things out with his dad before he left, so now there was one less problem to worry about. They had talked at length that night and he had promised him that he would be back for good within two years.

She had heard her parents talking about going to Chennai in December for the Music Festival and she could have sworn she overheard them mention the possibility of her taking some time off work and going with them. Geeta had feigned ignorance and never asked them if their plans were confirmed. *What I don't enquire about, I don't know,* she convinced herself.

A month later, when she had her nose buried in a legal document, her mother popped the question and asked her if she could come with them to India.

"It would be nice for Appa and I if you could be there. We could do a short pilgrimage and attend some kacheris."

She was so engrossed in her work that the truth tumbled out of her mouth: "I can't, I'm going to London."

The silence that followed was deafening and for once Geeta gave thanks to her grandfather's clock for tick-tocking. She concentrated on the clock and watched her mother's face harden. *Oh, you stupid, stupid fool,* she reprimanded herself.

She finally looked up to face Parvathi and boldly said, "Yes, I will be in London for three weeks in December. I have an extra week of leave from last year and I thought it would be great to spend it there in winter."

She felt falsely brave. Her mother always had a way of undoing her by remaining stock still and doing absolutely nothing.

I hate it when she does that to me, she thought.

"And when were you going to tell me this, Geeta?" Parvathi asked in a stony voice. "After you had left?"

Spiteful and mean, thought Geeta.

"Well, it's only September and December is still such a long way off. So what's the big deal anyway? I've earned my leave and I will spend it when and where I want!" With that, she stormed out of the living room and seconds later slammed her bedroom door.

"I hate living here. I fucking hate it!" she screamed at her reflection in the mirror. *All my friends lead independent lives, even those who still live with their parents. And look at me,* she jabbed herself, *still afraid to tell them I'm going out at night. What kind of a coward am I?* Geeta decided that she was not going to be cowed. She would stand her ground and she would be on that flight, even if it killed her.

The next three months were tedious for Geeta and her parents. The tension was viscous. Every time one of them tried to cut it, it seeped back together, gelling even stronger than before. She made every excuse not to have meals with them and her parents in turn hurried and had their dinner early in the evening to avoid her. She came home late most nights and when she was home early, kept to her room. She had taken up pilates and had made going to the gym a regular routine. All this extra work paid off because by the time December came around, Geeta was looking well-toned and fit.

Her flight arrived on time just after day break. There was still a dark sky over London and she shuddered at the thought of the bitter cold. They had been told that the ground temperature was 2 degrees Celsius. She had come sufficiently prepared for winter – thermals, pashmina and a bright orange winter coat.

In the last hour during MH001's descent into Heathrow, Geeta had spent critical time in the lavatory, slavishly applying all sorts of creams that promised to 'awaken', 'rejuvenate' and 'brighten' her skin. She hadn't slept very well so she dabbed on concealer to hide her dark circles. She attempted to brush her hair but it defied all her strokes and stood high on her head, crackling with electric impulses. With a final spray of her favourite Jo Malone perfume and with a swift swish action of her lipstick, Geeta was finally ready to meet Ken.

She spotted him in the melee of relatives and friends waiting for passengers to come through the door. He looked fresh and she knew he would smell even better. All of a sudden she became conscious of her ruffled hair and crumpled clothes. She needn't have worried because he grabbed her and buried his face in her neck the minute she walked past the barricade.

Winter in London was everything she remembered it to be: bitterly cold, wet and dark. All her memories of London came rushing back like a long, forgotten secret. People with heads bent low, wrapped in scarves, hands shielded in gloves pushed deep into pockets, knee high boots making cold contact with the dirty squishy ground, the sound of commuters footfalls as they burrowed into the depths of underground stations to start their long journey home. And yet, it was magical too - the streets were lit with strands of twinkling necklaces, winking at the eager shoppers working through their Christmas lists.

She, in turn, had her head held high. She was in love, in a city that she loved, with the man she loved. Ken had taken time off work and they spent the rest of the day strolling down High Street Kensington, visiting old, favourite haunts, delighting in the fact that the Boots on the High Street still assaulted the olfactory sense with its pungent combination of perfumes.

They had tea at The Muffin Man and Geeta ordered her favourite passion cake and a pot of Earl Grey tea. They held hands across the small round tables squeezed so close together and spoke in Malay so that the older couple sitting right next to them wouldn't understand their conversation. Nights were spent catching up on the plays and musicals she had missed in the years she was at home in KL.

She felt like a child who had discovered snow for the first time and kept insisting on going outdoors every time the weather turned. She loved to feel the snow crunch beneath her feet. *The sound of potato chips,* she thought happily.

They were a couple in love and it was a welcome relief not to have to hide it. They held hands and stopped in the middle of crowded Oxford Street to share languorous kisses. She would wake in the middle of the night and reach out for him. She would wake him softly, kissing his ears and his face and they would make love slowly, each touching the other as if it were the first time. He loved the way her hair fell about her face, framing her perfectly. He took her nipple in his mouth and teased it until she felt she would burst. She climbed on top of him and took him in her, their entire focus was each other, each wanting the other to have the greater pleasure.

After their love-making, they lay with their bodies entwined, stroking each other in silence. This was when Geeta always cried. The worry, guilt and stress of her relationship with Ken overwhelmed her.

They celebrated Ken's birthday with Ken's aunt, Kye Li and her husband Steven at The River Cafe in Fulham. She was his father's younger sister and she had settled down in London, successfully running an art gallery.

Uncle Steven was Ken's favourite uncle. He was a fat and burly Scotsman with a wicked sense of humour. In the early days, it took Ken quite a while to understand what he was saying, the Scottish accent so thick. It was unfortunate that they only saw each other once a year at Chinese New Year when the two of them travelled back to Malaysia, until of course Ken moved to live in London. Now they spent many an evening imbibing Uncle Steven's favourite Laphroaig, which he swore was far superior to Kah Sing's Lagavulin. "The peatier, the meatier," he used to tease Ken.

Their early married life had been a blur of parties and nights out at clubs and, as a result, they kept postponing having children. When they were finally ready to exchange their dancing shoes for diapers, it was too late, so they happily indulged their favourite nephew instead.

Geeta enjoyed their company, especially listening to Uncle Steven regale them with stories of his experiences as a cardiovascular surgeon. He had retired from practice at Guys Hospital and now spent most days at his wife's gallery. They were all relaxed and enjoying the food, the conversation was frivolous, peppered with bits of gossip of what some of their colourful relatives were up to. Reluctant to end the night, they extended it with a night cap at The Dukes Bar. After one too many gin martinis, they hung to each other for dear life on the pavement to avoid collapsing in a giggling, drunken heap.

As Geeta and Ken only had a week left until the New Year with each other, they decided they would be hedonistic and spend it in a whirl of happiness and indulgence. They went shopping together and would split up in Selfridges, both in search of little gifts for each other. Every evening, they would unwrap one present each as they would each other and spend hours in front of the fire, making love, talking, playing games and laughing. The night before Geeta was due to leave, they went to The Glasshouse, an understated restaurant in Kew, that in Ken's opinion served the best duck breast. They spoke of the future in the present and Geeta knew that this was the man she would marry, this was the man she would grow old with and this was the man she would fight for.

When Ken passed her an envelope across the table, she took it with a puzzled look on her face.

"What's this?" she asked him.

"Open it and see," he said.

Geeta squealed in delight when she read the destination on the two business class tickets and immediately fell silent.

"I can't go. I've got to be back in KL. I have work waiting for me on my desk as we speak. I can't buzz off for another week!"

"You have little faith in me," said Ken with a smile. "I've sorted it all out. I've called Satnam and worked it out. He's okayed you taking an extra week, so you're not going home and we, my darling, are off to the Masai Mara tomorrow afternoon. We better get home and pack!"

Geeta hugged him, unable to speak. Words betrayed her, but then they were useless to her now anyway. She didn't need them to tell this man what he meant to her. He knew already.

13
15 MILES SOUTH OF IPOH
30TH JUNE 1942

The jungle is never friendly at night. It is the colours of pitch dark and blackout meshed together. It hangs from the trees like an invisible net waiting to wrap up unsuspecting intruders, loitering around in its muddy womb. Kah Hoe was its baby. He felt no fear. He was comfortable and comforted by the dark. He had walked away from the clearing, leaving his comrades behind. He needed to be alone for just a little while. The only thing he took for company was his packet of cigarettes. It offered him some light and calmed his nerves.

His unit had gone on a mission the night before, to blow up a bridge near Menglembu. On the way there, they ran into a Japanese patrol and there was an exchange of fire. Kah Hoe had made his first kill. He had shot a Japanese soldier not more than 20 years of age, right through his eye. One of his comrades had been shot twice in the leg - in the thigh and ankle. He had to be carried on a bamboo stretcher back to the clearing, the bullets still buried deep in his flesh. He was in shock and couldn't stop shaking.

Kah Hoe's mind kept racing back to that moment when he pulled the trigger and watched the soldier's breath escape at the other end of his gun. He could still see the soldier in all his youth crumple like a limp sheet to the ground, where the earth thirstily drank his blood. He could not rid his mind of that image, no matter how hard he tried. He instinctively knew that the soldier's death would revisit him like an unwelcome acquaintance from the past, for the rest of his life.

How my life has changed. A good life, a bad life and now an ugly existence. Each day is marked by the grating sound of razor sharp bayonets in practice combat and the dull thud of bodies falling to the ground as we go through our routine. Is this what I have reduced myself to? I can imagine filling out a job application. Previous work experience: Maiming and killing. Perfect requirements for a job in commerce.

His new home was a clearing in the forest, some 15 miles south of Ipoh. There were fifteen of them, rough and toughened by the excruciating circumstances and conditions of living in the camp. They were part of the 5th Malayan Peoples Anti-Japanese Army. When they first arrived, it had been harrowing just trying to make it through the dense thicket. It took them hours to clear a pathway, hacking through spindly bamboo trees and fattened branches. Then they had to fight off the mosquitoes, the silent enemy which could reduce the toughest of men to shivering and quivering victims of malaria.

Soon, makeshift huts sprouted out of the damp earth. The search for attap to use as roofs was futile and in the end they had to make do with the bamboo they had tirelessly cut down. Hidden this deep in the jungle, the immense canopies of the ancient trees cut off sunlight, keeping the camp dark, damp and unbearably humid.

Kah Hoe watched his cigarette shrink as he sucked hard on it, wishing it was a woman he was working so hard on. His thoughts were haphazard, all over the place and in different time zones. Bob's face kept appearing before him like a bad dream. *He betrayed Pa and Uncle Swamy's friendship. We used all our contacts to try and trace Pa but no one knew where he was detained and whether he was dead or alive. How we suffered, poor Mama - neither waking nor sleeping, in limbo. Those fucking bastards. For what they have done to him, they deserve everything we give back to them. One less Jap in this world, thanks to me,* he thought drily.

Kah Hoe's hatred for the Japanese simmered like a stew in a cauldron. Every day he added a new ingredient or spice to it. He stirred it with a heavy hand of revulsion and anger until all that was left was a strong and bitter potion. His concoction finally spilled over when the Kempetei rounded up all Chinese men suspected of being involved in anti-Japanese activity, then shot and beheaded them in cold blood. They gave it a name, 'Sook Ching' or 'purification through purge'.

He pressed his cigarette stub into the grass and wearily lifted his body. There was much to be done and his alone time had helped to clear his head. Chan's wounds were worrying them all. It was obvious that he needed medical attention urgently but how were they going to get him any help? Ah Seng, one of his comrades had heard of a contact person who was reliable and trustworthy who knew of a sympathetic doctor in Ipoh. They needed to find him fast if they were going to keep Chan alive.

He headed straight for Ah Seng when he got back to the camp. A few of them were already deep in conversation and he saw a stocky middle-aged man whose face he didn't recognise. All that he could glean from the intense discussion was that there was a safe house in Papan where they could get medical attention. It was manned by a supportive couple, a doctor and his wife. "I'll be back in about six hours. I need to make the arrangements," said the stocky man as he disappeared into the thick forest.

It was almost day break when he returned. The camp listened to the intricate arrangements he had made for this dangerous and treacherous journey. "Ok, I have worked everything out. We leave now on foot. Two of you will carry him out on a stretcher to the edge of the jungle. Once you get to the trunk road, there will be a vegetable lorry waiting to transport you to the safe house. You wait there till nightfall and only then head to the Doctor's house."

Speed and urgency were critical and Kah Hoe and Khim

were assigned to look after Chan. The journey was tough. The damp leaves that had fallen the night before made the forest floor slippery and there were many times when they nearly dropped Chan. He was already running a very high temperature and becoming delirious.

When they finally made it to the edge of the forest by morning, they were blinded by the intense rays of the sun, having hidden for so long in the dank and dark like mushrooms. As promised, a lorry was waiting for them. The driver had made a bed between the vegetables for Chan. From the depths of the vegetables, the lorry driver yanked out two bicycles for Kah Hoe and Khim to cycle to Papan.

"It's too dangerous to travel together," he explained. "Keep to the smaller roads and meet at the safe house." With those curt instructions, he swung himself into his lorry and disappeared in a cloud of dust. *Stay alive Chan,* Kah Hoe willed.

Kah Hoe and Khim followed the lorry driver's instructions and cycled separately to the designated safe house. They patiently waited until it was dark before making their way to No. 74 Main Street, the home of Dr Kathigasu and his Eurasian wife, Sybil. They went to the back door and knocked out the pattern they were given. They were let in by a slight bespectacled man who introduced himself as Thean Fook.

"Bring them in, Moru," called a female voice from inside.

He led them to a room where Chan was already stretched out on a makeshift operating table. Kah Hoe and Khim stood back and watched as Sybil prepared the anaesthetic. Once Chan had slipped off into a deep slumber, Dr Kathigasu worked on his wounds. The bullet in Chan's thigh had embedded itself comfortably in his muscle and Dr Kathigasu deftly removed the bullet and dressed the wound before he turned his attention to Chan's ankle. That wound had already turned septic and the bullet had shattered some smaller bones. It took the couple a while before they could differentiate bullet from bone. After some prodding they were finally able to find what they were after. They cleaned out the wound and there was a palpable sigh of relief in the treatment room.

"Here's one as a souvenir," declared Sybil, holding up the mangled lead in a pair of tweezers. "Moru, please make sure you bring him back here from the safe house every day to change his dressing," said Sybil.

Thanking the good doctor and his wife profusely, Kah Hoe and Khim allowed Thean Fook to show them out. They had to return to their camp that night itself and share the good news. At the door, Kah Hoe suddenly turned to face the doctor's assistant. A thought had clouded his mind.

"Hey, why do they call you Moru? You said your name was Thean Fook," he asked suspiciously.

"Because I like to drink moru," he answered in a monotone, matter-of-fact voice.

Kah Hoe shook his head and chuckled inwardly. *How ironic that two Chinese boys from such different backgrounds would find common ground over moru.*

14
KUALA LUMPUR
30TH JUNE 1942

Elaine cut a desolate figure on the balcony of 912 Batu Road. Her shoulders were tense and she felt completely and utterly at a loss. The last she saw of Kah Hoe was nearly four months ago. It was soon after Chin Nam had been dumped unceremoniously on their doorstep. The servant had seen a truck pull up and the soldiers kick a large sack to the ground. Only after they drove away, did she realise that it was a body. She approached it cautiously wondering if it was dead or alive. It took her several seconds before she recognised the body as her master's. Her screams sounded alien even to her.

Elaine was the first to reach her. She was so overwhelmed by what she saw before her. She covered her mouth to stop herself from gagging at the sight of her crumpled husband but instead, she threw up right next to him. The sound of the two women howling carried on the breeze and had sent Vairavar running towards them. He had to peel Elaine off Chin Nam's body and slap the servant to stop her beating her breasts.

"Tak da mati! Tak da mati!" he screamed at the both of them. They cried for Kah Hoe to help. Between them they finally managed to carry the beaten body inside.

What was left of Chin Nam's face was mush and pulp, his body a broken wreck. There were bruises and welts all over him. Not one bit of him had been spared. They had beaten him repeatedly, breaking several bones in his body, some more than once, that would eventually leave him limping and bent over for the rest of his life. It would be many weeks before he would be able to talk about his torture. And when he did, his voice would be devoid of emotion. It would seem as if he was narrating someone else's story, except for the steady stream of tears that rolled down his face.

In the days before he started talking, the whole household could only guess at how they must have tortured him.

"Pariahs, all pariahs," mumbled Vairavar to no one in particular. "I hope they face the same torture when this war is over. Karma will get these dogs," he went on.

"I can't bear to look at the blue black marks on his back," said the servant.

"Human beings can be most cruel," said Saras tearfully.

The nights were the toughest for Chin Nam. He would scream in agony, his body writhing in bed, fighting imaginary assailants. Most nights he would be woken up by Elaine who would change him out of his drenched clothes. She would lie in bed cradling him and assuring him he was safe now. But Chin Nam wouldn't feel safe for a very long time. The servants would sometimes find him cowering in a corner, his head buried in his hands, begging for mercy.

His wounds were slowly turning dark and angry. His fingernails had all been pulled out leaving black stumps in its place. Every day, Elaine and Saras would gently peel off the layers of gauze and patiently clean and dress his wounds. Chin Nam would always close his eyes when they unwrapped his fingers, wincing in pain and unwilling to face his physical deformities. He was too afraid to look at himself in the mirror and Elaine had to cover the mirrors in their bathroom and bedroom.

So much was going through her head as she stood on that balcony. Elaine had lost so much weight and her face looked tired and gaunt. She prayed for Kah Hoe's safety every day, just as she had done for her husband.

How cruel war is. There are never any winners, only losers, misery and untold agony. Unbearable pain and such deep loss. Chin Nam's spirit will never be the same. The sparkle and light have gone from his eyes. He had so much fire in his belly, so many dreams and aspirations. And now Kah Hoe has gone off and we don't know if he's dead or alive. I never thought my life would end up like this. If father could see me now, he would be so sad.

But God does provide in times of need. Swamy and Saras have been my guardian angels. How will I ever be able to repay them for all their kindness? Dear God, I pray you protect them from any harm. We have suffered enough. I don't think I can take any more pain. I am parched of tears. But what will become of my son? Will he come home alive or will I have to bury my young? Kah Sing has been my pillar of strength. The boy has remarkable grit, like his father. Who would have thought my 9 year old would be so industrious, buying produce at the market and providing a delivery service for a small fee. True entrepreneurship! Chin Nam would be so proud of him. I wonder if Chin Nam knows what's going on around him. How will he react if he finds out that his beloved Chin Nam and Co has been taken over by the very animals that ruined him?

Every evening Swamy would return home and sit with Chin Nam. He would talk to him about his work and share small anecdotes. He himself had been through several changes. The military had taken over Victoria Institution but retained him as a clerk. Like other civil servants, he was forced to learn 'Nippon-Go' and hated every minute of it. Swamy knew that ultimately he had no choice. He knew that it meant staying alive and taking home a meagre salary to feed his family, immediate and extended.

As night fell on 912 Batu Road, the lights went on in the bedrooms while the living room succumbed to the shadows. Eventually, the night sounds took over, drowning out the whispered pillow talk, silent prayers, voices reading and Tamil songs caressing the night.

15
PENANG
30TH JUNE 1942

Sleep had stopped visiting Tochi in the last two weeks. It happened suddenly and insidiously, first one night and then the next and the next. He would lie awake from dusk until the first light broke through the sky and he heard the distant sound of the muezzin, calling the faithful to prayer. He tried many different tactics – he read till 1am, had a stiff nightcap, then warm milk with turmeric. He tried each remedy individually and when that didn't work, he combined them. When that didn't help, he resigned himself to his fate: to lie awake rationalising with his demons to leave him be. This morning at 4am, he made his way to the prayer room and pleaded with God to clear his head of the confusion that had settled there.

Tochi sat facing the Granth Sahib, the 11th Guru and Living God, cross-legged on the floor in total deference to the Almighty. The events of the last year played before him like a movie in slow motion. Scene by scene, his mind replayed the tumultuous period in not just Malaya's history, but his own too. He remembered how the British had scurried like vermin escaping in the night and how he had been disheartened, no... disappointed and disgusted. So much so that he had even rejoiced at the arrival of the Japanese, singing their praises to his friends who were wary of them.

Tochi was learning to speak 'Nippon-Go'. So earnest was he in this new endeavour that he even joined the Speak Nippon-Go Association. He listened to Japanese music at home and could even sing the Japanese national anthem, Kimigayo. The change for Tochi was drastic but he welcomed it with hopeful, open arms. His usual salutation of, "Good Morning, Mr. Yap," had become, "Ohayo, Yap-san." He learnt the Japanese tradition of bowing, the more superior the status of the Japanese, the deeper the bow. Every morning, when Tochi went to the clinic, he took part in the mass exercise drills with great gusto, hoping to get his day off to a good start. The drills were conducted in tune to music on Radio Taisho.

Tochi had embraced the Japanese way of life, much to the irritation of his wife. Even at home, he insisted on listening to the news in Japanese and encouraged Dalip to speak in Japanese when possible. There had been many a fight in their household when Dalip had refused to speak the language. She had come to see a big change in her husband. It was not just the Japanese who had enchanted Tochi. He had also joined the Indian Independence League, which was committed to wresting power from the British and declaring India's independence with Japanese support.

Things eventually came to a head one evening when Tochi returned from a rally by Rash Behari Bose that was organised to support India's independence movement and to increase donations to the League. An intoxicated Tochi had stumbled home with a few of his League friends. He knew Dalip wouldn't be happy to see him in his current state and figured that a few extra allies in tow would help soften the blow. He was so far from the truth. Dalip was already seething when she opened the door but worked hard to keep her anger in check. She managed a cold "Hello" and a forced smile for his friends.

As she busied herself in the kitchen making the guests a pot of tea, she heard one of them ask Tochi how much he had pledged to the League. "$30," he whispered loudly enough for

Dalip to catch.

Storming out of the kitchen empty-handed she exploded, "$30! That's nearly a whole month's salary!"

The men looked at her in horror but knew better than to offer an excuse.

"People are going without food, children are starving and you go and give $30 to a bloody useless group of men preaching and ranting about independence in India! Why do you care about a country so far away! You will just replace the British with the Japanese. Do you honestly think we will get self-rule? Have you lost your mind? Do you know what I could do with that money? How could you be so stupid and irresponsible?" she yelled. "If it's not the Indian cause you are campaigning, you're sucking up to the wretched Japs! Everything in this house now is bloody Japanese. I hate it! You want me to speak the damn language and you have the gall to ask me to cook their tasteless food! Go to hell - you, the Japanese and all your friends here," she yelled.

"Ay, where do you think all those tins of sardines, butter, condensed milk and soap come from, ah? What, you think you look up to the sky and it drops from the heavens, huh?" Tochi drunkenly looked at his friends, winking for support. They had been stunned into silence by Dalip's outburst and made their hasty excuses to leave. It wouldn't be wise to be caught associating with an anti-Japanese protestor as they all knew the consequences that could follow. They mumbled their "good-byes" and slunk off like reprimanded school boys. Dalip threw the kitchen towel on the floor and stormed off.

Tochi wasn't blind to the brutality of the Japanese. He knew of the cruelty inflicted by them in Singapore where they murdered thousands of Chinese. He didn't have to look that far. At home in Penang, the Japanese had stormed Chung Ling High School, one of the island's top educational institutions that drew its students from as far away as Indonesia and Thailand. Soldiers had marched into the school and accused the teachers and students of collaborating with the enemy. They rounded up over 100 teachers and students and executed them. One morning outside the Clinic, Tochi had witnessed the Japanese roughly shove a group of Chinese men at rifle-point into a corner. Two spies, their faces covered by ominous black hoods, collaborators with the Japanese, pointed out several men, claiming them to be anti-Japanese. They were then loaded like cattle onto a waiting truck, probably never to be seen again.

Tochi had come to hate the walk to the market. In the past it was one of his favourite errands, stopping to talk to old friends along the way. Now, he kept his head bent low and tried not to look up at the beaten and decapitated heads of men looking down at him from the poles they were staked on. He always said his prayers for the departed souls as he hurried past. *If I just keep my mouth shut, work hard and learn Japanese, they cannot touch my family,* Tochi constantly told himself. *The British abandoned us, the Japanese have liberated us, I have to think of my family's future.* He repeated this over and over again to himself and each time, his heart ached a little more and his sleep became more restless.

On a quiet afternoon when work at the Clinic was slow, Tochi was enjoying a cup of thick black coffee with his old school friend, Kim Seng. The genial chatter in the coffeeshop suddenly turned to silence when a Japanese officer strode in. Cups clattered on saucers and chairs scraped on the floor as patrons immediately shot to their feet, ready to bow. This was an automatic action for Tochi who was already staring at the tiled floor. Kim Seng defiantly sat still, watching the soldiers intently.

Immediately the officer yanked Kim Seng off his stool and hit him hard in the gut. Tochi watched as his friend fell to the floor but didn't move a muscle. The officer barked an order to his entourage and smelling blood and an easy prey, they leapt on Kim Seng, two holding him up while another punched him over and over again in the head and stomach. Tochi immediately drew himself up to his full height and pleaded with the officer in Nippon-Go.

"Shut your fucking mouth, you black monkey. You think you can speak a few words of our language and you can tell me what to do?" the officer sneered. He then slapped Tochi hard across the face and spat straight into his eyes. "Show this black monkey how we discipline those who do not bow." The minutes that followed were the longest in Tochi's life as he watched his dear friend Kim Seng viciously punched and kicked senseless. Second by second, time crept by and blow upon blow fell upon a now unconscious and badly bleeding Kim Seng. A kaleidoscope of violence multiplied hundreds of times through the tears in Tochi's eyes.

Tears were still running down his face when the soldiers finally tired themselves out. The officer turned to the motionless patrons, barked an order and left. Tochi feared for the life of his friend and prayed very hard that he would make it to the hospital alive. And with help from the now not-so-motionless patrons, they managed to get Kim Seng to hospital quickly.

Kim Seng had suffered critical internal injuries including broken ribs and a punctured lung. He was lucky to be alive, the doctors declared. All night long, Tochi sat by Kim Seng's bed waiting for his friend to open his swollen eyes. *I'm so sorry Kim Seng, I shouldn't have opened my stupid mouth,* Tochi hung his head in shame at the recollection. *Dear God, let this man live, dear God, let this man live,* he prayed on repeat.

This was one of the unfortunate string of events that had brought on Tochi's insomnia and plagued his conscience. He tried rationalising with himself that things were still looking good for his family. They had access to little luxuries and they weren't harassed like some of his other friends. Yet something was changing inside. The brutality that Kim Seng had suffered had nearly ended his life. It tortured him to see the constant carnage at the Clinic and he wrangled with his conscience every single night. Watching his innocent, beautiful Chinese baby fast asleep in his cot, oblivious to the killing, the blood and the constant brutality, the truth dawned on him - his new overlords were a cruel, cruel people who were neither interested in bringing freedom nor self-rule to Malaya.

He repeated the words that would always give him comfort, that would wrap him up in their meaning and from which he drew strength. It was his first breath and he knew it would also be his last....

Ik o'nkaar
Sat – naam

"God is One
Truth is His Name"

Tochi heard the cockerel proudly announce daylight, a new day was just beginning.

16
AN EMAIL TO KEN
KUALA LUMPUR, 2009

31 Jan 2009
From: Geeta Ramesh
Sent: Saturday, January 31, 2009 10.39 PM
To: Ken Tan [mailto:hotmale@hotmail.com]
Subject: Missing You

My darling,

It hasn't even been a month since I left you and it already feels like a lifetime. How I hate the parting and even worse, the many days that roll into each other – stretching it out, making it unbearable for me. I can't take it without you. It has become so clear to me that my happiness is dependent on you, my love. I want nothing more than to bury my face in your neck, to feel you wrap your arms around me and make me feel safe.

Enough of my lovesick whining! But I can't seem to help it – I love you so desperately. The days are not so bad because I am really caught up with work but the nights are tough. My mind keeps travelling back to the days we spent in London, strolling down High Street Ken, smooching, fighting over the last remnants of the cheese toasties! And Kenya, under the stars, in our tent. But the best of all was our love-making! I can smell you right now. I want to inhale you so that you become a part of me, a part of my breath. I want to run my fingers through your hair, feel your lips on mine and never let you go. Please promise me that this is the last time we will be apart from each other. I can't be separated from you, ever.

As you know, it's Chinese New Year and the office is closed for a whole week. My 'supposed' Punjabi boss is attempting to embrace his Chinese heritage! Isn't that how it will be for our children one day! God, how far ahead I am dreaming!

Darling, you aren't going to be very impressed with me – I haven't been able to summon the courage to tell my parents. Please don't be angry. Every time I want to say something, my throat constricts and I can't seem to find the words. Maybe it would be easier if you were here, then I could run to you and hide in your arms. I know, I can hear you say I am a cop out. Please darling, bear with me. I will tell them, I promise you. I am not willing to let you go, not for anyone in the world.

Well, enough said about what I need to do. We were at your dad's place for his open house party and it was awful. My parents came with me and it was so awkward; your dad was so warm and affectionate with me. He actually asked me when I was getting married so he could stop giving me ang pows. He did it in front of my parents and even winked at me! I wanted to curl up and die! The food was great and your dad in his usual thoughtful way had plenty of vegetarian food for us. How I missed you.

I spent most of the run up to Chinese New Year shopping and hanging out with my friends. I was hoping things would quieten down before the long weekend but as luck would have it, a huge and controversial brief landed on my table. Actually, I can't complain because it's quite interesting. It involves the arrest and detention of five suspected terrorists who are supposed to be a part of a group who call themselves the Jemaah Islamiah. This brief has got the whole office divided into two camps! One camp, headed by Rafizi, who is of the opinion that they should be locked up and the key thrown away! I keep reminding him that everyone deserves a right to representation and I keep pointing out to him that he is a lawyer! Isn't it strange how emotions can creep into the psyche to play havoc with common sense and objectiveness. Mind you, I am talking about a group of educated, professional individuals. For me, I truly do believe the right of every individual to a fair trial. They have alleged that these five had explosives and firearms. The joke is these buggers haven't proved a fucking thing! And what sucks is that in spite of there being no proof; they will be thrown in under the ISA. It stinks to high heaven.

Oh well, I'm visiting Emily tomorrow with the rest of the gang from the office – that will be fun, she has promised us lots of wine and good food! I'm not complaining. Remember my cousin Sowmya, the one who gave in to an arranged marriage? Well, it looks like it's working for her. She and her husband are moving to Sydney, so lucky her.

All right my love, I ought to finish this here or else I will never press send!

I love you for ever and ever...... and ever.

G XXX

P.S. I can't get the baboons and hippos from the Mara out of my head! Must be something to do with the state of our politics!

17
AN UNSUITABLE BOY
KUALA LUMPUR, 2009

It was just after midnight and all that Geeta had for company was a latte-coloured gecko, clicking away at her, disapproving of the late hour. She was oblivious to its presence, as she hunched over a stack of papers. Buried at the bottom of all the files and books was the dining table, still faintly smelling of the ghee that had seeped into its grain, forever staining it an oily brown.

She stood up, stretched her limbs and checked the time on her grandfather's clock. She was only halfway through her submission and she was already feeling brain dead. *Not an option right now,* she thought to herself. She headed for the kitchen to make herself her third cup of coffee for the night. *I'd much rather death by chocolate than by coffee. But I have to keep awake!* When she walked back to the dining room she was surprised to see her mother poring over her work as if looking for clues to her daughter's life.

"What are you doing up, Amma?"

"I woke up to go to the bathroom and I noticed the light still on downstairs so I thought I'd take a look. What are you working so hard on, kanne? When does this need to be ready? It's so late, you should be in bed. Can't it wait till tomorrow?"

So many questions, I don't need this now! I wish she'd go back to bed.

Parvathi had something to say to her daughter and they were both bristling with that knowledge. Not knowing where or how to begin, she absentmindedly tidied Geeta's papers into neat piles. With her burst of activity she didn't notice Geeta silently seething.

"You see Geeta, Appa and I hardly see you and there is something we have been wanting to tell you for awhile," she said in what she thought was a steady voice.

She's got to be kidding me! I am neck deep in my work, it's past midnight, I am dead beat and she wants to talk to me about something totally irrelevant, I am sure. Shanti, Geeta. Stay calm. Don't lose your cool!

Not getting any response from Geeta gave her mother a little more courage to carry on.

"There's been a proposal for you from Singapore. He's a good boy from a very good family. He's a doctor about your age and he's about to finish his specialist exams. He will soon be a cardiologist!" she declared with such pride.

If she had looked up from her hands, she would have seen Geeta exhaling fire.

"They have seen your photo and your horoscopes match and we would like you to just take a look at his photo and see what you think. If you could meet him just once, Appa and I will be happy," she pleaded.

"Ma, can you hear yourself? You are asking me to agree to an arranged marriage! Do you know just how ridiculous you sound? Don't you and Appa know by now that I will NOT agree to one? Have you not been hearing a thing I have been saying all along? Why did you give me an education only to clip my wings now, when I am ready to fly? There's no way I'm going to meet this fellow, Ma. You and Appa had better come to terms with that. I am not marrying a Brahmin boy to become subservient in his mother's house. I WILL NOT marry someone I don't love.

I can't do what Sowmya did. I'm sorry. I am not the daughter Sowmya is. I can never be someone other than me. Please don't bring this up with me again," Geeta was astonished at how calm she was.

"But what will we tell this boy's family? Please Geeta, for Appa's sake, at least meet him once ," pleaded Parvathi.

"What am I supposed to say when I meet him? That I'm sorry that my parents put you up to this? I'm sure you're a nice guy but I don't want to spend the rest of my life with you! Are you mad! Stop this right now, Ma. I don't want to talk about this ever again. Don't test me. And don't blackmail me by using Appa's name. That was an unfair thing to do."

"How dare you speak to me like that! Just because you are educated and a lawyer today doesn't give you the right to raise your voice at me in my house. Don't forget that you are who you are because of what we gave you. I will not allow you to speak ill of our traditions and customs. You think by studying in England you have become a vellakari. You had better take a good look in the mirror. You carry your father's name and you had better not bring shame to him! Learn to behave like the Indian you are, Geeta. None of these fancy Western ways. Too much freedom we have given you and for what! Ungrateful, you are. I am ashamed at how proud and arrogant you have become. Thank God your Athai isn't here to hear you speak like this. She would have had something harsh to say to you!" With that she turned around and walked upstairs, her back ramrod straight.

She couldn't stop the tears. Big fat salty tears wet her dry cracked lips. Regret for words hastily said in anger curdled in Geeta's stomach. She abandoned her work and dragged her feet up the stairs to her room.

She knew she wouldn't be able to sleep for some time so she pulled out her Tata's letters, eager for a distraction from the unpleasant confrontation. *If Tata were still alive, would he help me?* She wondered. *Would he approve of Ken?*

Dearest Appa,

How lovely, Appa, that your letter arrived on my birthday! That was a lovely present and the contents of your letter were truly surprising. I must add that it was a pleasant one! This girl Saraswathi is beautiful. I am compelled to use the adjective radiant, even! I am delighted that the astrologer has said that we are a perfect match. Have you and Amma met her? Is she soft spoken and graceful like Amma?

I was unable to contain myself and I have already spoken to my Headmaster about my impending kalyanam! He has agreed to me taking three months off so that I can come home to get married. I showed him Saraswathi's picture and he agreed that I shouldn't delay it any longer or she may accept someone else's proposal! Of course, the English have no idea that in our custom, once the intention has been spoken, it is blessed by the stars.

I am so excited at the prospect of seeing you and Amma that I have taken my calendar down and started crossing out the days. I hope she will be happy to come back with me to Malaya. There is much hope and potential for this country, Appa. As much as I miss Thanjavur and Madras, I am slowly growing to love this new home of mine. What I find amazing, is the diversity of people and cultures. I have made a few good friends and I have taken up some hobbies but reading is still on the top of my list. You will be most happy to know that I have started playing cricket again. Twice a week, some of the other teachers and I wear our whites and we do make a pretty sight.

The teachers and staff had a Christmas party last week. We had put up a Christmas tree and there were carollers singing all the carols! It was a good and lively gathering. There was a mass in the school chapel and we all attended it wearing our best clothes. I must say the atmosphere was peaceful and the experience pleasant. It was quite amazing that so many of us who were not Christians gathered in the chapel and bowed our heads in prayer, each praying according to our own faiths yet happy to be where we were. I couldn't help but wonder why we fuss so much about the caste system. People from different races sitting together was a beautiful lesson in humanity. Don't you think so, Appa?

I will write to you or maybe even send you a telegram to give you details of my arrival. I am going to book my passage soon. Tell Amma to start preparing all my favourite 'uzhuhais - vadu manga and thoku!'

My namaskarams to Amma and you.

Your loving son,
Rangaswamy

Geeta put the letter down with a huge sigh. She contemplated her Tata's excitement; the complete antithesis to how she was feeling. She knew just as Tata knew his arranged marriage would be the start of new beginnings, the same for her would spell the beginning of the end. The time for procrastination was over. *I will write them a letter and tell them that I have lost my heart to another. My deceit has to stop.*

18
A LETTER TO APPA AND AMMA
KUALA LUMPUR, 2009

Dearest Appa and Amma,

First and foremost, I owe you both an apology for my outburst last night. No matter what, I should never have raised my voice with you Amma, and for that I am very sorry. But I do think the time has come for me to iron things out with the both of you. Over the last six months we have become so distant. You have your dinner before I come home and when I get back, I end up spending most of my time in my room. To think we used to sit together in the living room and I used to tell you both about my day and we would chat about politics and the extended family. Truth be told, I miss that. How did we lose that so easily? It's as if we are strangers living under the same roof!

But I think I need to tell you how I feel. Appa and Amma, you both know my thoughts on the subject of arranged marriages. I have never hidden my dislike for it. You know how vocal I was about Sowmya's wedding. Sometimes I don't understand what you want from me. You both always said how important an education was and you were so keen on an English education for me. You raised me to be independent and broad minded, to be able to discuss politics or social issues of the day and on the flip side you still want me to think like a traditional Indian (might I add Brahmin) girl and agree to an arranged marriage!

Somehow, I am unable to reconcile the two. I have been given every opportunity and I have taken every challenge that has come my way. I have never cowed in fear but have always looked on them as challenges. Isn't that what you taught me, Pa? How do you expect me to marry someone who the astrologer says I will be compatible with? Doesn't it sound just a little ludicrous in this day and age? Even Brahmins in India are becoming more broad-minded. In fact, don't you have some friend whose daughter married someone she met on the internet?

I want to say this very clearly: I will not agree to an arranged marriage. I don't believe in it, I don't believe in the caste system and I will not be coerced into one. I am still a traditional girl at heart; I have a great respect for our culture but I don't agree with some of the practices. Just because I don't agree to an arranged marriage doesn't mean I don't love you or that I disrespect you. But I do feel that you both too should respect me for who I am and for the choices I make. I am 28 and I would like to decide who I am going to marry. I want to be happy with the choices I make with my life, especially one as important as my marriage partner. Pa, I can't wake up every morning to a person I hardly know. You both must understand it was a different time for the two of you and many others. But I want to be in love with the person I marry. I don't know if you can understand that.

Since I am pouring my heart out, I want to tell you both that there is someone in my life. I know you both are going to be very upset and angry but I sincerely hope that you will find it in your heart to understand my feelings. I have been seeing Ken, Uncle Kah Sing's son. He's a good man, Ma. You know the family and they are good, honest, lovely people. He loves me and he wants to marry me. He's going to finish his project within a year or two and he will be back to take over from Uncle Kah Sing. Please don't be angry and try to understand. I've wanted to tell you but I haven't had the courage. But I think the time has come for me to be honest

102

with you. I would like to be able to talk about it without tears and anger. You both are very important to me and I don't want to lose you. Please try and see things from my perspective.

Much love,
Geeta

19
AMMA'S FURY, APPA'S FURY, GEETA'S FURY
KUALA LUMPUR, 2009

The letter sat on the prayer table like a bad omen. They knew it the moment they saw it. After last night's outburst, they expected it like they did the afternoon rain.

"There is absolutely no way I will accept this! It is out of the question. What is she thinking? Didn't we always tell her that she had to accept our customs and traditions? How can she go and do this? It's all this Western education that you were so crazy about! Education gives you a daughter who is stubborn, that's what it gives you! Ipo numba yenna pannaporam," wept Parvathi in despair. Ramesh was silent, busying himself with filling the oil lamps with ghee. Neither wanted to open the letter. Neither wished to read the contents and have it burned into their memory.

All Ramesh could hear was her incessant voice drowning out his own thoughts. He could feel his head filling up with her noise and he finally turned around and yelled for her to shut up.

"It's you. Ellamai on thappu, Parvathi. You should have taught her our customs. I worked every single day of my life and now you are telling me I didn't raise my daughter well? Nee yenggai irinthai? Yetho oru mami aathalai, at some pattu class or recital. Why didn't you take her for veena or bharatha natyam classes? Ipo nee ninindhe yennai thitriyai ni! Andhe yezheve letter, thorondhu padi."

Within minutes their faces went ashen and Ramesh's knuckles turned white. When she read the name 'Kah Sing', it was as if she were spitting venom.

"Shandala pavi," Ramesh spat with even more venom. "That bastard! I am sure he knows about this illicit affair and he must be laughing behind my back! I know one thing is clear to me. I will have nothing to do with that filthy lot and I will have nothing to do with Geeta. She does not exist and I don't want her name spoken in my presence." With that he turned and walked away.

Parvathi wrung the end of her sari and sobbed. She sat at the prayer table and cursed her life. "How could you do this to us? Nambe yennai thappu pannum" she berated Ambal. "What is it that we haven't done for you? A Chinese man, how could she insult us like this? Not even an Indian Hindu boy. Why are you making us suffer like this? The whole Brahmin community is going to laugh at us. Is that what you want? For us to hang our heads in shame? He says he doesn't want to have anything to do with Geeta. The truth of it is neither do I. She has betrayed us and let us down. I can't look at her without feeling disgusted." With that, Parvathi tore the letter into tiny white flecks and threw it in the bin to mingle with ghee-stained tissues.

Depression descended on the household. Three ghosts occupied the home, each staying clear of the other. Parvathi, so engrossed in her grief, had taken to sleeping in the guest room and Ramesh had neither the energy nor the interest in reeling her back. As for Geeta, she floated around the house like an apparition, taking care not to come into any contact with her non-speaking parents. There was no mention of the letter and she was too afraid to bring it up. She stayed at a friend's house over the weekend and no one even noticed her absence. The next Sunday lunch was cancelled. This time the maid made the phone calls, informing all Sunday-lunch-goers that her ma'am was down with the flu.

Geeta came home early on Monday because she wasn't

feeling well. She so wished she could turn back but it was too late. Both her parents were sitting in the living room and she felt like she had walked into the early tremors of an earthquake. Their fear and anger were ready to erupt and now Geeta stood there, at the epicentre. There was no turning back as she stood there absorbing all the hate that was swiftly directed at her.

"Paavi!" Ramesh shouted.

Geeta's jaw dropped. She had meant to greet him but no words would come out.

"How dare you stand there and look at me in the face! Aren't you ashamed of yourself? You have behaved like a cheap slut and now you try and look innocent!"

Parvathi was silently crying yet trying to hush her husband. He turned to her and told her to shut up as he pushed her away.

The sight of her parents bickering brought Geeta back to her fiery senses, "How dare you call me a slut!" she retorted, her head pounding from a poisonous combination of headache and anger. "You were never willing to listen to me. You and Amma were always caught up in your self-righteous Brahmin crap. You can never see the good in others. If they are not Brahmin then they can't amount to much! Can you imagine that! You have lived in this country all your life and you talk like this! Even the Brahmins in India are more tolerant than you both. I am ashamed of this awful caste system. How can you two take such pride in belonging to a caste that looks down on other people!"

"Don't you talk to your Appa like that!" yelled Parvathi.

"Well, it's time we had this out and it's time you heard some home truths," Geeta spat back.

"He betrayed me! He was supposed to be a friend and you have brought shame to this family," yelled Ramesh.

"How have they betrayed you and how have I shamed this family? By wanting to marry a man who is not a Brahmin?" Geeta laughed out loud. "You would rather I marry a Brahmin from another country who may be a good-for-nothing or serial killer than see me happy with my life. How selfish can you both be – to think that only you know what's good for me and that my happiness is immaterial? Only maintaining your face in your

106

small-minded community will make you happy. How can you say they betrayed you? Tata would be devastated to hear you speak like this. Tata and Uncle Kah Sing's father were as close as brothers. They stood by each other and helped each other during difficult times. To think you will forsake a generation of friendship because I want to marry the grandson! How shallow you are!"

"My father took them in during the war and this is how they repay us for our kindness? By stealing one of our own! Some friend he is! He is nothing more than a common thief and I want you to have nothing to do with that family. That is final!"

"Well, I have news for you. I am marrying Ken with or without your blessings! I love him and that's not about to change."

"Get out of my house," hissed Ramesh, through clenched teeth. "Get out and don't come back until you come to your senses."

"Don't worry, I wouldn't want to stay here a moment longer," Geeta retorted defiantly.

At that moment, she decided to go to her one ally in this whole world – Krishna Chitappa. Still seething, Geeta chucked whatever clothes she could into a suitcase, grabbed the box that sat at the foot of her bed and stormed out of the house. Her parents stood in different corners of the living room neither seeing nor hearing, so blinded and deafened were they by their hate and angst.

She only allowed herself to cry when she saw the look of concern on Krishna Chitappa's face. He knew this was coming; it was just a matter of time that his little Geeta would fight back against all that was expected of her, just like he had tried to do all those many years ago.

20
PENANG
15TH NOVEMBER 1942

Tochi had become a chameleon overnight. On the streets and at work he still sang the praises of the Japanese. He continued to sing their songs and continued to speak their language. He was even promoted to Hospital Assistant at the General Hospital. He seemed to have flourished during the Occupation. The Japanese liked him. They made an example of him to other locals, pointing out his love of all things Japanese and his willingness to embrace their culture. Why, they even asked him to tutor at the Speak Nippon-Go Association.

Behind closed doors though, Tochi shed his Japanese veneer. They had driven him to hate them. He would stand in his bathroom and scoop cold water on his body, scrubbing it down until his skin turned a bright red. He knew he had to keep the pretence going. He had a mission and that meant being courteous and pleasant to the people he had grown to despise. His loyalty to the Japanese had earned him several special rights. He had become good friends with the Kumiais – the officials who were in charge of the distribution of commodities and foodstuff. Tochi had access to basic necessities like soap, razor blades, medicines, tins of sardines and butter. He was even able

108

to procure ladies underwear and silk for those who so desired these.

But the biggest earner in Tochi's basket of goods were cigarettes. He carefully nurtured a thriving little business from home, selling these now precious luxuries to people who could afford them. He gave the profits away to families that had been robbed of their fathers and had little means of making ends meet. Several of his Chinese friends helped him identify such families through the traditional Chinese clan associations. Money was discreetly passed on from one willing hand to needy mouths. This would be Tochi's salvation for some time to come.

Tochi was a creature of habit and habit decreed that he visit the Gurdwara every Sunday. It was always the same comforting routine and he looked forward to seeing familiar faces. During these uncertain times, it was nice to have some certainties in life. And this was certainly one of them. He was at the temple by 10.30 in the morning and after greeting the elders Sat Sri Akal, he made his way to the kitchen and helped himself to a small stainless steel cup of tea, the very tea he had been surreptitiously supplying to the temple. He missed the usual breakfast fare of chapattis, dhall and pickle. *What a treat it would be for all these old people to have just one chapati each,* he thought to himself.

The conversations around him were conducted in hushed tones. Most heads were bowed in prayer. Everyone had a request for the Almighty and Tochi was willing to bet his last dollar that the common prayer was for the war to end and the exit of the Japanese. Tochi was deep in prayer when an unfamiliar voice startled him, "Hello Terlochan." Tochi turned to face the stranger and greeted him back.

"I don't think we have met before," he said to the kind face that wore age well.

"No, you don't know me. I am from Ipoh. If you don't mind I would like to talk to you in private. I hear that you help Chinese families."

"No," said Tochi immediately, glancing around nervously. "I don't know where you heard this from but it's not true. I'm sorry," he said with a frown etching across his forehead.

"I know your friend Hong Huat and he told me that I could speak to you freely," the stranger continued.

Tochi's frown instantly ironed itself out as he relaxed at the mention of their mutual friend's name. Hong Huat was one of Tochi's closest and most trusted confidants in his Robin Hood endeavours. If the stranger knew Hong Huat, then he was someone Tochi could trust.

Tochi carefully scanned the area to make sure that no one was listening to their conversation. When he felt it safe to respond, he whispered, "Come to my house tonight. I live at 88 Sri Bahari Road and my wife will not be at home. Make sure it's dark before you leave and that you are not being followed."

It was late when the stranger finally rapped on Tochi's door. Tochi let him in silently and led him to the dimly lit living room.

"You know my name, brother, but I didn't catch yours."

"My name is Gurchan. Formerly of the Malayan Police Force and last based in Ipoh before the war."

"Can I offer you a scotch, Gurchan?" Tochi asked with a smile as he shook Gurchan's large hand.

"I have heard many things about you, Mr Terlochan, but a bottle of Johnnie Walker has got to be the most laudable thing about you!" replied Gurchan with a hearty laugh.

"Please, my friends call me Tochi," he responded. With pleasantries exchanged and drinks poured, the two men finally sat down to discuss the business at hand.

"Tochi, do you have any idea how the war is progressing in Europe and in Malaya?" Gurchan asked, his steely gaze holding Tochi's full attention.

"I have no access to a wireless. As you know, these were all confiscated by the Japs. Of course, there is the Penang Shinbum but everything they print is simply propaganda. The bits of news I hear from my colleagues at the Hospital usually contradict the newspaper reports, so…" Tochi's voice trailed off.

Truth be told, he had very little idea of the events playing out beyond Penang's shores and he felt embarrassed to admit as much to his guest. He sighed almost to himself, "If it weren't for

110

Singa's posters, I think I'd be even more in the dark."

Gurchan raised a quizzical eyebrow over his whiskey tumbler.

"The Singa posters," Tochi explained, "usually appear every fortnight or so on walls, lamp posts and other public places. Updates on the war, how the Japs are being battered by the MPAJA. These posters are usually only up for a few hours before the Japs tear these down. He's a brave man this Singa, whoever he is." Tochi watched Gurchan chuckle to himself.

"I wouldn't bestow on him such an honour. It is totally misplaced," he said quietly.

Tochi jumped up from his chair and pointed a trembling finger at Gurchan.

"You are Singa, aren't you?" he said unable to hide his excitement. "How could I have been so stupid? You are Singh-a, the lion, aren't you?"

Gurchan smiled, "Singa is more than one person. But you are partially right, I am the courier."

Pouring out another peg of whiskey for them both, Gurchan managed to quell the excitement and finish what he had started.

"I need some help putting up the posters. Would you be willing to help? I am only asking you because I was told I could trust you. You need to give me an honest answer. If you can't, then we will forget we ever had this conversation".

Tochi's response was effusive and spontaneous. "Of course, of course you can count on me! It will be an honour to be a part of your brave effort."

By the time their conversation had run dry, well into the wee hours of the morning, so had the once full bottle of Johnnie Walker. It lay on its side just like the two men sprawled across the floor.

21
KUALA LUMPUR
15TH NOVEMBER 1942

Swamy had learnt to live with the bile that rose frequently to the surface of his palate. It had been nine months since he started working for the Japanese and he was desperately trying to make the best of it. It felt like a long drawn and painful pregnancy with no easy labour in sight. His Nippon-Go was improving rapidly as were his public relation skills. He had mastered the art of saying 'ohayo san' while smiling and bowing down low – all in one seamless action that started with his face and ended at his waist.

His English skills endeared him to the Japanese - not to be mistaken with affection – and they had one very important job for Swamy. Every day he was tasked with listening to the BBC News Service and other English news channels to provide a summary of current events. The fact that he was Indian also worked in his favour as the Japanese distrusted the Chinese and trusted the Indians a little more. Swamy was therefore on the verge of becoming an 'insider' as he was often asked to decipher and translate documents that were left behind by the British.

Swamy's favourite assignment was tuning in to the relevant radio stations and soaking up the news. He would store the information in his head, carefully carry it home and regurgitate it to his family and Chin Nam. He was extremely careful about passing the news on and warned his family not to repeat a word outside of 912. The fear of Japanese cruelty far outweighed the excitement of any good news.

Swamy loved returning home after a stressful day working for the Japanese. Stepping into his home, he thought he felt fresh strands of grey hair inching through his scalp to find their place under the Japanese sun. There was hard work that Swamy needed to carry out at home as well, as Chin Nam had suffered enormous physical and mental damage. While his physical scars were slowly healing, his mental scars frazzled like sour mango on the tongue. Even so, his healing had left him with three fingers missing; gangrene had insidiously set in where they had pulled out his nails.

Elaine's patience was slowly starting to pay off. With hour upon hour of sitting with him, talking to him, reading to him and with Swamy's and Saras' optimistic spirits, Chin Nam was now able to sit at the dining table and take part in short spurts of conversation. Often he retracted into his world of still silence, with the salty tears that ran down his face the only testament that he was physically alive.

Swamy's route home was typically the same. He loved the freedom of clambering onto his big, sturdy and dependable black bicycle and riding away from Victoria Institution to his safe haven. He always looked out for his favourite trees along the way. One was the fully grown frangipani tree crowned with its heavy bloom of fragrant white flowers, the other was the majestic red flame of the forest that stood on the corner of Batu Road. To him, these ancient trees marked the spirit of resilience in the face of adversity.

He always took the corner at a tight enough angle just to feel the thrill race through his body and he always laughed out loud at exactly the same spot. He hopped off his bicycle at the garden gate and walked up his drive, marvelling at the amazing tenacity of nature. His mango tree had beautiful green jewels hanging from its branches. *I must remind Saras to either leave them and let them ripen or pluck them and make some mangga thokku.* He could never say the name of the pickle without setting his taste buds a-tingling.

He thought he saw a shadow sitting at the top of the front steps. Well, more like a runt of a man. From where he was, the visitor looked rake thin, yes, with yellow skin and covered in scabs. It wasn't until he walked closer and peered at the man that he saw the vague similarity between the skeleton on the steps and the rambunctious Kah Hoe of the past.

"My God!" cried out Swamy. "Is that really you, Kah Hoe?"

Kah Hoe nodded in agreement either from exhaustion or the inability to speak. Swamy was so pleased to see him but afraid to slap him in a friendly fashion on the back for fear that his bones might crumble.

"Have your parents seen you? How long have you been sitting here? When did you come home? Where have you been that you look like this?"

The questions tumbled out of his mouth faster than he could ask them. "Come on, come on, son. Let's go in," Swamy said with sudden urgency, turning to look behind him to see if there was anyone watching. "It could be dangerous for you to be out here."

With Kah Hoe's mysterious appearance, the Rangaswamy kitchen took on a bustle quite unlike any other weeknight; it seemed as if even the pots and pans celebrated the return of a loved son. The children certainly knew 'koko' was back and they were telling anyone who might listen from their soft toys to the furniture. In the midst of all this hullabaloo, Elaine was making futile attempts to 'shush' down the noise, while she flailed her arms at the same time. She was fearful that the sound of loud voices from their house would alert the Japanese to her son's return.

There was more food on the dining table tonight and all members of the household sat huddled and squished together. Hands were flying in every direction trying to reach for the rice, the thin vegetable broth (which in another life might have been called a sambar), some crunchy, stir-fried vegetables (perfect for the Chinese palate) and an absolute must-have for the Indians –

plain yogurt. Swamy wondered how long the happy faces at the table would remain so.

As soon as the dining table was quickly cleared, the children didn't need any further cues from their parents and they trotted dutifully upstairs, leaving the adults to talk without distraction or disruption.

Everyone immediately turned to Kah Hoe; there were millions of questions brimming in four pairs of eyes. Their words tripped over each other as they came spilling out in 'why', 'how', 'where have you', 'how could you'. Finally, Swamy cleared his throat and everyone else fell silent.

"Kah Hoe," he began in a solemn voice, "We all know you said you were going to join the Anti-Japanese Army but the last eight months have been nothing short of traumatic for all of us. I know it couldn't have been easy for you too. So tell us everything that has happened to you."

The four pairs of eager eyes stayed glued to the thin and tired 'boy' that sat before them.

"It was what they did to Papa that drove me to the Anti-Japanese Army. I went to see Ah Seng's father. You remember him, don't you, Ma?" he said turning to Elaine. "Ah Seng joined the guerilla a couple of years ago and his dad was the only person I could go to. He was initially unwilling to help me. He asked me why the son of Tan Chin Nam would want to leave the comfort of his home and put himself in the path of danger. I had to convince him that the enemy had tortured my father and at that point I wanted revenge."

"He told me that Ah Seng had come back to KL and had undergone training at the Chunjin School. The British were working with the Communists and were training the guerrillas to form an Anti-Japanese Army. They were training in Singapore and in KL. Ah Seng had been fortunate enough to be a part of this. So, his father promised to try and place me with one of those groups in the jungle."

Kah Hoe drew in a deep breath to say what he needed to say.

"I am back here for a specific reason." He turned to Swamy and added, "Uncle Swamy, we need your help since you work

115

with the Japanese Military. It would help greatly if we had advance knowledge of their movements."

He was glad it was out and now he heard his Uncle Swamy suck in all the remaining air in the room. Swamy was silent for less than a brief moment, before declaring, "I will."

Elaine was the first to speak in a surprisingly strong voice that came from the depths of her soul.

"Kah Hoe, how can you expect Uncle Swamy to give you that kind of information! That is ridiculous and you are being very ungrateful! This man," she waved her hand at Swamy, "has put his life and that of his family at risk for us and you are asking him for more? Have you lost your mind son? Look at your father, I don't want Uncle Swamy or you to meet with the same fate. You cannot expect him to do anymore."

With that she stood up to leave the room when Chin Nam interrupted and spoke for the first time that night.

"No, Elaine, Swamy has to do it for all of us, for Malaya. We all make sacrifices in life and, whether we like it or not, we are sometimes faced with hard choices. We must all stand up to these bastards and do what little we can. I know Swamy will agree with me."

With that he lapsed back into silence, tired from the effort of speaking.

22
WHITE LILIES
KUALA LUMPUR, 2009

It was a busy week at work for Geeta and for the first time in awhile, she wanted to go 'home' to Krishna Chitappa's house early. She knew she could unwind with him, each of them sipping some cold, cold white wine just how they both liked it.

This Friday, Geeta turned down all offers for a quick after-work drink. She had planned a simple meal for her uncle and she needed to stop off at the grocer's on the way home. She listed the ingredients in her head, *lemongrass, pumpkin, zucchini, a small bottle of olive oil, a packet of pasta, twelve ripe tomatoes, a carton of fresh cream (full fat, of course) and some dried chillies. Oh, and some roses,* she reminded herself.

She let herself in to find the house empty with a note on the side table telling her he would be home by 8pm. She put on an Aretha Franklin CD and got started. First, bruising the lemongrass stalks and then sautéing these on a low fire until the first notes of lemongrass tickled her nose. She left her trademark lemongrass oil to steep in a corner like a spoilt child and attacked the pumpkin, squaring off its round, plump edges.

If only I could do this in my parents' home, she pondered with a tinge of regret. *Oh well, positive thoughts Geeta,* she chided herself. *Just enjoy the moment.*

Her meal was done in an hour and she stood back and

smiled. She had set the table with what her uncle had and added her own little touch by arranging some roses on the dining table. All she needed to do was put the pasta on to boil when her uncle got home.

The cooking smells greeted Krishna Chitappa even before he could get to the door.

"My, my, that smells marvellous, Geeta! I can't wait to tuck in. I'm absolutely famished!" he announced to his beaming niece.

They were halfway through the pasta and nearly done with their first bottle of wine when Krishna Chitappa asked her.

"So tell me, do you love this boy?"

She smiled a little smile at his question because to have used Ken's name would have meant betraying his older brother.

"You can call him Ken, Chitappa! You do know the family and KEN, you know. Just because you don't say his name doesn't make it less real!"

He raised his hands in defense and repeated the question, this time filling in the blank where the 'boy's' name should be.

"I do," she said at last. "At first I tried to fight the feeling and I told myself that it was only on my part and it was nothing but infatuation. And then I had to deny it to myself that he was keen too. That was the most difficult. It was Ken who finally stopped me in my tracks one day and confronted me. He confessed his feelings for me and asked me if I, by any chance, felt the same. I found it so hard to deny it any more." Her tears rolled down with a will of their own.

"Hey, we'll work something out. You trust me, right? Have I ever let my favourite niece down?"

She shook her head from left to right as she wiped her eyes on her sleeve.

After dinner they graduated to a bottle of port when Geeta found the courage to ask her uncle the taboo question.

"Chitappa, why didn't you ever marry?"

She wanted to swallow her words as soon as they flew out of her mouth.

Krishna Chitappa looked into his half empty glass of port as

118

if hoping to find a simple answer within the silky maroon liquid. He looked up at her and said almost to himself, "Where do I begin?"

Geeta waited patiently as he collected his thoughts. He rubbed his right wrist over his left knuckles, the way he always did when he was deep in thought.

"You know I have never spoken about this to the younger generation. You are the first. I was in love with Satnam's sister. Yes, don't look so surprised, the same Satnam you work for.

"Satnam and I have been friends for a long, long time. We were both in London together – he read Law and I studied Medicine. We happened to be in the same halls of residence and we hit it off, although we were a few years apart. We've been good friends ever since.

"When Satnam came back, he practised in Penang but was sent to KL to start a branch of the Penang firm. After I returned, we would catch up for drinks now and then. That's when I first met his sister, Surinder, only a few months later. She wasn't beautiful in your conventional way but she had a presence and a quiet strength that I liked. I pursued her! I knew it would be difficult but I was willing to give it my all. How naïve I was.

"I thought I could take on my parents and family and I thought she could resist her parents. I was stupid to believe that. My parents threatened to cut me off, I told them that I didn't care. Her parents were worse. They told her she would be ostracized, left penniless and they would discontinue her education. Satnam tried to intercede on her behalf to his parents but they wouldn't relent. Sometimes Geeta, the best of people are unable to see past their prejudices. I guess everyone has their blind spot. And for them, like my parents, it was race and religion. Man's greatest folly, that one people is less than another - less pure, less holy, less enlightened. Yet, all I wanted was the road less travelled. I would have been content with less.

"Her parents immediately married her off and they stopped her from finishing her studies. She refused to see me and even Satnam sat me down and told me it was hopeless. The unfortunate thing for me was that I loved her deeply and completely. From what I gathered from Satnam, she was broken and unhappy. The man her family married her off to was much older and he used to beat her up. He died a long time ago in a car accident. She has three children and she has raised them herself, with Satnam's help of course."

"But how could her parents have such double standards especially as Uncle Satnam is Chinese! How could they possibly say no to you! Didn't she bring that up with them? Why didn't she fight harder? I mean, how could they not see the ridiculousness of it all!" Geeta demanded angrily. "Have you kept in touch with her?"

"I did see her at her husband's funeral and we had lunch once after that but it was different for both of us. Too much had happened. There was too much water under that bridge. We thought that maybe it would be nice if we could keep in touch. We tried. But it was always a little too strained, especially for her. She was so used to her husband telling her what to do that she found it difficult to make the decision to be happy again. She had become very fatalistic and had only one aim, one passion – to see her children educated well.

"I can't blame her. I tried to explain to her that she had a right to happiness but she was too bitter. I don't think she wanted to be reminded of the past. And I was the past. So I didn't pursue it." he finished. "She loved white lilies," he said quietly more to himself than Geeta. "And to this day I am always reminded of her when I see white lilies,"

"I still think you should see her. That was so long ago. You are both so much older now and why should either of you care what people say. You have a right to be happy too! I'm not suggesting that you marry her but at least be friends. It's nice to have a companion, a soul mate if you like. You must, Krishna Chitappa! This might be your only chance," Geeta pressed.

Krishna Chitappa gave her a wry smile. "You follow your heart, 'kanne'. Don't let others tell you what and who will make you happy. Don't let love pass you by. It might be your one chance. If you love Ken and can't imagine your life without him, then do it! Love is too precious and too rare. When you find it,

120

keep it close to your heart. Ok. Enough of all this. Let's read one of those lovely letters you brought with you. This is certainly an opportune time," he said with a laugh.

4th August 1927

Dearest Appa,

Sorry for the silence as much has happened in the last few months. I wonder if you recall from one of my earlier letters that there was an opening in Kuala Lumpur for the position of senior teacher at Victoria Institution (one of Malaya's leading schools!). You will be delighted to know that I was interviewed and I was offered the position!

I am very glad for this new teaching position as it comes with a decent pay increase! At least now I will be able to think about buying a house. But let me tell you who I met just two weeks into my new role - you will not believe it when I tell you! Yesterday, our great Gurudev Rabindranath Tagore visited the school. I couldn't believe my good fortune! Meeting a Nobel Laureate and one from India!

It was such an event that even the British Resident (he is the Queen's representative, no less) was in attendance.

He spoke at length about the importance and virtues of children. He elaborated that the idealistic youth would help attain world peace and happiness. He hoped that when they grew up, they wouldn't forget virtues like happiness, love and kindness. Without these values, he warned that war and disharmony would reign.

What a gracious man, Appa! He even read us a poem from The Crescent Moon. The poem that touched my heart is called The Merchant. It made me think of home and how much I miss you all. Here it is in full. When you read it you will understand what I mean.

The Merchant

"Imagine, mother, that you are to stay at home and I am to travel to strange lands.

Imagine that my boat is ready at the landing fully laden.
Now think well, mother, before you say what I shall bring for
you when I come back.
Mother, do you want heaps and heaps of gold?
There, by the banks of golden streams, fields are full of golden
harvest.
And in the shade of the forest path the golden champa flowers
drop on the ground.
I will gather them all for you in many hundred baskets.
Mother, do you want pearls big as the raindrops of autumn?

I shall cross to the pearl island shore. There in the early
morning, light pearls tremble on the meadow flowers, pearls
drop on the grass and pearls are scattered on the sand in spray
by the wild sea-waves.

My brother shall have a pair of horses with wings to fly among
the clouds.
For father, I shall bring a magic pen that, without his knowing,
will write itself.

For you mother, I must have the casket and jewel that cost
seven kings their kingdoms."

Isn't it beautiful?
By the way, I have by the Grace of Ambal some beautiful news
for you and Amma. Saraswathi is in the family way. You will be
'tata' and 'patti' in eight months, God willing.
My namaskarams to you and Amma.

Your loving son,
Rangaswamy

P.S. I must tell you about this precocious young talent by the name
of Lall Singh. He is the Captain of the school cricket team. I think
if he lived back home he'd probably be on the India team!

23
THE COUSINS
KUALA LUMPUR, 2009

Sandhya was the 'keeper of the faith.' Among the second generation, she was the matriarch. If Parvathi was not around, it was to Sandhya that everyone went to with queries about festivals and religious ceremonies. She had learnt this art at the elbow of her mother. She was well versed with reading the panjagam, working out the good days, bad days, good times and ill-fated times that were tabulated in the saffron yellow Hindu almanac.

The well-being of the Rangaswamy Iyer family was a subject close to her heart. So when the wind carried the nasty news about Geeta and that Chinese boy (she couldn't bring herself to use his name), she knew she had to step in and mend things.

Her first call had been to Manjula, the loud speaker for the younger cousins. Manjula and Sandhya were chalk and cheese. The former believed in the freedom of choice and yet had been pushed to make choices which she was uncomfortable with, along the way.

The two sisters arranged to see Geeta at Bobo's Bangsar. Geeta had picked the place because she wanted to feel safe and in familiar surroundings, especially as they were going to be talking about 'uncomfortable things' like boyfriends and relationships and arranged marriages. The way Geeta figured it, there would be three different points-of-view – Sandhya's was the voice for the Brahmin cause, Manjula's would be the voice for the 'hedging, agnostic' Brahmin who was a little unsure of which side of the fence she really was on, and then of course there was Geeta; firmly pro-choice and anti-establishment, 'atheist Brahmin'.

Geeta was the first to arrive. She wanted to be seated and ensured she had her escape route planned. She didn't want to walk in late and face two pairs of eyes burning holes into her.

She was nursing a frappucino when her cousins walked in. They both ordered the same drink as Geeta and with palms and elbows on the table, they started the most important discussion of all.

Geeta put on an air of nonchalance. Sandhya had an air of, "I am here to solve this problem, so let's get on with it." Manjula looked a little dreamy and far away. Sandhya took a long slurp from her drink to draw in her strength and bombarded Geeta, "So what is this I hear about you and this boy?" she asked without quite planning her sentence.

"To start with, his name is Ken, like you don't know. And I am GOING OUT with him. We are dating and I have every intention of marrying him. And let me guess, you both have come here as emissaries of my parents to convince me otherwise!" Geeta exhaled all those words in one breath.

"Geeta, we have come to talk to you to find out how serious you are and where you think this is going. I would be lying if I said we aren't going to try and talk you out of it, but we've come with good intentions. Please don't look at us like we're the enemy," soothed Manjula.

Here they are trying to play good cop, bad cop! My two cousins, hah!

"Geeta, you need to give something as important as this a lot of thought. This is your life you are talking about. Once you make a mistake like this, the damage is irreparable," said Sandhya.

"What makes you both think that I haven't given this any thought? Do you know just how much of my time I have spent worrying about the repercussions, about whether all I was feeling was infatuation or that maybe I was the only one that was feeling that way. I prayed for the longest time that Ken wouldn't feel the same way and when he told me he did, I knew the difficult task ahead of me. Do you understand that feeling? Do you know the sleepless nights I have had, the umpteen conversations I've made up in my head between Appa, Amma and me? I used to day-dream and hope against hope that they would be cool about it and accept it without a fight, but who was I kidding! And to think my two cousins are now sitting here and trying to tell me that I haven't given it any thought what I feel for this man is not just wrong but thoughtless. Manjula, I can't believe you prescribe to this! I thought you believed that we should make our own choices?"

Geeta was trying very hard to keep her voice down but she wasn't succeeding and before long there were curious glances coming their way.

"Geeta, what we are here to tell you is that you can't just dismiss how your parents feel. Arranged-marriages are all they know and to them it is tried and tested. Of course, they are concerned about the rest of the Brahmin community and what people will say, but that's HOW it is for them. You know that only too well. There is something to be said for marrying our own kind. Language and customs and religion don't become issues. Especially in a country like ours, it's important to feel like we belong in our own community," explained Sandhya.

"Well I don't quite care what the rest of the Brahmin community thinks or says, but even in a warped sense, I can understand how Periappa and Periamma feel. What Sandhya says is true in that is all they know and that is all they understand. You bring to them a problem that they have no answer and control over. They only know how to resist and fight it," added Manjula. "Unfortunately Geeta, I understand exactly what you are saying and I sympathise with you but I also feel for your parents and can see that the pain they are feeling is real. None of it is made up. That's the truth of it. I would hate to be where you are sitting right now, you must be going through hell," she added sympathetically.

"How can we continue living in the 21st century and still cling to these archaic ideas? Someone please explain to me! Just look at some of our second cousins. Haven't their parents moved with the times when some of their children insisted on marrying vellakarans! But look at us! Sitting here in modern Malaysia and holding tight to some customs and traditions that make no sense in today's world. How can my mother tell me with a sense of superiority, that her mother would never let the shadow of a non-Brahmin cross her while she was eating. How utterly ridiculous!! How can you, for one moment think that it's okay to treat someone like that? Doesn't it sound insane and shouldn't we be ashamed of it? What is the point of a 'broad' education when at the end of the day, you burrow yourself into your little all-inclusive-reclusive-Tanjore-Iyer world, faking to be liberal-open-minded-diaspora Indian. Do you want to be treated the way Patti was when she was widowed? To have your head shaved bald and made to wear a white sari for the rest of her life? I bet bloody NOT!

"So how can you discount what I am feeling, in favour of predictions a man who hasn't an inkling of who I am or what I choose to be with whom I choose to be? Does it say anyway on your precious chart that Ken makes me laugh, that he can finish my sentence, that I know when he is nervous or am I to play a game of chance with my life, to take a gamble with my happiness. I will not martyr myself for my parents' false sense of pride and achievement. They will have to learn to shed theirs and wear mine. I am not a puppet and they are not my puppet masters. All through my life they nagged me about studying hard and doing well and going to a good university and becoming independent. Whatever for! Why can't they be happy that Ken truly loves me? You both know him reasonably well. What's wrong with him apart from the fact that he is Chinese. If he was Brahmin wouldn't you all agree he's a great catch? He's warm, he's generous, he's funny, he's good looking, he holds a good job and is rich. The only thing not going for him is his race and that sucks.

"I'm sorry but there's nothing more I want to say on this. You tell my parents that I'm not willing to throw my happiness away for the sake of this inequitable community I was born into."

Geeta strode out of Bobo's, her emotions all knotted in a tight ball of resolute anger. She was certain that she was doing the right thing, that all her doubts had immediately dissolved.

She drove back to Krishna Chitappa's house with the radio blaring. She seethed and sighed and huffed and puffed about the entire hour she spent with her cousins. *How very condescending! Did they honestly think I would crumble and give in? My mind is well and truly made up. I love my man and he loves me. That's all that matters. What did Krishna Chitappa say to me… I won't let love slip by me. I know deep, deep in my heart that it's Ken I want to grow old with. He makes me so happy.*

It wasn't until she got to her room that she realized that she had forgotten to take her mobile phone. There were three messages from Shilpa reminding her about Karen's house warming, 'Tonight at 8!' "Oh shit!" she yelled out loud.

She stripped and looked at herself in the mirror with a critical eye, considering if she was attractive. *Well,* spoke her critical eye, *that depends. If you look at your features individually, I would say your nose was a little wide and your mouth a bit too big. But your eyes, Geeta, any man would sink in them.*

That's not so bad. I like my hair too. Why didn't you say anything about my hair? She asked a little irritated.

You cut me off! I was going to say any man would love to run his fingers through your thick hair. But it is your neck that men will want to bury their faces in, Geeta. It is graceful and long and smooth, it begs to be caressed. And if only men knew how you like to be touched there, the way you slump in a heap. I know you well. I know how your body reacts to Ken when he touches you. You are like clay in his hands. He is a potter, isn't he, Geeta? That is why you love his hands best, because when they touch, you come alive, said her critical eye provocatively.

By the time Geeta reached Karen's house, it was 9pm. The

music alone would have led her there and she was hard pressed to find a place to park. She had decided to wear her black trousers with the sexy new black top she had recently bought. In her strappy black heels and red toe nails, she cut a striking figure.

"Bloody hell, what took you so long!" yelled Karen over the din of talking voices and drunken singing.

"I'm sorry sweetheart, I was delayed with something else, but I am so glad to be here!" enthused Geeta.

"As you should be!!" muttered Karen with a smile. "What would you like to drink?" she asked.

"A gin & tonic of course. Tanqueray Rangpor with a wedge of lime," said a familiar voice from behind that made her go weak at her knees. She spun round and saw Ken standing there.

24
PENANG
20TH MAY 1943

Sometimes even Tochi wasn't sure which hat he had on. Like a child caught up in his own world of play-acting, he changed roles at the drop of the proverbial hat. Some days he was a courier with wads of cash stashed away in various parts of his clothes or body; other days he was Gurchan's willing accomplice as they cycled around town surreptitiously putting up Singa posters. And yet at other times it appeared that Tochi was a purchasing officer, ordering fine comestibles such as bacon and cheese for the Japanese (ironically, in true British style). So if anyone was to stop Tochi while he was peddling rapidly up and down the streets, he may be forgiven for hesitating when asked, "Where are you going?"

Over the past few months, Tochi had been helping Gurchan put up his posters in various parts of town. These famous posters carried news of the war and kept the people informed on how the tide was gradually turning against the Axis powers. The latest instalments had revealed how the British had won a decisive battle at El Alamein in North Africa and how Hitler's troops had been slaughtered in the Battle of Stalingrad. Almost overnight, there was the intoxicating scent of fresh hope in the air. People walked about with their heads held a little higher, more unafraid and a refusal to bow to the Japanese for now they knew the truth and not the lies the Japanese had been feeding them.

The Singa posters drew Malayans, like bees to honey. People crowded around the posters that appeared almost out of nowhere in the dead of night and fed on the information like starved rats. Once they had tasted the truth, they yearned for more. It was on the periphery of a crowded group of people reading the latest poster that Tochi stood, basking in the powerful sense of hope that radiated around him.

Standing with the rest of the crowd, he marvelled and 'tsk-ed' and pretended to shake his head in wonder at the information that was plastered to the wall. "Who would be so brave to do this?" asked one voice.

Another voice answered, "Brave if they're not caught but stupid if they are!"

"Shh," said another, "Some of us are trying to memorise what's written. This is more valuable than the crown jewels!"

The news on the poster had offered the huddled bodies valuable insights to the progress of the war; news that would be further shared and spread by word of mouth. Tochi felt the crowd's relief, an emotion that couldn't be contained anymore.

On every street and every corner, the same questions were being asked, "Which group is responsible for these posters?" Most people thought it was the work of the anti-Japanese guerilla fighters who were hiding in the jungle.

"I wonder how they come out at night and paste so many of these posters without getting caught?"

"It's amazing the Japanese haven't captured any of them."

"How are they printing all this information and how are they getting it?"

Tochi knew the answers to all these questions and more. All he did was smile softly to himself.

If only you knew it was the brainchild of one very brave man acting almost single-handedly by the name of Gurchan Singh, thought Tochi to himself.

This was how Gurchan did it:

He visited Penang once a month where he usually stayed for a week. His trip always tied in with the Penang Turf Club races. There were supposed to be seven races but due to the lack of suitable transport, there weren't enough horses in Penang. To keep the punters happy, the Japanese Governor had agreed to allow cycling races at the Club. As fate would have it, Gurchan was in charge of these cycling races and was given a permanent travel pass that permitted him to travel from Ipoh to Penang unhindered. Each month he would travel north on his bicycle with his posters tightly rolled up and hidden away in his secret hiding place.

Gurchan would usually peddle into town the day before the races and in order not to attract too much attention, he stayed at the Gurdwara on Brick Kiln Road. As was the usual plan, Gurchan came to Tochi's house for supper where the two of them enjoyed a meal of chapatis and dhall made earlier by Dalip. She too, had her own evening plans with her sisters. In fact, Tochi always encouraged her to visit her sisters when Gurchan was in town. Thinking her husband kind and considerate, Dalip always jumped at the monthly opportunity.

It was while Gurchan was mopping up the remnants of his dhall with the last piece of chapati that Tochi asked him how he managed to carry his posters with him even though he was still subject to inspection at all the checkpoints between Ipoh and Penang.

"I do it with great trepidation," he explained. "But I hold the ace card," he said tapping his shirt pocket. "I carry the Japanese Governor's letter according me permission to travel and that is the first thing I show them when they stop me. After that, they treat me like a very important person and wave me on my way," he explained. "But I tell you, if they ever found out about my secret hiding place, I would be dead meat."

With that, Gurchan stood up, made his way to the sink to wash his hands, opened the back door and wheeled his bicycle in. What Gurchan proceeded to show Tochi was nothing short of an act of pure genius. Gurchan turned his bicycle over and out plonked eight tiny bamboo cylinders about six inches long and one inch in diameter. These he hid in the upright bar of his bicycle. There was a cork at the bottom that prevented anything from falling out. In each of these bamboo cylinders were at least eight posters, waiting to be unleashed on a hungry audience. With Gurchan's secret finally revealed, all that Tochi could do was to give his friend a standing ovation.

Gurchan carefully unrolled one poster and the two of them read it.

ALLIED H.Q. COMMUNIQUE NO. 216 of the 20th May 1943. ALLIED FIGHT FOR FREEDOM. ALLIED FIGHT AGAINST AGGRESSION.

Today's news is tomorrow's history. This news bulletin originates from somewhere in Malaya, giving the true news round-up of the world. Tell your friends about the news you have read today in this communiqué, so that they may know that the news as given by the Japs in the local Press is untrue. If you are a freedom-loving person, you will not hesitate to pass on this news and watch for more tomorrow. For this co-operation of yours, we thank you.

You know of the total destruction of Rommel's Africa Korps. Well, the entire North Africa has been taken by the Allieds. The Germans in Tunisia have surrendered leaving the Allied forces in North Africa totally dominant. Soon, Italy will be for the taking.

British air heroes have taken on the Industrial heartland of Germany. Two hydro-electric dams in Eder and Mohne have been ruptured by RAF Lancaster bombers. Extensively flooding of German towns!

And the best news is that Yamamoto is dead! The chief architect of the Pearl Harbour attack has received his just end. He was shot down by an American ambush in the Solomon Islands.

Freedom-loving people! The time is now ripe for you to give up co-operating with the Japs. What have they done for us? They are a cruel and unjust race. Stop bowing to them!

The tide is turning!
SINGA

They carefully rolled up the posters, hid them in their clothes and bade each other luck, as each man set off alone into the darkness. Three hours later, they returned home tired and happy to see each other. As was customary with all their midnight capers, they were joined by a third gentleman in spirit.

25
LOCATION: TOP SECRET
20TH MAY 1943

Sharp pellets of rain pounded the earth. The guerillas who had gathered at the mouth of the tunnel near the royal town of Kuala Kangsar in Perak were thankful for the downpour. The torrential rain would slow down the train that was due to approach the tunnel at 11.15pm; when it would chug along, huffing and puffing up the slope. The sheets of rain were a much welcome dark cloak and conspirator which would shield the guerillas from prying eyes as they unloaded log after log of rubber trees at one end of the tunnel; an arduous and backbreaking task.

The scent of petrichor filled the air, hitting their noses as immediately as the dry, sun baked, ochre earth drank it thirstily, quickly sealing its cracks. By the time the thirty or so guerrillas had finished piling the logs, the rain had made itself a nice watery home at the mouth of the tunnel, waiting patiently for the train and all its human cargo.

The guerrillas had hatched and plotted for two weeks. Kah Hoe had carefully carried Swamy's information back to the resistance fighters. Several heads sat bent over the plans in the dead of night. Voices rose and fell in agreement and disagreement and it was only after several days of going back and forth that a plan was finally hatched to ambush the train near the Kuala Kangsar tunnel. To ensure that the train driver would have enough time to stop the train from hitting the logs, these were to be set on fire.

Once the train came to a halt, more logs would be placed at the other end of the tunnel, effectively sealing the train inside it. On either side of the tracks in the tunnel, gelignite bombs with pressure switches would be placed under soil and rocks. The quantity of gelignite bombs would be sufficient only to maim or kill without affecting the structural integrity of the tunnel.

The train was audible now. The rhythm of the engine matched the rhythm of the guerillas' hearts. Beads of sweat broke out on their foreheads and hands clenched harder around rifles. Soon the moment of truth would be upon them.

It happened so quickly, in a matter of mere seconds. The screeching sound of wheels grating on metal, desperate to come to a sudden halt caused sparks to fly. Fortunately, with the train making its slow ascent up the hill, its impact with the burning rubber logs that lay dead in its path was minimal.

The guerrillas sprung into action. As planned, four groups took their positions in the tunnel while others quickly piled more logs at the entrance. As was expected, the Japanese soldiers jumped out of the train to investigate the ruckus and set off the hidden explosives in a hail of deafening and blinding detonations. In the blink of an eye, the tunnel was a jigsaw puzzle of body parts.

The agitated Japanese soldiers left on the train were swiftly dealt with by the guerillas who unleashed their brand of welcome on them – deadly handshakes in the form of grenades thrown into each passenger carriage. It wasn't until they were certain that all the Japanese were dead that the guerrillas cleared the logs that had kissed the nose of the train. With a gun held to his head, the driver shifted the train into gear and slowly moved it out of the tunnel to allow the guerilas a closer inspection of the sealed wagons.

The sound of the screeching wagon doors being drawn apart filled the air and was replaced by a stench so vile that it

135

caused many standing around to retch and throw up. Behind the heavy doors lay bodies that had forgotten how to stand, that had forgotten what moonlight or daylight looked like, that had grown accustomed to the smell of faeces and urine, and the flies that covered their sore-infested bodies.

One by one, the prisoners of war stumbled, crawled and dragged themselves off the train and when the last one hit the ground with a soft thud, one of the guerrillas announced, "250 in total. 80 kwai lohs and the rest Chinese."

As they were divided into their respective groups, a small Chinese man with slicked back black hair that he wore away from his forehead asked who was in charge of the British POWs.

A tall, thin man came forward with an outstretched hand, "I am Lieutenant-Colonel Ridglee".

"And I am Chin Peng", said the guerilla leader.

26

LOVEBIRDS
PANGKOR LAUT, 2009

Geeta's smile was drawn in permanent ink. It was tough talking with a mouth stretched so wide but she managed, demanding to know why Ken was in KL and how he had kept it a secret from her. She looked accusingly at Karen who simply held her hands up in defense.

"I was sworn to secrecy," she said, enjoying seeing her friend look so happy. "It gets even better, Geeta. I have reservations for the four of us and Saskea to go to Pangkor Laut tomorrow."

Before Geeta could record any sort of protest, she quickly added, "I've spoken to your secretary, she's going to cover for you. Relax, you have no cases and nothing urgent on. Even Satnam will be outstation for a case in Ipoh, so all you need to do girl, is pack!" said Karen.

"I can't believe you guys. How long have you two been planning this behind my back?" she asked giddy with happiness.

"Oh gosh, who cares, G? Aren't you just happy that I'm here? Would you rather I wasn't?" Ken asked her with a glint in his eye.

Geeta hugged Ken, shaking her head incredulously. She floated through the rest of the night, in a continuous daze of drinking, gazing and grinning.

It was an early wake up call for her. Ken, Brian, Karen and Saskea were at Krishna Chitappa's at 5am sharp. Saskea was gurgling in her car seat, totally enamoured with the butterfly mobile in front of her. Geeta had been up till nearly 2am, first deciding what to take, then trying on the clothes she had decided on, then throwing stuff out of her bag in frustration. Finally out of sheer exhaustion, she chucked in a mish mash of outfits.

The happy group had planned to reach Lumut in time to catch the first ferry to Pangkor Laut, a small island off the main Pangkor island. In the early morning mist, the drive up the North-South Expressway was smooth and Karen had thoughtfully prepared a large thermos of steaming Nescafe thickened with condensed milk. Served in plastic tumblers, everyone sipped the coffee with loud 'ahs' and slurps of approval. "Pure genius you are, my dear," declared Brian.

At precisely 7.35am, Brian parked his SUV at the car park allotted to the Pangkor Laut Resort. The 45 minute ferry ride turned out to be a huge source of delight for little Saskea who squealed when she felt the rush of the breeze on her face.

Geeta found herself a quiet spot on the ferry with only her private thoughts for company. Looking out at the clear blue sky and water she couldn't help but think, *this place is God's earth, a little bit of paradise right here. Hopefully it remains like this, silky green waters rushing up to shore to meet white, white sand. If only I can make this moment last forever and ever. To feel free of worry and stress, just to be at one with nature.*

Schools of white fish swimming around the pier greeted the guests as they disembarked. Young children yelped with delight at the sight of these little wonders and their mothers had to hold tight as some of the them rushed to the pier's edge to reach for them. Geeta and Ken were booked into a hill villa a couple of rows away from Karen and Brian's villa.

"Let's meet at 6.30 at Chapman's Bar for cocktails" said Brian, figuring that Ken and Geeta would want to spend some quiet time together.

The happy couple spent the good part of the afternoon by the adult pool, swimming, lazing and drinking plenty of fresh coconut water. They both had a soak in their outdoor bath before getting dressed and making their way to Emerald Bay where the bar was located.

Karen, Brian and Saskea were already there, the two adults nursing a cocktail each while Saskea sat in her stroller, happily blowing spit bubbles. Geeta ordered her favourite pre-dinner gin and tonic while Ken had a cold beer. They looked rested and happy and they all turned expectantly to Geeta, as if she were the storyteller for the evening.

"Okayyyy....Why are all three of you looking at me as if I am hiding a secret?" asked Geeta.

"Hey, sweetie" said Karen in her softest voice. "We're your closest and dearest friends, we don't just care about you, we are also worried about you. You haven't said much to me about what you're going through. I haven't prodded you either because I thought you needed time to gather yourself but I think it is time for you to fill in the gaps."

Geeta fell silent and her smile was replaced with a thin lip line.

"I don't know where to start. Ken knows most of what has happened. Soon after the first argument with my parents, I moved out. I couldn't handle the tension in the house, the way we were all trying so hard to avoid each other. I ate out or came home very late for dinner so my parents would eat early and retire to their room.

"I spoke to my uncle and asked him if he would mind having me as a guest for a while. I told my mother that I was going to stay with him and she wasn't happy about that either. But, heck, I needed to get away and I think they needed some time without me too.

"I have spoken to my mother since, on the phone but she invariably gets angry or starts her emotional blackmail and that really pisses me off! She's been calling my brothers in England and the States and complaining to them about how ungrateful and how inconsiderate I am. They have called me too and I told them my side of the story. It's been an emotional roller-coaster for sure. They even told me to move back in and slowly work things out but they have no clue how hard it is. Suresh is a little more understanding. He's told my mother to give me some time and space, but Ravi thinks I am being a little selfish."

She continued, "You know, I am past caring what anyone thinks of me. If I do what my parents want then I am miserable and I don't want to be miserable. I want to have my own life and be happy. But the saddest thing is that my father hasn't spoken to me at all since I moved out. When I asked my mother how he was, she would say he didn't want to talk to me. And it's true, he's not said a word about it to my brothers either and that's really upsetting. I don't know how long we are going to carry on like this but for now I am definitely not moving back in."

There was a long silence broken only by the sound of ice jostling in their glasses. Even Saskea thought it best if she waited politely before gurgling a reply.

"Ok, now that I've got it off my chest, can we please enjoy the rest of this holiday? I don't want to see any faces moping around this beautiful island. So, Mister Smart Alec," she turned to Ken, "Why is this bar called Chapman's Bar? I know you're dying to tell me".

Ken smiled. "It was named after Spencer Chapman, who wrote *The Jungle is Neutral.*"

Seeing Geeta's blank look, he continued, "He was a member of the British resistance against the Japanese during the war. He cooperated with the Communists to fight the Japanese and he hid in the jungle here, right on Pangkor. In fact, Chapman actually swam from Emerald Bay to a waiting submarine to escape from Malaya. On that note, let's get dinner, I'm starving."

The four and a half of them took a buggy back to the Resort and walked the long gang plank to Uncle Lim's restaurant. The rest of the evening was relaxed and easy. Saskea entertained them all with her laughter and baby talk. Karen caught Geeta and Ken looking at each other and then at Saskea longingly. *They do deserve to be together*, she thought.

"I haven't seen two other people more in love than these two," she whispered to Brian later that night.

27
KEN AND KRISHNA
KUALA LUMPUR, 2009

The journey home was a more subdued affair. They were all tired from the sun and drink, and apart from poor Brian who was driving, the other heads kept rolling from one side to the other. Ken had offered to share the driving with him but after fifteen minutes into the journey, he put his head back and drove straight into slumber. Geeta tried reading her *Living Etc* magazine but couldn't get past 'Best Finds' before she too closed her eyes, hugging the magazine close to her. Karen busied herself with Saskea's milk and once the little one had been fed, she too promptly fell into a deep sleep, her little body moving up and down with her breathing. Karen stayed awake to keep Brian company but he persuaded her to take a nap while the little one was still fast asleep.

By the time they reached KL, it was nearly four in the afternoon. Geeta was the first to be dropped off and she was thankful the house was empty. All of a sudden, she felt the heavy burden of her parents, her relationship, her living in someone else's home and it all seemed to descend on her like a heavy boulder.

When Ken got home, he realised he had missed a number of calls. Six new messages his handphone announced. The one message that had him stand up ramrod straight was from G's Uncle Krishna. It was an invitation for drinks at the Long Bar, the Royal Selangor Club at 7.30pm sharp the following evening – just the two of them. He politely called him back and accepted.

I can't avoid this any longer, he thought. *It has to be done and I might as well confront it now. Phew! Deep breaths, Ken,* he reminded himself.

Ken was fifteen minutes early at the Club. He had been a member since he was a young boy and he loved the old world charm about it. No doubt, the renovation had left him peeved because they had dug up the beautiful old tiles outside the Long Bar only to replace them with shining, slippery marble. The very tiles that had survived colonial times, when cricketers dressed in their whites would stand on the verandah and gaze out onto the green padang, watching the action.

The Royal Selangor Club was fondly called The Spotted Dog and one legend has it that the Police Commissioner's wife used to bring her dalmatian to the Club with her. The other legend was that the Selangor Club unlike the Lake Club allowed a certain strata of locals in. Hence, the black spots. The Long Bar, was and still is a 'men-only' bar and tradition dictates that if the wife of a Club member should so much as place her foot in the Bar, her husband would have to buy a round of drinks for all.

Ken was seated at Lall's Corner, looking at the old pictures as a distraction from feeling too nervous, when Krishna walked in. Krishna greeted him with a warm smile and a firm handshake, that instantly put Ken at ease. He ordered two glasses of single malt, each with one cube of ice; it was only after their drinks arrived that the serious conversation began.

"You must realize by now that I am on your side," said Krishna. "Geeta, as you know, now lives with me much to the chagrin of her parents but then they know better than to broach the subject with me. Right now, it's a case of I know they know and they know I know but no one wants to admit it! For the moment, I think it suits us all fine as none of us wants to open

142

Pandora's box and then have to deal with the harsh words and the hurt.

"Unfortunately, we can't go on pretending like there isn't this huge package sitting in the middle of all our lives, waiting to be opened. So I thought I might take matters into my own hands. I will be speaking to Geeta's parents soon but I thought I would like to have a chat with you first, just so I can get a feel and a better understanding of what your intentions are, if I may put it so bluntly," he added.

Before Ken could open his mouth, he continued.

"There is no denying that there are huge issues facing you and Geeta. I am not here to sit in judgment of you. But I will call a spade a spade and I shan't gloss over anything that I feel will be an issue with her parents. First is the fact that you are Chinese and she is Indian. Her parents come from very, very traditional backgrounds. They both had a very traditional upbringing, as I did, but we are not here to talk about me. They don't know anything other than the Brahmin way. They did what their parents expected of them, just as their parents before them did.

"My brother was the perfect son. He was every parent's dream. He never disobeyed them, was always polite, a voracious reader and deeply religious from a very young age. The words 'I can't do it' were not in his vocabulary. So when he got married and then had three children, he thought it would be the same for him too. His three children would do as they were told; study hard and get their professional degrees, have arranged marriages and then have beautiful Brahmin babies!

"Well, his two sons have done nearly all of that sans the arranged marriage bit, but neither has dropped a bomb shell about marrying someone from outside the community. That pleasure has fallen like a thud on Geeta's lap. Well, I'll tell you this, Ken," said Krishna leaning forward in his chair.

"When Geeta was a child, she would never allow anyone to tell her that she couldn't do something because she was a girl. She would have a hissy fit and get her way in the end. From climbing rambutan trees with her brothers to playing marbles, she was the best. Right then, I knew that she would test her parents at every stage of her life. And she did! They wanted her to do an Economics degree locally, but she wanted to read Law in England. And invariably, what Geeta wanted, Geeta got. Until now.

"Now they feel that they need to make a stand and they need to be united and hold on to all that they have ever known – their religion, their community and their race and caste. Geeta has turned out to be their living nightmare. All Brahmin parents' worst fear is that their child will end up marrying outside, not just their caste, but their race.

"So as much as I say that I am on your side, I also sympathise with them. Their world as they know it is about to fall apart right before their very eyes and to them the deepest pain is that it's being caused by one of their own. To them, it is an avoidable pain.

"The other huge issue is religion, Ken. Geeta comes from a staunch Hindu family. Your family is Catholic, aren't they? Are you a Catholic too?" enquired Krishna.

Ken was silent for a couple of seconds before answering, not too sure how his answer might reflect on him.

"Well, I don't believe in religion. If you ask me if I believe in God, I'd have to say I don't know. To me, religion has caused the world pain and suffering. People fight and kill in the name of religion and unfortunately, more harm than good has come from it.

"To have faith and belief is one thing, but to go about and profess that one religion is superior to another and then to push it down someone else's throat and worse, to belittle him for it, is unacceptable to me. I don't need religion to tell me what's right and what's wrong. For me, if I have done no one harm and I have not hurt the feelings of another, that is prayer enough. If you think about it Uncle Krishna, if half the world is Christian and the other half is Hindu, there is already a fundamental flaw in that premise because Christians don't believe in rebirth while the Hindus do. That means someone is wrong. But who? They both believe so strongly in their religion and that is the truth. Do you see it from my perspective? But that doesn't mean that I

144

disrespect a person who has strong religious beliefs. It's just that it's not for me," said Ken.

"Geeta and I have talked a lot about this. For all her 'modern' ways, for want of a better word, I know she is religious. And I have told her that I will do what is necessary to make her happy. If she insists on a traditional Hindu wedding, I will give it to her. We've even talked about our children. On that score, I have assured her that she can raise them as Hindus but they must be allowed to make up their own minds when they reach a certain age. It's not like we are two starry-eyed teenagers looking at the future through rose-hued glasses. We have spent hours talking about all the issues that may affect her. But there is one thing we both know for sure; we love each other deeply. I cannot see the rest of my life without her in every scene. And quite frankly, I will not," said Ken.

Krishna listened silently and was pleased that the boy had had the courage to speak his mind. "All right Ken. I think you have confirmed what I knew all along. Leave it with me. Let me come up with a strategy before I approach my brother and sister-in-law. I have to be tactful and gentle. But believe me, I will try and knock some sense into them," he said, with a laugh.

As he prepared to leave, gathering up his mobile and car keys, Ken turned to Krishna and asked him about the corner that was dedicated to Lall Singh.

"Oh, he was a phenomenon in the old days" Krishna remarked. "He was the only Malaysian ever to play test cricket. He played for India in 1932 during India's first tour of England, he even played at Lords. It's an amazing story actually, since he didn't have the means to buy a ticket to the UK, the local Indian community passed the hat around and sponsored his entire trip. When he eventually returned to KL, he ended up becoming the Club's ground keeper," explained Krishna.

This is something to share with G. I just have to keep her curiosity away from actually stepping foot in the Long Bar!

28
RAMESH VS KRISHNA
KUALA LUMPUR, 2009

The two brothers knew they would have to meet sooner or later; there were plenty of words that needed to be said and many words would undoubtedly cause hurt and pain. And so they procrastinated… both avoiding making that all-important phone call.

Then one Sunday morning after Krishna had read and re-read the newspapers, he decided that this cat-and-mouse game had to end. He dialed his brother's number hoping that Parvathi would answer it and tell him that Ramesh had gone out. Ramesh answered the phone while he was still daydreaming and was caught off guard when he heard his brother's slightly strained and tired voice.

"Uh, hello Anna," said Krishna.

"Yes, Krishna," said the terse voice at the other end as soon as he recognised Krishna's voice.

"I think we need to talk. Are you free today? Is Manni home now?"

When Ramesh told him that Parvathi was at a 'paatu' class, Krishna sighed a breath of relief and told him he was coming over shortly.

Krishna rehearsed his conversation with his brother on his drive over. He loved him dearly even if they had very different opinions on many things. He didn't want to say anything in haste that he might regret. Krishna knew that his brother had never acted out of malice. It was nothing short of pure brotherly love and concern but there were decisions that Krishna still regretted today. His life played back slowly like a black and white silent movie in his rear view mirror.

So many things I would have done differently. So many things I should have said to the people who mattered and I never summoned the nerve to do it. So many wasted opportunities when I could have righted my wrongs and yet I didn't. I have much to be ashamed of. My life would have been very different if I had had the balls to stand up for what I believed in. I can't see Geeta repeat my mistakes. She has so much more courage than I! She has taken a stand and has conviction in her love for this young man. Good for you, Geeta. His thoughts came to an abrupt halt when he found himself outside his brother's house.

With two tumblers of water dividing them at the dining table drawing battle lines, the brothers assessed each other silently for a little while. Krishna broke the awkward silence.

"Anna, we need to sort out Geeta's situation," (he didn't want to use the word problem because he didn't view it that way). "I know you and Manni are very upset because she is staying with me and you see me as a traitor to our side. I felt it best that she stay with me. At least, we all have peace of mind that she's not in some stranger's house. She's a lovely girl, Anna, and you should be so proud of her. She has shown such tenacity and faith in her convictions. That alone must tell you both how much Ken means to her. I know this is difficult for you and Manni, but you must try and understand how equally difficult it is for her. She has lost her heart to a boy from another race. That is her only crime. Ken is a steady, hardworking, honest and kind man. Can we not be happy with that? Would you rather her end up being alone like me?" said Krishna.

"Can you stop right there, Krishna? Have you lost all common sense! Are you asking me to put my feet up, laugh and clap and agree to what Geeta is asking for? Are you that mad? I will NOT have her marry a Chinese man! That is out of the question. We are Brahmins! How will I ever show my face in the Samajam if I allow my daughter to marry outside our race, not just caste, but race," retorted Ramesh.

"Don't you see that you will lose her? She is determined to marry this boy whether you and Manni like it or not! Is that what you want? Truly, dig deep into your heart and tell me you will be happy to lose your only daughter. And for what? Just because you can't hold your head in this small-minded cloistered Brahmin community. How can you be so affected by what people will say? You are an educated and cultured man and to hear you say those same words that I heard all those years ago makes me very sad. Nothing has changed. You haven't learnt to move with the times. Look around you, Anna. How many of our relatives in India are marrying European boys and moving! They are all getting on with their lives and not sitting and wondering what Ramesh in Malaysia is thinking about a mixed race marriage. Why do you care what the people in the Samajam will say! They aren't Geeta. They are not interested in her happiness, only in gossip and small talk."

"That is precisely why I want my children to marry Brahmins. How many are we in this country? If we don't hold on to our customs and traditions, what will we end up being? Another drop in a multitude of mixed races, watered down like insipid rasam! Will you be happy with that? Because I won't. I will not have future generations of this family contaminated with the blood of others. I don't care if you don't agree. I have nothing to say to you and you should leave," Ramesh said raising his voice and waving his hand in the air. "And if you are going to dig up all your old stories, I have no interest in listening to them," he added for good measure.

"What a hurtful thing to say to me! All these years I have lived a lonely and lonesome life and what good has that done me! I should have had the guts and gumption that Geeta has and stood up to the family back then. Instead, I succumbed to all the emotional blackmail and the rubbish about our standing in our community and the shame I would have brought on our family name. What happiness has that given me? Huh, you tell me? I am a miserable man, partly thanks to you! I know I have only myself to blame at the end of the day but you did me no favours. I will not allow you to ruin Geeta's life. She deserves to be happy and if she has found love, then good for her! I will encourage her to continue to be strong and resilient in the face of all this emotional hocus-pocus. You will all have to learn to deal with her decisions and make the best of it. Its 2009 for God's sake – wake up and join the living and stop living in this archaic world only you live in!" yelled Krishna.

"What I did for you was out of love, Krishna. Don't turn it around and make it seem like I intended to be mean. You and that woman would never have survived the pressure and tension of a mixed marriage. Have you forgotten the threats and the fear they drove into their daughter's head! Don't you remember the emotional blackmail her parents put her through? The melodrama of her mother committing suicide – would you have been able to cope? If she had indeed gone through with it, I doubt your marriage would have survived. You wouldn't be able to live with blood on your hands and that is exactly how you would have looked at it. I know you so well. The guilt would have stained and tainted your relationship and it would have followed you everywhere like a shadow. You were too decent to let something like that happen. You weren't a coward. You did the right thing, by her, by you and by us. What you are asking of us is very difficult. This is the only way we know. This IS our way," said Ramesh quietly.

"But this is not India, Anna, and this is a different generation of people. You need to bear in mind that you gave her a Western education with all the freedom of living abroad and fending for herself and that she is a product of her generation. And now she is a successful lawyer, holding her own and yet she chooses to live at home with you. Don't you think she is tempted to stay out on her own? She does it only out of deference and love for you and Manni. But to ask her to give up her freedom of choice is asking too much. She has fought against falling in love with this boy, that much I can tell you, but how do you tell your heart not to feel what it feels? I tried it, Anna, and I paid the bitter price for it. You don't want her to go through life feeling unfulfilled, always wondering what life would have been. Life is too short for too many 'ifs'. At least, think it over and talk to Manni. Talk to the boys too. I'm sure they'll have something to say about this. Listen to them and talk to Geeta. She will be very willing to talk to you both but you must hear her out and try not to be any more judgmental than you already have been," Krishna said with a sad smile.

"I'm sorry, Krishna. I can never accept this and neither will Manni. This is not how it was supposed to be. She always knew our customs and our value system. But she has deliberately forsaken us with her arrogance. I am doing what is best for her just as I did for you."

"You know, Anna, on the way here I kept telling myself that I didn't want to say things that we might both regret and re-hash old stories. But there has always been an empty void in my life and I have more regrets than I care to count. And truth be told, you had a big part to play in the way my life has turned out. I did not want to be alone at my age. I would have liked all that you have. But instead, you drive your only daughter away because of your belief system. Trust me, Anna, you don't want her to be alone and bitter. You should count your blessings instead of tallying your liabilities. One day I would like to correct the mistakes I have made in my life. I hope I get a second chance," said Krishna and with that he left his brother's home.

29
PERAK
31ˢᵀ DECEMBER 1943

There was a gentle breeze blowing where Kah Hoe sat, some 2,000 feet above sea level on a hill called Blantan. He looked out across the plains, his eyes following the liquid line of the Perak River. The weak sun lit the verdant green around him for a short time before slinking hurriedly into the horizon. The hill was soon engulfed in darkness and the houses in Bidor and Tapah began to blink to life.

It was a time of deep introspection for Kah Hoe. Tomorrow would mark another year in the jungle for him. Would the future offer renewed hope or just a repetition of the bleak days which had passed, like a scratched record repeating itself over and over? The gaunt faces of the prisoners still haunted him. He couldn't understand why, after all the massacres that he had personally witnessed; it was the memory of their faces that would wake him up in the dead of night. Had they not intervened all those months ago, those POWs on the train would have most certainly met their maker on Burma's death railway.

Kah Hoe had made great progress with the guerillas. Chin Peng had taken Kah Hoe into his confidence but there was always a fine yet distinct line between him and the rest of the men. He was English speaking and educated, he came from a different class and his father's affiliation to the Kuomintang in China was an open secret. Naturally, the guerillas were a little wary of him at the best of times and Kah Hoe invariably felt left out.

But things started to change for him in October when the first group of Force 136 troops arrived. The men had made the slow journey to Malaya from Ceylon underwater, in a Dutch submarine. They were primarily made up of Kuomintang supporters and were English speaking. They were the same people as Kah Hoe and there was noticeable relief written all over his face when they trooped into the camp after days of stealthily trekking through the jungle to Blantan. The first code-named 'Gustavus' teams were led by John Davis and Richard Broome; a week before Christmas Day, Spencer Chapman arrived at the camp to reunite with his old comrades, Broome and Davis.

The British soldiers weren't the only newcomers to the Blantan camp. Another submarine arrived shortly after carrying a Chinese agent by the name of Tan Choon Lim. He was undoubtedly an important person in the resistance effort as Chin Peng himself, accompanied by a small group, met the Chinese agent and led him back to their mountain base. However, unbeknownst to Chin Peng, Choon Lim's true identity was none other than the legendary Lim Bo Seng, the infamous leader in the Malayan effort to support the Kuomintang. Kah Hoe had met the man once with his father during a fund-raising dinner for the China Relief Fund. As Kah Hoe watched introductions being made around the camp, he wisely decided to make himself scarce.

After the newcomers had settled in for a couple of quiet weeks, it was apparent that Kah Hoe and Davis had struck up a special friendship. The two of them could spend hours in each other's company, sharing laughs and jokes and a deep common interest in books, from the classics, to fiction and non-fiction.

In fact, the camp in Blantan would easily have been classified as 'comfortable'. The food that was prepared by the Chinese cooks was more than palatable, almost delicious. Kah Hoe and Davis both loved the outdoors and they would often spend hours trekking into the jungle. To pass the time, Davis who was a keen boxer, would dare any young and able-bodied man to spar with him, much to the delight of the rest of the camp.

Their banter wasn't always lighthearted. In their more serious sessions, Kah Hoe learned of how Force 136 came into being. When Singapore finally fell, Davis and some of his British officers fled. They managed to escape to Bombay and they soon realized they would not be able to return to Malaya without being captured by the Japanese. It was in India where Davis and Broome were first introduced to Lim Bo Seng. Together they hatched a plan to return to Malaya and carry out armed resistance against the Japanese with the aid of Chinese volunteers. Lim Bo Seng made a trip to Chungking and managed to convince Chinese youth from Malaya who were studying there to sign up for the cause. Thanks to Bo Seng's efforts, there was a swell in the number of anti-Japanese youth ready to return to their motherland to take up arms.

Kah Hoe sat on the precipice pulling at the wild grass that made him itch and scratch. He was amazed at how acute his sense of hearing had become since joining the guerillas. He turned around quickly only to see John Davis walking up the hill.

"How's it going, John?" asked Kah Hoe.

"It's going pretty good actually. Chin Peng and Lai are being a little dogmatic but I think it's all coming together. There seems to be a common understanding amongst everyone here," replied Davis.

Kah Hoe stood up, stretched his achy limbs and set off for sentry duty, closely followed by a swarm of bloodthirsty mosquitoes.

As Kah Hoe neared the camp, he could make out the faint happy sounds of laughter and clapping. *All that's missing is cake and ice cream,* he thought wryly as he approached. Cornering one of his gleeful comrades, Kah Hoe managed to extract some useful intelligence on the evening's festivities - an agreement had finally been reached between the MPAJA and the Allied Forces to work cohesively to defeat the Japanese. The MPAJA agreed to come under the command of the Allied Forces who in return would provide training, weapons and equipment.

Maybe this will be a better year after all.

30
PENANG
31ˢᵀ DECEMBER 1943

The bar top was heaving from the weight of pounding hairy arms and leaning women looking coyly at the men who had their arms wrapped around them. There were different scenes being played out simultaneously and all of them at varying pitches and levels; men were talking over each other, some women were giggling, others were chatting, some exhibitionists were locked in passionate embraces with Japanese soldiers and others rumba-ed with their drinking glasses.

It was New Year's Eve and the Officers' Mess on Farquhar Street was teeming with activity. In its previous life, the Mess was a beautiful colonial home with polished wooden floors and necklaces of chandeliers that dangled from the ceilings. Since the Japanese took it over, the overstuffed settees and the chintz curtains had been replaced by stark practical tables and chairs. The lustre and glamour had long left the mansion. But tonight it reclaimed some of its lost charm as the living room was transformed into a modern sitting room with comfortable chairs that had appeared out of nowhere.

Gurchan and Tochi walked coolly into the living room. It felt alien to them and in spite of all their bravado, they were both uncomfortable being there. Colonel Suzuki greeted them along with a couple of Chinese comfort girls who hung from his arms like walking aids. Gurchan's initial unease was dispelled instantly, as the Colonel seemed genuinely happy to see him. It was obvious that they had all been drinking quite heavily as the two girls, Kelly and Molly couldn't stop giggling. Colonel Suzuki left both the girls to entertain the two Sikh men as he followed a Japanese soldier who moments ago had whispered something into his ear.

The conversation between the four of them was lighthearted as they compared notes on the type of music they were interested in. When Colonel Suzuki returned, the banter quickly shifted to military matters; Gurchan and Tochi's backs both stiffened involuntarily. They looked at each other out of the corner of their eyes, giving each other unspoken instructions to tread carefully.

Colonel Suzuki explained that part of his job was intelligence work while the other aspect of it was to act as the liaison officer between the Japanese Service and the Indian Independence League. Kelly and Molly kept leaving the table to top up everyone's drinks before eventually settling down. It was Molly who brought up the recent spate of anti-Japanese activities that had taken place all over the island. Gurchan couldn't help feeling that this was a fishing expedition that had been cleverly arranged.

"How come there are so many Communists here in Penang?" asked Molly.

"These bloody Communists are a waste of time. We, the people of Nippon are trying our best to exterminate these vermin and we will behead them when we find them," said Suzuki very matter of fact.

"How can you say that about them?" asked Kelly. "You Nippon people don't treat them with any respect. You soldiers rape their women and act like sex maniacs. And you expect them to welcome you with open arms ah?" she exclaimed with arms in the air.

Gurchan and Tochi were shocked, sure that she was going to be punished right there in front of everyone. But to their astonishment, Colonel Suzuki looked at her and grinned!

"Ay, these soldiers have been fighting very hard to give these women their freedom. They should be grateful and be happy to pay them back in kind. That is not called rape! We don't think that is inhumane at all!" he said with a smirk.

"Yes, but in this country we don't treat our mothers, sisters and wives like dogs. What your soldiers do is inhuman. No wonder the Chinese and other Malayans hate you," declared an equally drunk Molly.

Colonel Suzuki turned and patted Molly on her knee as he sweetly reminded her that they had killed many political agitators and that they would continue to kill them as they raised their ugly heads.

Gurchan decided that it might not be such a good idea to sit quiet as the Colonel may take it as a sign of acquiescence so he bravely intercepted the two with a question of his own.

"Suzuki-san, have you caught these political agitators red-handed?" Suzuki had an incredulous look on his face.

"Of course! And we kill them. These agitators are ungrateful and they don't deserve to live! It's really quite simple."

"I agree with you, Suzuki-san. These Communists have no understanding of what you are doing for us. But what exactly has been happening in Penang these past few months? I've been a little out of touch," admitted Gurchan innocently.

Suzuki laughed out loud. "Are you telling me that you have not heard people say things about the Japanese?"

"No," declared Gurchan, feigning surprise, "Not until just now."

Kelly who had been watching Gurchan closely couldn't contain herself and she burst out, "Eh, you and your friends are dreaming ah! How you can say you got not hear people don't like Japanese ah! Outside ah, (as she pointed to the street), people all saying 'balik orang Jepun! I think ah, you sleeping under tempurung leh! Better you bangun!"

"No, I only mix with sporting people who don't get involved

157

in politics lah," replied Gurchan.

A quick glance at Tochi confirmed what both men had suspected – the Molly and Kelly double act was precisely just that. Both men knew that they had to tread very carefully to avoid the Colonel's trap.

"I think such people must be punished and taught a lesson," added Tochi. "They shouldn't be allowed to threaten the peace of this beautiful land".

"Are you saying I should be punished?" asked Kelly drawling coyly.

"Yes, I most certainly do", replied Tochi. "But we all know you are only joking, right? You're just trying to make Suzuki-san angry for the fun of it!"

There was silence for a moment and then Suzuki diffused it with a laugh.

"You cheeky darling," he said to Kelly as he kissed her.

Tochi and Gurchan exhaled slowly.

They had barely recovered when Suzuki suddenly turned to Gurchan and said in a low, cool tone, "There are some disturbing elements I would like to get my hands on. I believe they are young Chinese boys, troublemakers, going around pasting anti-Japanese propaganda posters all over the island. Have you heard or seen them?"

"No, I haven't," said Gurchan. He turned to Tochi and asked him the same question.

"No", said Tochi, "Neither have I. Have you seen them or their posters?"

"As a matter of fact I have a copy of the latest poster right here. It's written in English and its signed off Sin Kah. I believe they are an organization, a Chinese organization, I'm sure of it," Suzuki added with a distant look in his eyes. "I'd like to catch the young boys who go around spreading all these untruths."

Gurchan couldn't believe how brave he was feeling when he asked, "If you have a copy here, I'd be happy to look at it and keep my eye out for these hooligans. Vandals, that's what they are. Up to no good!"

"Yes, yes! That will be good if you can look out for them.

You can be my eyes and ears. More people looking out for them the better. Come, follow me, I'll show you the one I have in my room," said Suzuki.

Colonel Suzuki showed Gurchan four new sheets that he pulled out from his drawer. Gurchan pretended to read these for the first time. "But these don't look like they were pasted."

"No, these weren't," said Suzuki. "These came by post. It looks like these criminals are trying to demoralize us Japanese as well. Ha! How foolish of them!"

Gurchan continued to scrutinize the paper, "I don't think this reads as Sin Kah," said Gurchan. "It looks more like Singa, Suzuki-san," insisted Gurchan.

"I don't think so! I think they are trying to mislead us!" said Suzuki raising his voice. "What can Singa mean and why are you so convinced it's not Sin Kah?" he asked frowning at Gurchan.

"Look at it carefully, Suzuki-san. Singa means lion in Malay. See, the heading reads Allied H.Q. Communique." Before Gurchan could complete what he was saying, Suzuki butted in.

"Are you telling me this is the British Lion?"

"I think so, Suzuki-san. It seems to me that this must be the work of the British forces in the jungles and those rats are using Chinese, Malay and Indian agents to distribute them. Isn't the lion their symbol?" added Gurchan for good measure.

"No, no, I am telling you it's the Chinese and they are trying to throw us off the scent by using this Singa word," insisted Suzuki.

"Sin Kah means ploperty in Chinese," slurred Kelly.

"It's no matter, Kelly. I will try and find these rascals and I will report back to Suzuki-san and then you can do the necessary. These buggers must be wiped out," said Gurchan, with a sweep of his hand.

"You are a good man with true Nippon spirit," said Suzuki, amicably whacking Gurchan on the back.

It was way past midnight and the alcohol had lightened everyone's mood, Gurchan and Tochi included. So when Colonel Suzuki suggested that they all head to a cabaret to dance, there was a round of approval. They waited for Suzuki to lead the way as he staggered out the front door with his Kelly-Molly duo clinging to him. He had his arm squarely on Kelly's round bottom and she made no effort to remove it.

31

KUALA LUMPUR
31ST DECEMBER 1943

It was six in the evening and the birds had returned from t[
day's activities to settle on the power line; resting, chattering
muttering about the day's events, extolling the high point]
their feathery friends.

Inside, Rangaswamy was seated in his straight-bac[
wooden chair, its rattan seat sagging from the years of his sitt[
in prayer. He was at his prayer table, prayer beads in one h[
and eyes focused on the picture of his favourite deity. The g[
lamps flickered and danced their approval of the meditation
progress. He recited Ambal's name 108 times and went on
pray for all who were near and dear. He also prayed for those
didn't care much for - the Japanese and their speedy departu[
from Malaya.

As he came to the end of his prayers, he allowed the oth[
sounds in the house to invade his space. The pleasing sound
children's banter, the hollow sound of ever silver pots clangi[
against each other and as Swamy had grown accustomed to, t[
quiet sound of Chin Nam reading with his mouth and not h[

eyes. He whispered the words as if he were afraid that those would be lost forever if not spoken out loud.

Swamy was lost in reflection. Like a lost soul weaving his way through the past, Swamy's thoughts mapped their way through a mental filing system of images and sounds that had buried themselves deep in his subconscious. The image he was searching for was the one of Kah Hoe sitting on the steps of his house, looking dishevelled and gaunt and yet the distinct air of hope and anxiety the boy carried with him.

Swamy counted many blessings, but for the moment, the one he was most grateful for was his photographic memory. To stumble upon valuable information on nearly a daily basis and not be able to retain it would have been an utter shame and waste.

He had walked into his superior's office late one evening and there it was laid out on the table, like a prostitute baring intimate details for all to see. It was a schedule for the prisoners of war who were to be transported to the infamous Death Railway in Burma. Swamy remembered the stealthy late night meeting with one of Kah Hoe's runners to whom he passed this information. He had felt a deep sense of pride when the news that the POWs had been saved from certain death had filtered back to him. He had left his own indelible but invisible mark on history.

So accurate was Swamy's information that the guerillas salivated for more, like hyenas that had tasted blood. The second time had been a little different and more difficult for Swamy. He had gleaned information that led to the assassination of a high-ranking Japanese military officer. It had taken him weeks to rationalize that it was necessary to trade the life of one man who had become synonymous with torture and killing, to save the lives of hundreds of others. So, when Swamy passed on the information about the convoy that was making its way to Tanjung Malim, he knew that there would be blood on his hands.

There were times when Swamy felt like a total fraud. He would sometimes stand in front of his mirror and contemplate the two faces he had learnt to wear – mask off and mask on. It

sometimes frightened him, the man in the mirror and it was always Chin Nam who allayed his fears, reassuring him that he was in a unique position, albeit a dangerous one, but one that could tip favourably for Malaya.

His efforts in convincing the Japanese that he was 'one of them' had paid off handsomely when he was sent to attend a rally in Singapore at the Cathay Cinema where Subhas Chandra Bose announced the formation of the provisional government of Free India and declared himself the Head of State. For all his hatred for the Japanese and his scepticism of what Chandra Bose might have to say, Swamy was completely in awe of the eloquence of his rhetoric and the charisma of this larger-than-life man.

Swamy dragged his mind back to the present. Food had become scarce. Their ration cards were only for essentials like rice, flour and sugar, and the queue for these went on for hours reducing people who were irate enough to jostle and shove at the earliest opportunity. Thankfully, they were vegetarian and were able to get by on the produce they grew in their garden. Raman and Kah Heong had taken on the job of tilling the land behind 912. The boys were rewarded with beautiful tomatoes, kangkung, spinach, sweet potato leaves, tapioca and even some brinjals. Invariably, by the very nature of its hurried growth, it was the tapioca that gave them the most sustenance.

Kah Sing and Ramesh in turn had found their own endeavour. They would wander into people's homes and make them an offer they could scarce refuse, paying them money for their small possessions - fountain pens, watches and clocks - and selling these on to the Japanese who craved these like sweets. Their profits greatly contributed to the household kitty. Lavanya, much to her chagrin, was resigned to kitchen duty, helping her expecting mother with the preparation of meals. Everyone did their little bit to keep the inhabitants of 912 fed and watered.

Above all, Swamy's happiest moments were derived from watching his dear, dear friend, Chin Nam, make a slow but sure recovery. What had started off as an arduous journey had resulted in some quite remarkable signs of improvement. Elaine had worked so hard with him and allowed him all the temper tantrums of a tempestuous three year old. But she had also been firm when she knew she had to be, with his exercise and her insistence that he begin to talk a little at a time instead of pointing to something he wanted.

By the eve of the New Year, Chin Nam could take small steps without shuffling his feet as if they were in shackles and he had started to have short conversations with Swamy. That would be Swamy's high point as he reflected on the year that had brought them nothing but hardship and pain. Yet in a twisted way, it had elevated two good friends to a brotherhood that transcended blood and marrow.

32
LETTER TO KEN
KUALA LUMPUR, 2009

Geeta rarely used her fine Italian writing paper but she felt the letter she was about to write to Ken warranted only the finest stationery. She had a head full of wobbly jelly thoughts which she rationally attempted to sort into their respective jelly moulds. Much to her irritation, she only came up with a neapolitan-like concoction.

Focus, she chided herself. *Start at the very beginning and tell it step by step.* She took a deep breath and finally put pen to paper.

12/10/2009

My darling,

My mind is in such a mess, I don't know where to start. As much as I promised myself to be systematic and logical, I find my thoughts disorganised and scrambled as I sit down to write to you.

So much has happened in the last two weeks, so much unpleasantness, hate (I know it's a strong word) and bitterness that in the end, it is all very sad, really.

165

I wish I had something new to report, but from the tone of this letter, you will know how things went. Krishna Chitappa went to see my father, hoping to talk some sense into him. He told him he was being a bigot with double standards, to which my father proudly agreed he was.

He is adamant about not accepting or recognising our relationship. I think he feels that if he continues being belligerent and stubborn, that it will wear me down and that I will give in. It hasn't occurred to him that we are cut from the same cloth and that I can be equally single minded.

I have been sitting under a cloud of depression and at times even hopelessness; because even though I know I have Chitappa on my side, it feels like a battle I am fighting alone and it's a lonely place.

It would be so much easier if you were here with me. Nearly every night before I fall asleep, I lie in bed and think about us - how long we've known each other, friends first and then lovers. You have known me since I was born and who would have predicted that we would end up together. You have been in nearly every frame of my growing-up photos - every birthday party (up until you left for boarding school), family picnics, dinner. I can't pick any significant moment in my life without seeing you reflected in it.

What should have been a celebration in us bringing our two families together has become the very wedge that is driving it apart. I have spent so many sleepless nights worrying about us. How I long for the simplicity of our childhood friendship, the uncomplicated, carefree and innocent days when no one bothered what we were up to or where we were. I remember begging you to play pick up sticks with me, because you called it 'girlie'!

Had anyone held a crystal ball up to my face and shown us together, walking along Kensington High Street with your arm around my shoulder or of us lying together after a languorous afternoon of love-making, I would have accused them of witchcraft! Who would have expected or believed that the little Tamil girl in two pigtails would end up with the slightly portly Chinese boy with slick, side parted hair, stuck down by a touch of Brylcream. It would have been as unexpected as the proverbial fox and the crow getting married.

But here WE are, Ken, the fox and the crow. It would be so easy for me to accept defeat and do my parents' bidding but all our combined memories married through a friendship spanning generations would die a certain and sudden death. Our families will never come through this even if we end our relationship.

I am NOT willing to give up on us. Everything that is good about me is because of you. You make me a better version of myself, put me on even keel and lift me in the best possible way. You are always all that I need and I love you desperately.

G xxx

P.S. Here's an update on the local political scene and this case I am working on. Recently, three assemblymen from PKR defected to become "independent." For taking that leap, they now go by the moniker "The Three Frogs." Their new found loyalty has shifted the balance of power in Perak.

The Chief Minister's office was deemed "vacated" as he had lost the confidence of the majority of the House and this has sparked a constitutional crisis in Perak. The legal question is whether the Chief Minister can be removed only by a vote of no confidence at the assembly or whether the Sultan can make that decision. Not an easy point to do research on, but it is such a thrilling case to be involved in. Uncle Satnam has been asked to lead the team for the Chief Minister.

33
HEARTACHE
KUALA LUMPUR, 2009

If Geeta's mobile phone could speak, it would have told the multitude of people who called her that she was in court. But all it could do was take message after message, desperately asking her to return their calls.

When she walked out of the freezing courtroom that Thursday lunch time and turned her phone on, she was embarrassed at the number of times her phone beeped rudely at her. The first message was from her father telling her in a voice that was surprisingly calm, that her mother had been admitted to hospital. She had had chest pains while cooking lunch and he had rushed her to The National Heart Institute. She was in Block D, Room 409. Geeta stood rooted to the spot as she tried to absorb this information. She immediately called her office and told them she wasn't coming in; she had to steady her nerves before making the call to her father.

He sounded distant on the phone and she sounded too matter of fact (much to her own surprise); she told him that she was on her way. Traffic was gridlocked and by the time she made it down the hospital's narrow basement carpark, she was more than a little ruffled.

Her father was alone in the room. He had turned the air conditioning off and the room was still, as if all the air had been wrung out of it. She could pick up the faint scent of her mother's lavender powder. This was the first time father and daughter had been alone after Geeta had moved out. He barely nodded his head at her.

"Where is Amma?" she asked him.

"They've taken her to run some tests," was his curt reply, head bent, making it clear he wanted to make no eye contact.

Geeta prepared herself for an onslaught of more mono-syllabic answers. "What tests are they doing? Did she have a heart attack or was it just chest pains?" she persisted.

"What do you mean by JUST chest pains, huh? Do you want to see her dead from a heart attack? Is that when you will be happy? Do you have any idea how she has been suffering since you so selfishly dropped that bombshell on us and then walked out. Your mother hasn't slept in weeks and she hasn't been eating well. Most times she is crying and she doesn't want to go out in case she sees someone she knows. She's ashamed, do you know that? Do you understand the pain you have put her through or are you so self-centred that you can't see beyond your precious self!"

It took a lot of strength for Geeta not to retaliate. She knew her fight with her parents was far from over and she had been bracing herself all the way to the hospital. She reminded herself not to say anything rash and not to be defensive, but she could feel her anger snaking its way up and choking her. She could feel the blood pounding in her head, she had to get out so she turned quickly on her heel and stormed out of the room. She only realised the hot tears on her cheeks when she walked out of the hospital; the hot, humid air on the other side steam rolling into her.

Once she had calmed down, she returned to the nurse's station where she made enquiries about her mother's whereabouts and condition. As she was talking to the doctor, she felt a light tap on her shoulder. She turned around expecting another fight and was instead relieved to see a friendly face looking back at her.

169

"I heard about Periamma and I got here as soon as I could," Manjula said.

Geeta hugged her and felt her body slacken as she wept again into her cousin's shoulder.

"Ssh, stop crying now. You can't let Amma see you like this. You must be strong for both of them, as difficult as the circumstances may be," said Manjula.

"Am I really the reason why Amma is here? Have I been such an unkind daughter? Have I really been as selfish as Appa says I am? I couldn't bear it if anything should happen to her. I could never live with the guilt. Oh Manjula, what on earth am I going to do! I don't know how to solve this and I don't know what to do," cried Geeta.

"Hang on a minute, Geeta," she said in a stern voice. "We don't know how bad it is. Let's wait and speak to the doctor and see what the results are. Whatever the outcome, we will get through it. Your mother is a strong-willed woman. She may not look it but she has an iron will. She isn't going to be defeated by this! You know her fighting spirit. You can't afford to collapse in a heap like this in front of her. She is going to need your support and you will have to rise above all the anger and unhappiness and bitterness to be there for them. Your Appa isn't going to make it easier for you, but you have to be patient and try your best not to fight back when he says something you disagree with. Once we know Periamma's diagnosis, our focus has to be her health," she said as she gently led her back to the room.

"Well, the doctor said she's been taken to do a blood test and that we need to wait for the results. That will determine if she needs an angiogram. If she has a block or more than one block in her arteries, they will either have to put a stent in or in the worst case, she will need to have bypass surgery. So it's all hanging right now and I haven't spoken to Appa about it. In fact, he gave me an earful when I went in to her room just now."

"That's his way of dealing with the situation, Geeta. Don't take what he says to heart, forgive the pun, she attempted a frail joke. He needs to be in control and if he lets his guard down he will break down. Don't focus on his temper. Remember, your

170

mother is the issue here and we need to decide what is best for her. And for that, you and your father will have to get past your differences and work at getting her the best treatment and care. How long will it be before they bring her back?" asked Manjula.

"The nurse said it wouldn't be that long. She should be here anytime soon," replied Geeta.

"Come on," said Manjula kindly, "Let's go see what Appa's up to."

"Manju, please stay with me till I leave," implored Geeta.

"I will, as long as you stop crying and start being positive."

Geeta's father looked up expectantly when the door opened, hoping to see his wife being wheeled in, but was crestfallen to see Geeta and Manjula standing there.

"Hello, Periappa," said Manjula. "What are the doctors saying? What exactly happened?" she asked.

"Why don't you ask her what happened and why it happened," he said, waving in Geeta's direction. "She is the reason why her mother is here," he said bitterly.

"Listen, Periappa. Periamma will be brought back here anytime now and the last thing we want to do is make her uncomfortable. I have spoken to Geeta and she agrees that we need to focus on her recovery and her health issues, not continue this bickering. It's no good for her, for you or Geeta. Your differences need to be sorted out but this is not the place to do it. Please let's be adults about this and focus our energy on getting Periamma well and on her feet again. You know how much she hates to be idle and this recovery will be difficult for her. So, we have to ensure that she keeps her mind focused on getting better and back to her usual routine. Seeing you both like this is going to drive her into depression. You both are all she has here and you must come through for her. Is that understood?" There seemed to be a silent agreement when seconds later the door was held open and a gurney was wheeled in.

Geeta went to her mother and hugged her and against all her sensibilities, started to cry. Her mother stroked her head and said in her usual manner, "Che che, why are you crying, kanne? I am here, aren't I? Don't be silly, I will be fine," she said into the mop of hair that was buried and blubbering in her hospital gown. "All I felt was a little breathlessness and your Appa insisted I come and have it checked. It's nothing serious. They did an ECG and it was normal but they are being a little cautious because of Krishna Chitappa and have run some other tests," she said with the confidence only a mother can possess.

No one would have guessed that this was the first time mother and daughter were meeting after an estrangement. Parvathi talked about the goings-on in her life, subtly filling in the gaps for Geeta. Geeta was so struck by her mother's resilience and ability to rise above without a word of anger or accusation. She saw in her mother for the first time, a gentle and deep love for her child, she saw her mother's quiet strength in holding this family together, she saw her mother's healing hand in trying to fix some of the cracks and fissures in the relationship between father and daughter. The woman she thought was weak and without a voice was the bridge that would allow two very strong headed individuals, similar in spirit and temperament, find a wedge of space somewhere between understanding and tolerance.

Manjula, sensing that the time had come for the three of them to be alone to put right what should have been done earlier, made her excuses and left, giving Geeta a conspiratorial wink.

When it was time for Geeta to leave, her parents were fully filled in on the details of her work life, though they were all too careful not to tread on her personal life. She hugged and kissed her mother as tightly as the I.V. line would allow her and hugged her father fiercely as he hugged her back. She brushed the tears that were peeping out of the corner of her eyes and left with the promise to be back tomorrow morning with breakfast and the newspapers for both of them.

34
A GRIM CHOICE
KUALA LUMPUR, 2009

It was possibly Geeta's worst moment ever. Her journey from her mother's hospital room to the carpark was veiled in heavy regret. With feet leadened by the weight of her decision, the ghost of Geeta had come to take her place in this world. What she was about to do would affect her happiness and that of the man she loved. And yet on some level, her subconscious had decided that sacrificing her love would redeem her soul, giving them angel wings to rise above the embers of a lost love.

She scripted several versions of a break up line in her head, cancelling one to script over it; a mental palimpsest. Her heart raged war with her head. Her head forced her hand to write. A list of pros and a list of cons. Her head scored an extra point under the 'con' column. She hated her head for it. Geeta became an unwilling tenant in the living world. She preferred hovering over the soul world, but for her singular desire to speak to Ken, to hear his voice, to seek shelter, to hide, never to be discovered. Her world would soon resemble a parched landscape, cracking from neglect, lack of sustenance and love. It would crumble about her, her crackled memories and broken, void promises.

Her only sounding board was Krishna Chitappa and she wailed and howled into his shoulder. She cursed the entire Brahmin community, for its 'stupid and insanely selfish customs'. Her grief was so intense, all he could do was to hold her. This was no time for hollow words.

It took Geeta nearly an entire week before she could make the call to Ken; it took her a further three attempts to do so having hung up twice. He tried calling her back but she couldn't bring herself to answer it. She didn't know how she would react when she heard his voice.

She finally called him late one night, after she had finished half a bottle of wine. Armed with alcohol-induced bravery, she patiently waited for him to answer his phone.

Tears began to flow the moment she heard his voice. She closed her eyes tight in case her spilt tears leaked from her eyes to his listening ears. Her words were incoherent gibberish - "I can't do this anymore", "My mother is suffering because of me", "I am incredibly selfish and ungrateful" to "I can't make you happy if I marry you because I will always have guilt in me". Ken had to yell at her before he could get a word in sideways.

"What in the world are you trying to tell me!" he shouted down her earpiece. "Are you telling me it's over? I can't and won't accept your reasons. We've been through this so many times and we decided that I would both be strong for you. So your mother has chest pains and you run off the deep end and think you caused it? How far fetched is that! I will not allow you to do this to us, G. You cannot bury us under this ridiculous guilt" he said quietly.

"I don't know what else to do, Ken," she sobbed. "There's no doubt that our relationship has put a lot of stress on my parents' health and if anything happens to either of them, I couldn't live with myself."

"But you think it's okay to break my heart and yours? You are obviously upset. But what can I do so far away, huh? Get a hold of yourself. It's not like you didn't know what you were up against. Am I not worth anything to you? Grow up and take charge and control of your life, for God's sake. I would move mountains and give up my life for you and all you can give me is some pathetic shit like your parents might die on you. Listen to yourself! You caved in under pressure after all. Ha, all your bravado bullshit about how I was your moon and stars and now what? If this is what you want then screw you and your family! I'm glad I found out now and not two days before our wedding. Well, goodbye and good luck to you. I hope you're happy now," he yelled and hung up.

Geeta sat rooted to the floor. She was numb from all the crying and now her eyes were void of tears. She rocked back and forth, cradling her phone. Eventually, she managed to crawl into bed. The stack of her Tata's letters were illuminated by her bedside table, beckoning her like a salve.

26th April 1930

Dearest Appa,

Reading your last letter left me feeling sad and depressed. The guilt I carry with me now because I am not there with you and Amma especially during these trying times after Amma's fall has made me homesick. I hope with sufficient rest and with the proper medication, her hip will soon recover. For someone who is so used to keeping herself busy, she must hate being confined to her bed.

The depression has hit Malaya quite badly. Rubber prices have slumped and unemployment is on the rise. But don't worry, I am still in employment and even better, I am seriously considering buying a house. There is an English planter who has lost his job and is desperate to sell his house. I have had a look at it and it will make us a happy home. I will put in an offer sometime soon and, Ambal willing, 912 Batu Road will be our new address. I have checked with an astrologer here about the number and he has said it is suitable for my jadaham. Maybe you might want to ask Sankaran Ayer if the number is good. I am sure that you and Amma will like the house and I hope and pray that you both will be able to come and stay with us soon.

I want to share a funny experience with you Pa. I was reading Somerset Maughm's latest short story called 'The Letter'. The story is about a woman who murders her lover. She was a planter's wife and she lived on a rubber estate. Her husband had gone to Singapore and she was alone in her bungalow. She claimed to receive a surprise visitor, a planter from a neighbouring estate who apparently tried to molest her. She, in self-defense, took her husband's revolver and shot him dead. Her lawyer uncovers a copy of a letter, which she had sent to the man she shot asking him to come and spend a night as her husband was away. Unbeknownst to the planter's wife, the letter finds its way into the hands of the dead man's mistress! The accused's lawyer was surreptitiously shown a copy of the letter. He knew his client was doomed if this letter was made public! Well, to cut a long story short, the accused's husband paid the dead man's mistress a sum of money in return for the original letter and she was subsequently acquitted.

Why I am telling you this is because when I mentioned this story to a colleague of mine, he laughed and told me that it was based on a true story - a murder at the Victoria Institution itself! Imagine that, Appa. A murder in the very school I am teaching at. What headlines that must have made back then.

This is apparently what happened at my school – the wife of the acting principal shot dead a man who was a friend to both her and her husband. She claimed that he tried to force himself on her. She was convicted and sentenced to death but the Sultan of Selangor pardoned her on the condition that she left Malaya.

I had better stop myself here or I shall go on forever! Please convey my love to Amma and tell her that I pray to Ambal everyday that she bless you both with good health.

My fondest love,
Your son,
Rangaswamy

Wiping her tired eyes, she gently folded the letter and returned it to its pile. Surely this letter was a sign from her past that to keep her family together, she would have to leave Ken.

35
A LONELY SPARROW
KUALA LUMPUR, 2009

There wasn't even a conversation or a discussion about whether Geeta should return home. It seemed like the most natural thing to do, especially with her mother finally out of the hospital. She explained to Krishna Chitappa that her conscience couldn't rest, so one day she packed her bags and her guilt and moved back.

The familiar smells and sounds gathered her in their waiting arms and made her realize how much she had missed home. Her room was comforting; nothing had been moved and everything was just as she had left it. *A strange feeling. It's like I've been dead or missing and I have suddenly walked back into my old life to find everything the way it was, like in a movie,* she thought, running her hand over her dressing table.

Geeta felt drained, both physically and mentally. She felt miserable with her dismembered life which was falling apart.

I feel like someone has slowly and deliberately picked at the stitches and unravelled the threads of my life. A little bit at a time, peeling back layers of my flesh, until all that is left is a huge frayed hole in the middle of me. How drastically my life has changed.

I always thought I would have control over it simply because I thought I was smart and had a good, secure job. To think of those times when I scoffed at Sowmya and how she had allowed her parents to make choices for her and had given her grief for caving in. Who would have thought I would be in the same predicament. It's amazing how your parents can give you all the love and support and nurture you to be this independent woman and in the next breath take it all away. And why? Because they LOVE you! How ironic that they should take away my essence of happiness because they think they know what will make me happy. And am I any better off than Sowmya? I don't think so. At least, she never experienced the kind of love and oneness like I had with Ken. She'll never know what it is to lose someone who is a part of her soul. I feel like a widow. How crazy that must sound but that's the truth. An unmarried widow.

I wonder what Ken is up to? Is he hurting like me? What I wouldn't do to hold him right now and never let him go. But that's what I thought I could do. I never realized I would cave in under pressure. Ken is right. I am a coward. How badly I have treated him. I wouldn't blame him if he never wants to speak to me again.

But I can't bear the thought of not seeing his beautiful face or smelling him or pulling my body close to his and willing it to swallow me up. I should never have allowed myself to fall in love with him. Because I know I will never make another man happy when I can't give him all of me. There will always be some of me that will be reserved for the love I have lost, buried deep inside of me, like a scar that only I can see and touch just to remind me of my loss. What a price to pay. I know I will mourn him but there will be a day when I can lift my head and face the world. Maybe even hold my face up to the sun and challenge its brilliance. I know the pain will recede but the wound will throb a dull throb when I caress it, but most of all I hope that Ken will find it in his heart to forgive me.

She was sitting numb in front of her mirror, looking but not seeing, as tears streamed down her neck. Her nose was dripping its own sorrow and everything about Geeta spelled regret and sadness. She looked so lonely and lost that even reading one of her grandfather's letters now would have offered her little solace or help in finding her way back to the life she had before.

For the first time, her balm would be to write a letter instead of reading one. She stretched over to her bedside drawer, opened it and took out her writing paper that was waiting to receive her words.

06/11/2009

My dear Sowmya,

I know I haven't written you a proper letter in a long time but this moment seems to be most opportune.

I feel like my world is falling apart all around me and I am unable to do anything to stop it. I can see it crumble but I can't seem to stand up and tell the people who are hacking at it to go away. I want to run and hide and wake up to find it a bad dream.

As you must know, I moved out and went to stay with Krishna Chitappa because of the huge falling out I had with Appa and Amma. I was strangely at peace there because I could pretend that my life was good and everything was okay. Then Amma was admitted into hospital for chest pains and my world went topsy-turvy.

The short of it is that I have decided to end my relationship with Ken. I know what you must be thinking but I didn't know what else to do. Seeing Amma so fragile made me feel so selfish and the guilt was just too much for me. As you can imagine, Ken was angry and disappointed with me. He said all the things I already know; that I am weak and gullible and selfish. Our last conversation ended with him hanging up on me.

I have moved back home and am so miserable, Sowmya. I hate my life. I am so sorry I was so judgmental of you when you made your choices but I can understand it couldn't have been easy for you. But you're happy and you're growing to love Vivek and that's so good for you.

My life is a huge mess and I don't know where to start if I want to fix it. I feel so sorry for myself which I know is pathetic but I

179

don't know what to do. I am sorry for unburdening this on you but I needed to tell someone who wouldn't be able to tell me the obvious face-to-face.

Anyway, I've been promising you Amma's Puli Kachal recipe, so here it is:

Puli Kachal

Puli (size of a tennis ball)
6 dried chillies, cut small)
1 tbsp kadahu
1 ½ tsp salt
¼ tumbler raw peanuts (soak in hot water for a while and then peel)
¼ tumbler kadalai parappu (soak for about 10 minutes)
Drain peanuts and kadalai parappu of excess water

For the Podi:
In some gingelly oil, fry 1 ½ tbsp of vendiam until it just starts to turn colour. (Don't let it burn as it has a bitter taste when it does) and a 1 inch piece of perangayam.

Method:
Fry kadahu, peanuts and kadalai parappu in 4 tbsp or more of gingelly oil until it turns golden brown.
Add turmeric and fry for a while. Add 1 sprig of curry leaves.
Add puli thani and salt.
Let it thicken and add podi (approximately ½ to ¾ tsp)
Taste for salt.

Take care Sowmya. Sorry for sounding so morose but I hope you understand. Do write to me when you have the time.

Love,
Geeta

36
KEN'S CONUNDRUM
LONDON, 2009

For four nights in a row he had visited the same cocktail bar on Liverpool Street and had many of the same wretched drink – gin martinis, dry with a hint of vermouth. After the second day, the bartender neither raised an eyebrow nor asked him what he wanted to drink. Discreetly, a martini would appear before him and Ken would gaze into the liquid and down it. He sat staring into the empty glass expecting some answers at the bottom.

This isn't a fucking tea-leaf reading session, Ken, he thought to himself. *How could I have been so naïve? To think that a girl from a conservative Brahmin family would throw caution to the wind and run off into the sunset with me! Even if our families have been friends for more than a generation! Here I am, night after night, drowning my sorrows and for what? The awful truth is I love her. I love her so deeply I don't know where to begin to start un-loving her. She's in the breath that I inhale, she lives in my soul, I can't reach in and tear her out! She's mine and I am hers. There's no need for any logical reason, we just are. We belong together and I know she knows that. I wonder what she is doing now? Is she grieving like me or has she hardened her heart and blocked out the pain and the hurt? I'm like a blithering, blustering, love sick fool! But I can't lose her. Oh, fuck this shit!*

"Pablo, another martini and I'll be out of your hair!" he yelled across to the bartender.

He was on his second sip when he felt a hand gently touch his shoulder. He turned around to see Mikhail, his colleague and close buddy standing behind him.

"Hey bro", said Mikhail, "I could smell your trail all the way back to the office! Is that a martini you're having?" he asked amiably.

Ken nodded in agreement.

"I'll have the same," he said to the bartender. "Shall we have a plate of jamon?" he asked Ken.

Ken shrugged a whatever.

"Let's put some food into you buddy, and then you can sit here in silence. Or you can shit on me about what a bitch she is or we can play noughts and crosses. Whatever you choose," said Mikhail.

"I'm totally fucked up, Mikhail. You don't want to hear it," said Ken.

"Try me. I haven't got to be back early tonight, so I'm all ears."

Ken took another sip and started to tell Mikhail all that had happened. He cursed her family and her community and he cursed her too. "I don't know how to start pulling myself out of this rut. I know I need to but I don't know how. She means, I mean she meant everything to me. She was in every thought I had about my future. How do you suddenly start making plans for just one! I've forgotten how to do the whole single thing. Isn't that bizarre? Here I am in fucking London and I don't know what to do with myself," rattled Ken.

"You need to get yourself laid man, if you don't mind me saying this," said Mikhail.

"Are you out of your fucking mind?! Why the fuck would I want to go and do that? Like my life isn't complicated enough.

182

I have no desire to chat up women at some sleazy bar and what would I say to her; excuse me, would you like to sleep with me because my girlfriend just dumped me and I feel like shit! Yeah, there's a chat up line that should work wonders," Ken rolled his eyes at Mikhail.

"I'm not bloody asking you to jump into a serious relationship! For God's sake, I think what you need is a really good, mind blowing screw! Just let your frustrations and your hurt out. You know the saying, fuck it out of your system!" he said smiling at his own cleverness.

"You know that's the problem with guys like you, Mikhail. You will never find someone to build a relationship with. Have you any idea what it's like to love someone so completely that you would lay your life down for her? Of course you wouldn't because you've moved on to the next girl even before you know her name. How do you do it? To tell you the truth, I envy you. Maybe you're right. Maybe I should go out and have a one-night stand and see how I feel."

"That's the spirit! Look, I don't want to get emotionally attached to some chick. I'm in it for the fun and I don't pretend to walk her down the garden path either. I make it very clear what my intentions are so there isn't any drama. Look what all that emotional crap got you. You can't sleep at night, you can barely work, you're a bloody zombie. This is the end of you wallowing and feeling sorry for yourself. From tomorrow on, you're going to be positive about what's happened to you. Maybe it is the best thing that happened. Can you imagine if you had married her without their consent? And they disowned her? That's a heavy load to carry. What the fuck would you have done then, man? Things always happen for a reason, bro. This obviously was doomed from the start. I mean man, who needs in-laws who can't get over their own prejudices. It's the 21st century bro. You're better off without the hassle. You get yourself cleaned up and try and put this behind you and I'll find you some hot chicks. Cheers brother, to a new era and a new awakening!" With those words, the two of them guzzled the remains of their martinis, paid the bill and stumbled out onto the noisy street.

When Ken woke up the sun was streaming through his window. The pounding in his head reminded him that he had obviously drunk way too much the night before and had forgotten to take, his never-fail panacea, two Panadols. He was about to throw his duvet off when he heard noises coming from the kitchen. Before he could pull his boxers on, a tall vision in his bathrobe strolled into the bedroom carrying a tray of steaming hot coffee. *Oh shit,* he thought, *what the fuck have I done now?*

"Good morning," chirped the 5' 8" green eyed, blonde bombshell. "Coffee?"

"Uh, I don't mean to be rude, but who are you? And how did you get into my apartment?" asked a bewildered Ken.

She pouted and made a face at Ken before breaking into a big grin.

"Aw babe, how could you forget so quickly? Don't you remember coming to Ronnie Scott's last night? You came up to me and asked me if I wanted a drink and then we danced and you asked me to come home with you," she explained in a drawl he didn't care much for.

"What is your name?" he asked incredulously.

"Annika," she replied sweetly. "You don't remember that either! Do you remember us making love twice through the night or was it so unremarkable that you've forgotten that too! But tell me this, who is G?"

"Why are you asking?" he said defensively.

"Well, that's because you kept calling out the alphabet while you were fucking me and I kept thinking, gee, what a lucky girl she must be!" retorted Annika with a slight attempt at humour. "The only thing I can't figure out is why you slept with me when you are obviously in love with her?"

"I think you need to leave and I am terribly sorry if I seem callous and flippant. I am not that sort of person," he admitted, lifting his hands in surrender. "I don't know what came over me and I apologise."

"Hey listen, I was looking for a good time myself so no worries. I'll get changed and be out of here in no time. But, if you feel like talking about whatever, call me. I'll leave my number on your table," she said in a friendly enough tone. With that she got changed and quietly let herself out.

All the while, Ken sat on his bed with his head buried in his hands not knowing whether to laugh out loud at the incredulity of it all or slap himself for not remembering anything from last night.

37
TAPAH
30TH APRIL 1944

Kah Hoe had recused himself from the outside world. He was ensconced in a safe house in Tapah. It was like any other ubiquitous shophouse, with a coffee shop on the ground floor. During pre-war times, the food here was exceptional; one vendor sold lam mee and another hor fan. The hor fan stall was famous with both the locals and outstation visitors who flocked here for their weekly or monthly fix. But circumstances were different now, the noodle sellers had since disappeared, hiding in their homes; so the owner of the coffee shop had to be a little more creative. They still served their famous thick coffee and had added pan mee to the menu; a wartime twist on a Hokkien favourite. The reason the guerillas picked this particular shophouse was due to the high flow of human traffic that would allow them to blend effortlessly with the stream of people that passed through. The upstairs floor was rented out to supplement an already healthy income.

Kah Hoe had since become one of the disjointed fragments in this kaleidoscope. Different faces with different stories soldered together with the black coffee and soupy noodles but Kah Hoe kept his stories close to his heart. He kept to himself and encouraged only the occasional superficial conversation that was always peppered with untruths about himself.

He had not come to Tapah for rest and recreation but instead was here under unfortunate circumstances. The Japanese had captured Lim Bo Seng the previous month, when he had come to garner more support and funds for his comrades in the jungle. Kah Hoe was now his replacement.

The room upstairs was basic, with two mattresses on the floor in one corner. There was a formica table under one window that held an array of personal belongings, books and the odd cockroach in search of sustenance. There was a lone bulb to light the whole room, sufficient considering its compact size. There were two sets of windows; one set fronted the main road, giving Kah Hoe a clear and undisturbed view of the people who walked in and out of the coffee shop. The other window was at the back of the room and overlooked the back alley, affording the noisy alley cats some unwarranted stares.

Kah Hoe looked on as filthy water sloshed out from a big, blue tub that served as the wash basin for the dirty plates that came through the coffee shop. This dingy alley was also a playground, home and meal stop for stray cats and other vermin. This window would be Kah Hoe's ticket to freedom as the bars that appeared to be securely fastened, could be easily screwed on and off. In Kah Hoe's case, because of his gaunt and rake-thin frame, he needed only to unscrew three bars should he have to make a quick escape.

It wasn't long before heavy hands came pounding on the metal grill downstairs. Kah Hoe had taught his body not to fall into a deep sleep, so he had jumped out of bed on the first rattle. He also slept fully clothed, forever in anticipation of uninvited visitors. His instinct to survive kicked in instantly, as he made his way in the dark to the bars at the end of his room. In no time at all, Kah Hoe was on the roof, stealthily making his escape in the dead, dark night. He could hear both his heart pounding and the pounding of feet clad in army boots. He knew that he had a head start but he wasn't able to screw all three bars back and the Japanese would soon realize how he had made his getaway.

187

He sprang lightly from one tile to the next and kept willing the end of the roof to come into sight when he lost his footing and cut his shin on a broken tile. He grimaced and sucked in his breath, for he knew it was a reasonably bad cut but he knew he had to keep going. Kah Hoe could now hear the sound of footsteps and the shouting that followed and knew that the soldiers had figured out that he was on the roof. With every ounce of energy he had, he focused on the tiles ahead and not his injury. He hobbled until he came to the end of the row of shophouses. He knew there was a water pipe that would lead him down to street level and it would only be a short dash to the forest and hopefully freedom. Over the sound of the beating of his heart in his ears, he could tell from the commotion behind him that he was rapidly losing his lead.

Kah Hoe shimmied down the water pipe and landed awkwardly on his injured leg. He could feel the throbbing spread through his body and a weakness closing over him.

I have to be strong. I have to focus on staying alive. I have to live. I have to run! I can run. I can beat them. This is my jungle. I know it well even in the dark. I will be safe there. It will protect me.

It took every last ounce of strength for him to pick up his pace. The Japanese soldiers were still hot on his heels and were screaming at him to give up and surrender. Surrender was not a word that Kah Hoe subscribed to.

The safety of the jungle was only a few more steps away and Kah Hoe made one last burst for freedom. Lunging forward with his tired lungs gasping for air, he tripped over a large branch that was covered with mossy leaves from a recent rainfall. He fell with a clumsy crash, twisting his good leg. He tried to push himself up but immediately buckled under the pain. There was no time to get up, so using his upper body strength, he continued to drag himself along the jungle floor. He could hear the leaves behind him rustle as the ground resonated with the sound of boots, each footstep beating out his imminent capture. The enemy was upon him.

His capture was something that Kah Hoe had never imagined because that would have been defeat in his eyes. So when the Japanese soldiers descended on him like jackals to a carcass, he knew his time was up. One soldier pulled him by his hair nearly breaking his neck while another kicked him from behind. The pain in his legs was quickly replaced by the deep, deep shame and sense of defeat that came with being captured. Kah Hoe could taste the earth in his mouth as they slammed his face back into her bosom. They took their turns with him, each with their own personal style of abuse.

By the time the fifth soldier had stamped on him, he had lost track of which part of his body had been beaten out of shape. He could taste his own blood; tart and acidic. The soldiers lifted him by his arms and dragged him off, his legs dangling behind him leaving behind a trail of blood. All Kah Hoe could remember was the taste and smell of shame; a putrid mix of salty, bitter, metallic shame.

38
BATU GAJAH PRISON
1ST MAY 1944

Once his body had been beaten to a pulp, they had handcuffed him, to make doubly certain that he could not escape. The irony was that Kah Hoe was now a prisoner of his own wounds. Escaping his captors was far from his mind, as he lay almost lifeless. The soldiers had picked him up like a limp rag and thrown him into their truck. He would be dispensed with in time, of that he was certain, but how and where was still a secret.

The night was still jet-black and the army truck jaunted along the deserted road for what seemed like eternity. When they arrived at Batu Gajah Prison, he was dragged off and unceremoniously thrown into a cell. The few hours Kah Hoe spent there would be the only blissful hours he would have without anyone kicking, shouting and torturing him.

He slowly became conscious of his surroundings after hearing a blood-curdling scream outside his cell. He tried to pry his eyes open, but they were sealed shut under a crust of dried blood. The light in his cell was blinding and it made him wince in agony when he finally opened his eyes. He tried to move his legs but the sharp pain stopped him. He could feel his mouth and throat dry and parched, desperately in need of water.

The screaming started again, as if someone was lodged in his brain, yelling in his ear to be let out. Kah Hoe tried to focus on the memory of what had happened. The screaming was in a different language, that much he could make out. But where was he? Then he heard the sound of metal on metal and the sound jangled his nerves. It was the violence of the kick that made him bring his legs up to his chest and shake. Another kick and more screaming. He covered his face with his hands and this time he knew what was coming next. His senses returned fully to the present; he was a captured prisoner-of-war.

Kah Hoe's hands were pulled from his face by a kempei. He lifted him and forced him to kneel. The act was just one in a string of many to make him feel worthless and subservient. A misshapen metal plate was slid across the floor to Kah Hoe; the contents were three grey lumps of sweet potato and a mug of black tea. After the kempei left, Kah Hoe crumpled forward, his face inches away from his only meal for the day.

It took immense effort for him to bring both his hands together and slowly lift the mug to his lips. Even though the tea was cold, it burned his throat. He ate the sweet potatoes without caring that they were starting to rot. It was only after he ate, that he was able to take a closer look at his cell. His bed occupied one side of the wall; cobbled together with four planks of wood. His toilet was an old, broken nightsoil bucket at the other end of his cell. Kah Hoe would fast become acquainted with his new living quarters.

He and a few prisoners would be escorted every morning to have a bath at the parade square. They were allowed a few minutes to clean themselves and their nightsoil buckets before they made their way back to their cells. Kah Hoe and the other prisoners shuffled their feet under the weight of their beatings, to and from the open tap; their only form of exercise. The bodies of the prisoners were covered in a patchwork of scars and wounds, and the wounds that were healing would be persistently beaten until they split open, forming a bloody patch all over again.

Kah Hoe tried very hard to keep his mind focused on getting out of the Batu Gajah Prison alive. As was to be expected, news travelled fast through the prison grapevine and within days of Kah Hoe becoming lucid, he learnt that Lim Bo Seng was also a guest at this facility. The kempetai guards who had been patrolling their corridor for the first few days had left the prison, leaving the warders in charge and Kah Hoe made every effort to befriend them. He was single minded in his motive – to have at least one opportunity to talk to Bo Seng.

The one time that Kah Hoe was allowed to stop by Bo Seng's cell and talk to him left him feeling depressed and demoralized. Bo Seng had embarked on a hunger strike, ignoring the food that was placed in his cell. He insisted that his share be given to the other prisoners instead. So Kah Hoe stared at his friend in despair as he saw him lying on his bed dangerously gaunt and lifeless. Kah Hoe's pleas for him to eat and regain his strength fell squarely on deaf ears, as Bo Seng continued with his hunger strike.

He soon fell terribly ill and his loud groans of pain could be heard along the corridor. The other prisoners pleaded with the prison officers to get Bo Seng the medical attention he desperately needed.

Finally, the Chief Warden came to inspect what the fuss was all about and found a very weak Lim Bo Seng who didn't seem like he would last through the night. When Kah Hoe saw them carry Bo Seng out of his cell later that evening, he was relieved, believing that he would be taken to the hospital to be treated. Instead, they carried him to an empty room in a house that was right next door to the administration block. This was well known as the accommodation for dying prisoners and that was where they left Lim Bo Seng, to wait for death to pay him a visit. Kah Hoe knew he had died even before his friend's cries finally fell silent. The silence announcing to all, the felling of a legend, who had laid down his life for his country.

Bo Seng's death left Kah Hoe more defeated in spirit, and in a quick turn of events, the kempei turned all their energy, focus and attention on Kah Hoe. His torture became robust and they took pride in trying out their ingenious and cruel tactics on him.

They would come for him in the dead of night and at other

times, at the break of day. They would make him kneel on rough pieces of wood and tie him up so that he could neither move forward nor backwards and then apply electric shocks that would leave him shaking and jerking like a fish bartering for his life on land.

The torture the Japanese loved best was the water treatment, where they tied the prisoner down and forced water into his mouth and nose until he lay there unconscious. Then they would jump on the prisoner's stomach until all the water spurted out and start all over again. This was a gruesome game they played regularly with all the prisoners.

Kah Hoe was brutalized so severely that he was unconscious most of the time. During the rare moments of blurred consciousness, Kah Hoe's mind flitted back to different moments in his life; the young Kah Hoe was a frequent visitor and would sit by his older self and offer him comfort, stroke his hair and sing to him in a soft voice.

He would remind him of the times he tried to catch butterflies, running in the garden with a white net and the older Kah Hoe tried to tell him that it was a cruel thing to do, to capture and cage in jest. Kah Hoe remembered trying to dig a swimming pool in the garden with his siblings. *We used our spades and buckets! Do you remember Kah Sing and Kah Heong? How we drew lines with chalk all along the perimeter of the garden. Mama thought we were mad! And how Dino used to run around us wagging his tail like it was a huge game for him!*

No, Kah Sing! No, Kah Heong! Of course I haven't told anyone of our secret! It was a promise we all made to each other. We will take the secret about Dino to our graves. I haven't said a word to a soul. I know we were only having some fun and we were kids for heaven's sake. Even Dino knew that.

Kah Hoe's favourite visitor was his mother, and Elaine often came to visit now. She seemed to sense his loneliness and his need for peace. She was always the least in a hurry to leave. She always smelled the same, *was it lavender or lily of the valley?* Kah Hoe couldn't quite make it out. He would have to ask her. He needed to know. There were many things he wanted to ask her and he knew she would be ready with answers. *Why did she never speak about her father? Where were her siblings?* She had ghosts locked up in the deep recesses of her mind and he needed to meet them. He wanted to know how she had met his father. There were many questions swimming in Kah Hoe's beaten head and he knew his time was running out.

Not yet! He begged Death. *I need some answers. I need a little more time. Please! I implore you, don't be impatient. I will be yours forever but not just yet.*

Elaine lifted his head gently and made him a comfortable pillow on her lap. His cell felt brighter and less drab with her there. Her touch healed his wounds and her voice soothed his rankling nerves.

Mama, tell me, how did you meet Papa?

Elaine sat stroking his hair while she gathered her thoughts.

I just turned 18 and was a junior nurse at the local hospital when your father came in to have his appendix taken out. He was only 22 then and he was young and very handsome. I still remember the day so clearly. He came in with his mother and I was the nurse on duty in his ward. I was the one who had to give him his medication and take his temperature and I knew there was something special about him. I used to look forward to seeing him and before long I knew he liked seeing me too!

As soon as he had recovered, he came back nearly everyday to visit me at the hospital. He was so persistent that I eventually gave in and agreed to have lunch with him. And that's how it all started. Imagine if I hadn't! It would have been love's greatest tragedy.

We used to meet often and go to the cinema to watch the talkies. We became very good friends and it took us a few years before we finally decided to settle down. Your father wanted to be self-sufficient before he took on a wife, so we decided to wait. And I have had no regrets. I couldn't have married a better man. He was always very principled and devoted to us. The early years were a struggle as he was trying to build the company and secure a future for us. The Depression virtually destroyed his business but he managed to rebuild it. We had our share of hungry years but it was our struggle together as husband and wife and I was happy to be beside him.

Now you must rest, my darling and not talk so much. You need to regain your strength. We are all waiting excitedly for you to get out of this place and come home. Everyone is anxious to see you. You must not disappoint them. They have been planning your return so you must concentrate on getting better.

Kah Hoe drifted off into a restless sleep. He was in and out of consciousness almost floating around the room. His dog Dino came bounding up to him, pleading with his soulful eyes for Kah Hoe to play with him.

I'm too tired, Dino. Can't you see? I need to rest so I can get better and come home. How did you get in here anyway? You were always a crafty little dog. No, don't go, Dino. Just sit with me awhile. Let me hear you pant. Good dog, Dino. Here boy, let me give you a hug.

Kah Hoe's delirium lasted several days and even some of the prisoners alerted the Chief Warden to have Kah Hoe seen to by a doctor. No attention was paid to his strangled cries of pain. He could feel his body burning as if it were on fire and he begged for someone, anyone to come and put the fire out.

Please take me, Death... Death, where are you? You came to visit me so many times and I implored you to leave me here awhile. But I have had enough. I want to go home. Please take me home. Don't leave me here. Mama, why have you too left me here? Don't you love me? I need you, Mama. Take me home, Mama. Please, Mama, I promise you I will be good. I won't be naughty, really, Mama, I promise to study hard and make you proud of me. But just don't leave me here, Mama, not with the demons. They come for me when you are gone, they are cruel to me. Make them stop, Mama! Tears slipped out of the corners of his eyes, silently spreading his sadness across his cheeks.

Why aren't you coming to visit me, Papa? Where are you? Are you too busy? I am here, Papa. I can see you. Can't you see me? Carry me, Papa, I'm too tired to walk. I can see the car. Have you come to take me home? Is Mama here with you? Where is Pakcik? Is he driving us back? Where are the twins? I miss your noise. You want a piggy-back? Both at the same time!

When he came to, Kah Hoe was vaguely aware of someone holding his head up trying to give him some water. Most of it trickled down his chin. There were more noises now. The unfriendly sounds of people talking loudly. These weren't the soothing sounds of his mother. He wanted to sleep now and go back to the place that was calm, where his mother came to sit with him. He remembered it was green and it was soft, yes, it smelled like grass... wet grass! He was lying on it, warm and comfortable and his mama was there in the distance.

I'm here, Mama! Just lying on the grass. I'm coming, Mama. Give me a minute, I'm trying to stand up. It's too soft, I can't get up... I won't be long, Mama. Yes, I'll be home soon, I promise. No I won't leave you, ever.

The sky gathered all of Kah Hoe's anguish and pain; instead of blowing a gentle wind, it greedily sucked up all the air around him so choked with his grief. When the clouds had ballooned, they spat out blackened tears. The green earth knew, the nearby rivers knew and the jungle creatures knew, for Kah Hoe's suffering was theirs too. They drank it with a thirst - his life and his death... silently.

Kah Hoe's last breath was so light and effortless. He inhaled without an exhale; taking with him his promise of ever returning home.

39

PENANG

30ᵀᴴ JUNE 1944

The two turbaned silhouettes scurried along the darkened street, casting their magnified shadows on the white walls of the Convent Light Street. It was now home to the Japanese Navy and the two men had to be careful not to be spotted, for tucked underneath their baggy shirts were fresh Singa posters, proclaiming the latest news about the progress of the Allied forces.

The posters contained magical words that held the promise of the beginning of the end of the war. The Allied Forces had recently landed in Normandy in the north of France and on the Pacific front, US bombers had dropped their deadly parcels of explosives on the iron and steel factories in Kyushu. More than 100,000 US soldiers and marines had stormed Saipan.

They made their way around the perimeter, audacious enough in their quest as the School was heavily guarded. Because of Tochi's initial doubts, this night's escapade very nearly didn't happen. However, Gurchan insisted they rub the good news into Japanese noses by plastering their posters on the walls of their Naval HQ.

"I want those Japanese bastards to wake up in the morning and smell our posters! I want my words to scald their tongues as they read our news. It must be like poison to them. And our people will be visiting the school to read the writing on the wall!" laughed Gurchan.

"You are mad! How do you think we'll get away with it? It's foolish if we get caught after all our effort to remain anonymous, Gurchan! You can't be so reckless," answered Tochi.

In the end, Tochi lost the argument and in the days before the daring exercise, the pair studied the movements of the sentries that were positioned at the entrance of the base. They knew there were always two guards posted at all times and they also knew that there were two beds inconspicuously hidden behind the walls where they went to rest their tired heads.

Tonight was no exception.

Tochi and Gurchan moved with ease through the dark. They started sticking their posters with a nervous frenzy, afraid that their shadows would betray them. Nevertheless, they persisted and managed to glue three posters before a loud shout broke the silence like gunfire. Tochi and Gurchan dropped the rest of their posters and ran for their lives. The two sleeping guards jolted out of their slumber and started to give chase. Four pairs of feet pounding down the street. Tochi and Gurchan had no time to work out their escape route and were running on pure instinct.

They ran down Farquhar Street past Saint Xavier's Institution and as they approached Leith Street they stumbled upon bicycles, leaning against the wall of the Cheong Fatt Tze mansion. Tochi and Gurchan saw them at the same time and managed to steal a sideway glance at each other as they ran toward the two wheelers. They jumped on and rapidly pedalled off. Their sense of victory was short-lived as their pursuers had also found bicycles and were frantically pedalling after them.

Tochi and Gurchan could scarcely believe their bad luck. Their only consolation now, was the fact that they knew the quiet, dark streets of Penang better than their assailants. The soldiers kept yelling for them to stop and surrender, but this only provided more impetus for the two ahead, as they pedaled even faster. To anyone who may have been watching, it was a cycling race that outdid any of the races Gurchan had organised at the Turf Club! When Tochi turned back to check the progress of their pursuers, he was horrified to see four soldiers instead of the two they started out with.

"Saalle kuthe. Those bloody dogs have doubled in number. I hope we make it out of here alive!"

"We have to!" yelled back Gurchan. "We will! I will never let those pariah hands touch our turbans! Sat Sri Akal!" hollered Gurchan above the whirring of their bicycles.

There was little light from the streets but they knew that they would soon be on Northam Road. "Maybe we should chuck the cycles and run into the cemetery on foot," yelled Tochi.

"No way, Toch! We'll never make it with all the tombstones in our way" replied Gurchan, his voice straining against the whooshing of the wind.

Just up ahead of them was the Runnymede Hotel which had once been the home of Sir Stamford Raffles and in later years metamorphosed into a stunning hotel, boasting rooms with private bathrooms, a billiard room and even a postal office. But on a night like tonight, no one was paying her any attention, even if she stood out like a gleaming, white beacon of luxury and grandeur. The two Sikhs pedalled furiously down Penang's main thoroughfare; the heroes in their own treacherous, silent movie.

Finally, they reached the end of Northam Road on which Hardwick House stood gallant in one corner. This was the time for quick decision making and it was Gurchan who made the swift call.

"Let's dump the cycles and run the rest of the way. We can hide among the kampung houses and sampans."

This proved to be prescient as it was clearly the safer bet. There were many hiding places and it was easy to get lost in the maze of fishing nets and sampans.

Kelawai Road ran parallel to the beach and was lined with Malay kampung houses with attap roofs. The Malay and Indian fishermen had dragged their sampans and their nets to the shore; their fishing boats lay blanketed under a layer of palm fronds to prevent them from drying in the strong sun. The entire village was fast asleep, oblivious to the dangerous chase that was taking place in front of their homes.

The only inhabitants who had their sleep disturbed were of the four-legged variety. The dogs and cats that had made the kampung their home took their cue from the running feet and kick-started their own drama of barking, yelping and giving chase. But the sandman's potent dust lay like a magic spell over the villagers as they slept through it all.

The two Sikhs kept looking over their shoulders to see who was closer to them, the energetic dogs or the Japanese soldiers. They were pleased that the soldiers were coming in third in the race. The two men took a sharp left and headed towards Tanjung Tokong, loosely translated as the Cape of the Temple. The Tua Pek Kong Temple loomed like a large red brick monster; its entrance, a mouth wide open, waiting to swallow devotees into her cavernous bosom, heady with the woody scent of incense. They had to make a quick decision to either head for the hills behind the temple and rely on how fast their legs could run or turn into the labyrinth of fishing nets and boats and take their chances with the sea. With a sudden blast of inspiration, Tochi remembered a fragment of information.

"The Japanese don't like the water. Many can't swim!" he yelled to Gurchan. "We'll run to the beach and swim. I don't think they'll follow us. Let's pray they don't," he added.

Tochi and Gurchan dashed towards the sea without another backward look; crawling under the stilts of the kampung houses, trying to avoid the nets that were lying in the moonlight recovering from a long day of work drenched in the sun and water, hauling in writhing fish. If they had been able to see the soldiers, they would have clearly seen their worried looks at the realisation that the two crazy, turbaned men were heading out to sea. The two men heard loud yelling and could make out the heavy resonance of defeat in the Japanese voices.

In a matter of minutes, the two indomitable spirits who carried in them the strength and tenacity of their forefathers, hurled their shoes on the damp sand and ran into the sea like two lovers seeking some fun under the watchful gaze of the moon. One blue turban and one white turban jumped into the sea while the four men behind them stood on the beach shaking their fists in the air, wailing at them to come back. The two men swam further and further away from their nemeses, leaving behind their unravelled turbans to bob on the surface of the water.

40
HOROSCOPES AND DATES
KUALA LUMPUR, 2010

She took each day as it came, without fuss and without rejoicing, just with an acceptance that, like bitter medicine, it had to be swallowed and ingested. New Year had come and gone without much notice and when Chinese New Year rolled in, Geeta felt she had to visit Ken's dad, a habit she didn't have the heart to break. She felt a little odd and a little exposed as she walked into the familiar place that all of a sudden felt foreign and different. But Ken's dad put her at ease immediately.

"How lovely to see you, Geeta. You look as pretty as ever!" Geeta smiled at him warmly and gave him a hug that filled her with happiness.

"It's always nice to see you, Uncle Kah Sing", she replied.

She didn't stay very long but she was glad she had gone to visit. She felt overwhelmed with emotions as she drove home. She hadn't expected to feel so raw after all this while.

Geeta plunged back into work, convinced that it was her panacea. Fortunately, she was working on an extremely interesting brief with Satnam. He had been appointed to represent the Malaysian Bar as the lead counsel in a Royal

Commission of Inquiry which was investigating allegations of judicial misconduct. She spent her days and nights researching and trying to answer the difficult questions that kept popping up. The distraction was good for her and she had little time to think of much else.

So, her shock scored high on the reaction-richter scale when her mother announced to her one morning that there was a marriage enquiry for her.

Oh fuck! A marriage proposal pour moi! She who eats nails for breakfast (as that was how she was described by some of her colleagues)*! Anyway, didn't the whole community know I was going out with an 'outsider'. And yet, here it is, a marriage proposal. My word...am I such a catch or is he bloody desperate! Now what the hell am I going to do? Bugger this, I can feel the roller coaster ride starting all over again.*

Geeta glared at her mother. "Ma, your timing couldn't be worse. I'm rushed off my feet at work, I don't know if I'm in any state to see anyone," she flared at her mother.

"Does this mean you will meet him when things slow down a bit?" pursued her mother, with the renewed courage that her illness had accorded her.

"Whatever, Ma. I'll meet him if you want me to," mumbled Geeta as she lifted her briefcase off the dining chair. It was only when she started her car that the enormity of what she had agreed to sank in.

What the hell have I gone and done now? What the heck, Geeta... go with the flow. There's no law against meeting someone. He may be eye candy. Yeah, as if! I've yet to meet a hunk of a Brahmin who will get my pulse racing. But I'll never know unless I keep an open mind. And if he doesn't ring my bell, then hell, I'll just say so, she thought to herself.

Geeta was making a great effort to be positive and to put one foot ahead at a time. It had been six months since her break up with Ken and he had made no attempt to contact her; she had decided that it was best to let it be. She had spent too many nights crying herself to sleep that now, her body was parched of tears.

So that was why Geeta agreed to meet Keshav Narayanan, a thirty-three year old IT consultant who was working in Singapore. Her parents had agreed that they could meet sans parents in a neutral place with many exits (in case she came, she saw and had a need to flee). Coffee Hide in the city was the chosen venue and Saturday was D-day!

Geeta didn't want to overdo the dressing and neither did she want to make an effort to look too repulsive either. She settled for jeans with a white linen top and light make-up. With a spritz of Orange Blossom for 'something old', she made a quick escape, avoiding her parents' pleased looks. She was there before he arrived and she settled herself in a seat where she had a clear view of all those who walked in. She knew it was him even before he could scan the room in search of her.

He was tall, not thin, not fat, had reasonably broad shoulders and what she would describe as a nice face; not handsome not ugly. *He does have a presence. I would give him another look if I saw him walking on the street. Hmmmmm, not bad!*

He might as well have bumped into her thoughts as he confidently strode up to her and put his hand out, "You must be Geeta."

Geeta accepted his handshake and smiled back at him.

Nice hands. But Ken's are softer. She couldn't help the comparison. This was her first 'date' after Ken and he had set the bar very high. After an awkward silence, they settled down with their ice-blended drinks and attempted to make light conversation.

Geeta decided to be honest with him and told him that she was not a proponent of arranged marriages and that she was going against every grain in her body to agree to have an 'arranged meeting' in the first place. Keshav nodded in agreement and assured her that they were like-minded as he found the whole concept appalling. *Off to a good start!* she thought.

"So, what makes an eligible bachelor like you want to agree to meet like this," she asked him with a glint in her eyes.

"Geeta, I promised myself that I would be very honest with you so I'm going to give you all the dirt on me. I was going out

204

with an Armenian girl I met at work but neither her parents nor mine were thrilled with it. I tried to fight the wills of two old people and I lost. So did the girl I was going out with. Her parents were worse, they were ready to disown her and she gave in. So I decided to try the traditional method and see if there was any possibility of me meeting someone I might like. I, like you, hate the whole arranged marriage thing and I have fought my parents on this for a long time. There you have it," said Keshav, shrugging his shoulders.

Geeta couldn't have been more understanding. "Well, Keshav, its amazing how similar your story is to mine. I don't know how much you have gleaned about me from rumours that abound in the community. I was going out with a Chinese man and I wanted to marry him. But, like you, I had so much grief from my parents. She lifted her shoulders in despair. The pressure was too great and I felt the price was too high. Which explains why I'm still single. I didn't think I wanted to go down the dating road Brahmin style! This really isn't my idea of meeting the man I want to spend the rest of my life with. I've always spoken against this archaic system so vehemently and look, here I am sitting across a Tamil Brahmin man and if I might add, enjoying his company. Who would have thought that?" remarked Geeta.

Two hours and two coffees later, they had talked about their favourite books, the wines they enjoyed and movies that had made an impression on them, the burgeoning art scene in Malaysia, their favourite Malaysian artist, J. Anurendra, and their careers. Geeta found herself telling him about the interesting cases she was working on and he tried not to bore her too much with technical jargon from his IT world.

By the time they had finished their last drop of coffee, they had agreed that Indian authors ruled the day, disagreed about Rambo still being the action movie of their era (she felt that Indiana Jones earned that title) and he disagreed that white wine was superior to beer on tap.

"Listen, Geeta, if it's okay with you, I'd like to see you again. I think we could become friends. Only if that's cool with you. I don't want to impose myself on you. I'll be here till Sunday

205

so why don't we have dinner on Saturday night? No strings attached. Let's just go to a nice restaurant, share a bottle of wine or some beer and talk," said Keshav kindly.

Geeta dragged in the air in front of her face and found her mouth drawing itself into a smile. "Yes, dinner on Saturday night would be lovely."

When she returned from dinner that Saturday, Geeta refused to commit to a straightforward answer to her parents who were sitting in the living room, just as she had left them three hours ago; as if for some inexplicable reason, they had been UHU-glued to the sofa.

"How was it, kanne?" asked her mother tentatively.

"Chi, chi, ni onnam kekadhai, Parvathi" said Ramesh to his wife, telling her to leave Geeta alone.

Geeta looked at them, feeling sorry and irritable at the same time. They looked old to her, seated there, stuck together as a unit and not two separate beings. Each seemed to be lending the other strength as they waited with bated breath for her to say something positive.

"It was okay, ma. How can I say more than that? I just met the guy for two hours. I can't possibly make any character judgment. All I can say is, he was nice enough."

I can't believe this! Have I lost my marbles? He was nice. He was friendly and I think he's honest. He's got honest eyes. That's what I liked best about him. Dinner on Saturday? Maybe I was a little too quick to agree. But, at least he has a sense of humour and isn't old-fashioned with old fashioned ideas. But it all seems a little too soon. Should I cancel dinner? Oh, what am I going to do?

That night, when bedroom doors were closed to prying eyes and listening ears and when parents thought daughter was sleeping and daughter thought parents were sleeping, Geeta sat in bed with a legal pad perched on her knee and this is what it had written on it.

POSSIBLE PLUSES	COULD BE PEEVES
Honest eyes	
Nice hands	
Nice smile	*HE'S*
Funny, made me laugh out	*NOT*
loud a few times	*KEN*
Enjoys books! (Bonus point!)	
Modern	
Tall and pleasant looking	

She put her pen down and sobbed. Geeta cried fresh tears for a man whose memory she thought had faded. She was angry with herself for still grieving for Ken but she was unable to drag herself out of this rut she had dug. She had tried to break the spell by agreeing to see Keshav, as if having a drink and a conversation with another man would beat the 'Ken hex' out of her. She knew she had to move on but she didn't know how. Now she realized she did know but she wasn't ready to. Deep down in her heart, she still thought of Ken and her as 'we', a 'couple', and a 'pair'. She wasn't used to wearing just one sock. And like the stealthy moon, his shadow crept over her heart, eclipsing it from any possible liaison.

Across the passageway in Ramesh and Parvathi's room, with the ceiling fan oscillating at the lowest speed, barely moving the air around, they lay in the dark, whispering their hopes.

"Do you think she seemed vaguely interested? She didn't seem her usual antagonistic self," said Parvathi.

"Sssh…" said Ramesh. "We can only pray to Ambal that she shows Geeta the right path. At least she was willing to meet the boy. That in itself is a good sign. Let's hope, Parvathi. Maybe she will finally see sense."

With that they turned away from each other, hugging their renewed hope to sleep.

41
A WEEKEND WITH FRIENDS
BUKIT TINGGI, 2010

Confused and dejected was the best way to describe Geeta's mood when it came to her personal life. Fortunately for her, her work had been gradually moving from interesting to sublime. She had been working on the Royal Commission all last week and while she was exhausted from the research and preparation, she was heady from the sheer magnitude of the matter.

The following week, Geeta and Karen met for a drink and a long chat. She told Karen all about Keshav, that he was a nice personable fellow whom she may have met without any reservation if there had been no third party 'putting them together'. He was 'pleasant and interesting' but she didn't feel any chemistry. When she had met him for dinner, she smiled when she saw him but he didn't make her heart race. Ken had always made her heart beat faster. She confessed that she knew she was being unfair to Keshav and herself for not putting Ken out of her mind, but she couldn't help it, he was there with her at Coffee Hide and at dinner; even though she had actually enjoyed Keshav's company.

She was finding it increasingly difficult to believe that she and Ken were over. How was she ever going to move forward?

She had tried to immerse herself in her work and she had even made an effort to meet someone, but it was unfair to her and any other man that she may agree to meet. There was simply no comparison and in actual fact, she felt no desire to find a replacement for Ken. So when Karen invited her to go with her, Brian and Saskea to Bukit Tinggi for a weekend at her dad's country home, Geeta readily accepted her offer.

The day started out beautifully. Crisp blue skies and white, white clouds, a strong sun breaking through the blue and white to lend a blinding yellow; the perfect backdrop for a day at the park, beach or up on the hills. Karen and Brian were picking her up and she was all prepared with a good book and a couple of good bottles of white wine stashed away from her parents' eyes in her overnight suitcase. *More important than the clothes,* she thought.

She was so looking forward to getting away. Karen had described her dad's retreat as a respite; a real chill-out place and that's exactly what she wanted to do. Even before they hit the toll, Karen handed out wrapped-up sandwiches.

"Is this what happens when you become a mother?" laughed Geeta.

They were all packed in identical brown paper bags and marked with their names. The conversation was light and Geeta could tell that it was going to be a great weekend. She sat back and closed her eyes against the insistent sunlight, enjoying Lily Allen. *Holiday music, except she's singing about London. It always comes back to haunt me…*

By the time they reached Bukit Tinggi, it was noon and the house loomed out at them as they slowly made their way forward to meet it. It was perched on top of a hill; a vision of modern and contemporary design.

"Bloody hell, Karen. How come you've kept this place away from me!" remarked Geeta.

"Hey, I've been asking you to come here with us for ages but you kept telling me you were busy or not in the mood. Now you know why we try and run away here whenever we can."

The housekeeper, Thangamah was there at the door waiting

for them to arrive. Karen had to stop her in her tracks to give her a hug before she made a beeline for Saskea. Geeta just stood there taking it all in.

She turned around to grab the bags from the boot and they all marched in talking loudly as they did so.

Geeta soon learnt that there was a cook – Ah Lean, a robust looking woman who seemed to be a no-nonsense type of woman. Then, there were two maids, pint sized Indonesian girls who were always under the watchful eye of Thangamah, and Maniam, the gardener who doubled up as a driver when the family or friends came to stay.

Karen's father was an architect and this house he had designed was his designer baby. He knew what he didn't want – a mock Tudor-style house that was all the rage in the hill resorts, and so passé in his opinion. He wanted to embrace nature and not keep her out with brick walls and pokey windows. As a result, there were very few walls here. Most of the French doors opened out onto a front patio that hugged the front of the house. The living room floor had large smooth gray tiles. The furniture amounted to two three-seater sofas in powder white and two chili-red Arne Jacobsen swan chairs. Two tall metallic Spun lamps reached out from the floor and rose above the sofa like bodyguards, while a 1950s slim-line coffee table completed the look. The dining room sat at the other end of the living room, complete with a light coloured Scandinavian table and twelve Ghost chairs taking centre stage. There were fresh flowers and candles and family pictures that transformed what could have been stark and cold, into a warm and inviting space.

The kitchen was a large room with huge doors on one side that opened out to a side garden and a pebble-washed area big enough for outdoor entertaining. The kitchen was all-white; a large white island, white floors and white cupboards. Here too, were the same accents of red that were present in the living room. A red Kitchen Aid cake mixer and a coffee machine sat in one corner, waiting to whip up cake batter or gurgle some hot steaming fresh coffee to life. The star here was the red Smeg fridge that resembled a fat exclamation mark.

The rooms were beautifully laid out upstairs. A long corridor that offered views of the hills led to the rooms that were tucked away behind heavy white doors. Geeta's room was gorgeous. It had a double bed with starched white sheets and fluffy down pillows. Long pewter silk curtains brushed the floor and there were two French doors that led to a balcony large enough for a table with two chairs. Her view was spectacular; different shades of undulating green that seemed close enough to reach out and touch.

She barely had time to take in the beauty when there was a knock and one of the Indonesian maids announced that lunch was ready. It was set outside the kitchen under a bright orange umbrella. Ah Lean had prepared a light lunch – a vegetarian Thai salad with glass noodles.

"This is heaven on earth", she declared to Karen and Brian.

"We're so glad you're here, G. Brian and I have been talking about you and we feel it is so important for you to get away and recharge your batteries. We know how difficult things have been for you lately. But hey, let's not talk about anything too serious now. You must relax while you are here. Go for long walks or soak in your bath, whatever appeals to you!"

Everyone miraculously disappeared off in different directions after lunch with the promise to meet at 7pm on the front patio for drinks.

Geeta curled up with her book on the day bed that was made for exactly this. There was only the sound of her breathing and some birds clicking their approval. Her eyelids soon became weighty with sleep and she eventually put her book down to snatch forty plus plus winks.

Geeta had ample time to have a leisurely shower in a bathroom that she would best describe as fresh as lime zing. Lime green mosaic tiles greeted her feet, making them want to dance on them. *Icy chilled Sauvignon Blanc! Oh yum!* She quickly got dressed and made her way downstairs.

If the house looked lovely in the daylight, it looked stunning at night. The lamps bathed the furniture in a warm glow and there were candles that scented the air with a light jasmine fragrance. The arresting voice of Aaron Neville floated through the house. Brian and Karen were already there with the little mite looking out from her swing. They drank a toast to good health, Karen's dad and the wonderful place they were at.

"Ken should be here," said Geeta shocking the other two into silence. This was Geeta's way of letting the others know that she was ready to talk about him.

"Have you spoken to him at all?" asked Karen.

"No, it was only that one time when I tried to talk to him, but I hung up before he could answer the phone. I don't know what to say to him without it sounding cliché and without hurting him any further. I think this way at least he can get on with his life and hopefully move on. You know I keep thinking about him and I wonder what he's up to, whether he's met someone else. I even imagine that he's with someone else and that makes me really jealous and sad. I know I don't have a right to feel that way but I can't seem to help myself. To tell you the truth, I'm tired of thinking about him and I'm sick of being in this pit. I wish I could do something so drastic to climb out of this rut of self-pity. I know it's destructive but I haven't yet made my way to the surface. I guess I'll have to take each day at a time," said Geeta staring into her glass.

"Geeta, with all due respect, you have made a decision to go separate ways and that's because you felt you couldn't deal with the pressure from your parents. Obviously you still love Ken but you've got to live with that decision and move on," said Brian. "Unless of course, you want to tell your parents that you can't do this anymore and that the person you want to marry is Ken. But only you can make that decision. Only then can you start to feel like you can get your life back. Until you come to terms with the decision you have made, you will find no peace. Maybe it's time to put it to rest, put it behind you and give this poor guy Keshav a chance. You have seen him twice already. I don't envy you but you have made your bed and you have no choice but to lie in it. It sounds harsh but unfortunately, that's how it sometimes is."

When Geeta spoke, there was a quiet resolve that laced her voice.

"You know, you are right. I have made my mind up and you're right, I need to come to terms with it. I have to let go of the past and slowly learn to move on. I should start to look at things differently, more half-full instead of half-empty and hopefully I can move forward. Thank you Brian, sometimes I'm stuck so deep in my own sorrow I don't realise how I must sound and look to others. I think at the end of this break I will sit down with my parents and tell them that I am ready to take the next step forward."

42
SUNDAY LUNCH REVISITED
KUALA LUMPUR, 2010

If you listened closely enough, you could hear the crackle in the air in Ramesh Iyer's home. Talk was rife about the impending engagement party and although it had become common knowledge, no one dared to speak her name. Instead, nervous twitching, lifting of eyebrows and active nudging had replaced the easy flow of conversation.

This sort of behaviour was totally reasonable on this occasion because the person causing the nudging and eyebrow lifting was Geeta and everyone in her immediate and extended family knew that Geeta HATED being the topic of conversation and what was worse, everyone knew her distaste for arranged marriages was as strong as it was for capital punishment (there were some members of her family that felt she might have been a little more lenient with sending someone to the gallows than to a life sentence of preplanned nuptials).

The only one who dared to broach the topic in broad daylight was Krishna Chitappa. And he did so with brevity.

"When is the engagement fixed for?"

Everyone looked at everyone and someone said in a pipsqueak voice, " 20th of May".

"That's not too far off!" he exclaimed. "Isn't there lots to do and isn't it the girl's side that organizes it?" he asked, looking at Parvathi.

"No, it's the boy's side that's responsible for the Nischaithambul and the girl's side that looks after the wedding," she explained.

Geeta's face was hidden behind a paper wall of words. She wore her armour of resoluteness that protected her from the gaze of the several pairs of eyes that had burned holes through the newspaper.

"So, Manni, what do we need to do then?" persisted Krishna Chitappa.

"Well, it's all done in the Mapallai's home and we need to take a tambalam of vetallai and paaku, a shirt and pair of trousers for the groom, a sari for the bride and of course the ring for the groom."

"Geeta, have you been to look for a sari yet? Manni, is it all right for me to buy the sari for her?"

"It would be my pleasure. Geeta, would you like that?" he asked her gently.

She put her paper down and stared hard at her uncle and forced a smile and said, "I'd like that very much, Chitappa."

There was a sudden burst of voices and laughing and even light teasing that lifted the veil of awkwardness. Hands clapped and lips turned up in smiles and there was a general look of relief.

But only Krishna was watching close enough and listening hard enough to notice the sarcasm in Geeta's response and the sadness that had buried itself in the dark pupils of her liquid eyes. It was Krishna who felt the sense of grief he had experienced many years before. This time it seemed more intense than his loss all those years ago and it had come back to haunt him in a way that was far more unnerving. He wanted to reach out and take Geeta in his arms and comfort her, for only he could speak to her loneliness in such a crowded room. He stood up and walked out of the living room for he was too afraid that he might not be as strong as his niece.

Krishna made his way upstairs in search of his brother. He knocked on his door and went in to find his older brother bustling away at one of his favourite hobbies; sitting at his well-worn desk and underlining in red ink, a recent article he had cut out of a local daily. He closed the door quietly behind him and settled on a chair.

"Anna, I must speak to you about this engagement," he said without hesitation. "Are you sure Geeta has given it enough thought and she is not jumping into the fire for all the wrong reasons?"

Ramesh took his time before replying Krishna.

"Krishna, why are you bringing this up now when Geeta has come to her senses? She's seen the boy, met him and even had dinner with him. They've been communicating with each other over the phone and I agree that he is most suited for Geeta because he's a personable and broad-minded fellow. I think she's found the perfect match in him. Parvathi and I are so thankful it has come so far and I'm praying nothing or no one spoils it for her now," he said looking at his younger brother sternly.

"I think Geeta has realized that we have only her interests at heart and I am so glad that she has come to respect our ways and tradition. Krishna, don't you start on this whole issue again. I will not allow you to ruin it! The Nischaithambul is around the corner and there is much to be done so I'd appreciate it if you would lend your support and make sure that Geeta knows you are happy for her".

With that, Ramesh put his pen down and stood up to go down to lunch.

Krishna felt completely defeated. He had no choice now but to be supportive if this was indeed Geeta's decision and he knew he had to look cheerful without actually feeling it. So lunch went very well by all accounts and nothing more was said of the upcoming 'celebration'. Geeta was talking animatedly about Suresh's impending return home with his family and Manjula was working out how she could work out the Atkin's diet in a vegetarian context. Sandhya was talking to Lavanya Athai and Padma about Sowmya who was now happily settled in Sydney.

The little ones were hovering around the table in search of willing hands to pass them appalams and Ramesh was chatting to Raman about Carnatic music; Krishna was discussing cricket with the two Gopals. Everyone seemed to be happy and relaxed and soon the little pockets of conversation slowly expanded to include all at the table as it morphed to their favourite-topic-of-all-time – Malaysian politics. Today's discussion revolved around the recent Scorpene scandal where French submarines were purchased by Malaysia with alleged kickbacks disguised as commission payments which, according to the allegations, were channelled to the Prime Minister through his associate. This scandal was linked to the murder of a Mongolian interpreter who had acted as a translator when the deal was being discussed.

Geeta maintained her calm composure until everyone had left and her Athai had gone up to have her compulsory nap. She too scaled the stairs as if there were bricks attached to her back, as she felt the weight of the afternoon's events squarely pressing down on her. She closed the door to her room, locked it, sat on her bed and finally allowed herself to cry. The tears she wept were for herself and herself alone. Her sorrow was so alive and real and no matter how hard she had tried to bury it, it was there in every beat of her heart. The pain she felt now was fresh and raw and the salt from her tears made it burn. How would she ever be able to forget Ken? He had touched her in a way that she knew she would never allow anyone else to touch her. She was meant for him, he belonged to her and she belonged to him. He made her whole and complete and now with a life without him, she was unravelling before her very eyes. She was no good without him.

He makes my heart sing. Hearing his voice makes me tingle and kissing him reminds me of just how delicious he is. When I love him, I love every nerve and muscle in his body. They are mine as much as they are his, they belong to us and it gives me pleasure and comfort and strength that no one else can EVER give me. His love drives me and his goodness seeps into me and makes me feel warm and protected. Now I feel like a bird that has lost its wings, unable to escape this cage and fly.

She knew that she had promised to start anew but it was so, so difficult. *Oh God, give me the strength. Ken, let me go...*

She reached under her mattress for her source of comfort, a letter that she had saved there like a buoy, ready to keep her afloat... just barely...

2nd February 1933

Dearest Appa,

It's been awhile since my last letter and while I have many excuses, none of them will be valid in your eyes. I have good news for you and Amma! Saraswathi is in the family way again! My prayers to Ambal are that we be blessed with a pon kozhandai. She is just three months pregnant and I must say that she is feeling the strain of the pregnancy. The baby will be due in August and I am hoping to try and convince you both to come and visit us. Wouldn't that be lovely, Appa? Just imagine, you and Amma would be seeing your grandchildren for the first time. Nothing would make me happier.

I could take some time off from school and show you this wonderful country. You and Amma will be so happy with the life I have built here. Food is not a problem and there are temples that I could take you both to. Malaya has some beautiful places to visit too!

I know you don't enjoy travelling but it will be a pleasant enough journey and with Amma with you, it won't be so hard. I will send you both the passage the moment you agree to come. Just writing about it is making me very excited! Can you imagine when you arrive in Malaya? It's been too long, Appa – the last time I saw you was when I got married.

I pray that your reply will be a favourable one. It will surely put a smile on all our faces.

My namaskarams to Amma and my deep affection to you.

Your hopeful son,
Rangaswamy

I must move on. I will forget him. I will. I must. I can, she repeated to herself, like a mantra.

43
KUALA LUMPUR
9TH NOVEMBER 1944

The scream stuck half-way in her throat. As hard as she tried, it wouldn't escape; refusing to be released for fear that it wouldn't be able to hide or be suppressed once it left her body.

She could feel it gurgling up inside her, like an ocean churning, needing to spew its murky white froth on land. She was drowning in her own sorrow. She had had many conversations in her mind, she had prepared for the worst and put out worries and fears like she would a heated argument; she had reasoned with reason itself that this was the bigger calling. But who was here to console Elaine? A mother in her greatest moment of grief? Where was Reason? It had left her side very quickly and sent Sorrow and Anger as its emissaries. Both weren't strong enough to quell the fire that was raging in her soul.

News of Kah Hoe's death had reached Elaine's ear very tentatively and long after the incident. It had come to her twisted and torn, in snippets and drabs and she was trying to patch these back together; to give her a jigsaw picture in her mind as to what happened to her beloved Kah Hoe.

She tried to remember all the adjectives that Rangaswamy had used – brave, strong, courageous. *What use were all of them now that he was dead? Cold, blue, stone dead. Where had they buried him? Was he even buried? Did they clean him and put new clothes on him? Did anyone mourn him there in prison?*

These were questions Elaine asked herself when she was lucid and rational. At other times, she took to beating her chest and pulling her hair. She went in search of medicines to take, to snuff out her life just like they had done with Kah Hoe.

Was he watching her now? Can you feel my grief, Kah Hoe? Do you understand I need to see you and I can only do so if I come to you, because you will never come back to me! They took you away from your mama. Couldn't you tell them you promised me you'd come home? Did they not hear you?

No one at 912 Batu Road had any true understanding of the depth and width of Elaine's grief; it had grown larger than all of them; and the house was unable to contain it. It was in the food that they ate, it hung on the walls with the curtains and pictures, and they all took some of it with them to bed at night.

Chin Nam kept his grief mostly to himself. He felt guilty for not being dead instead of Kah Hoe. *Why didn't the Japanese kill me when they captured me? Instead they left me half the man I used to be and have taken my son instead. What kind of God allows this to happen? I am neither a good husband nor a good father. I can't protect those I love and look at me now, living in someone else's home and off their generosity. I am only existing.*

Elaine refused food. All that silent strength she had carried inside her when Chin Nam had come back beaten and broken, and when Kah Hoe had decided to join the guerillas, had abandoned her. She made no effort to try and stop it. She saw no need to be there for her other four children. It mattered not that they too were grieving their brother. In fact, Kah Heong was even heard saying that they were grieving for their mother as well, for they all felt like they had lost her. They tried to go to her and engage her in conversation but she would only turn the other way or worse still, just sit there and lend her tears her voice.

Wasn't I a good mother? Did I not love him enough? Did he have enough of my love in his last moments? Why did I let him go? I should have insisted he stay. He was my best. He was my first and now he's gone. I have failed him so badly. Would you forgive me, Kah Hoe? Can you give me a sign, please, I beg you.

Elaine refused Saras' company. She sat for hours in the garden under the mango tree wrapped in a thin cotton blanket sometimes not even realizing that it had become so hot that she was bathing in her own sweat. Her gaunt and small frame had become part of the landscape and for a long time after, Elaine would look to that same spot as Kah Hoe's burial ground. She would look back and remember that some of her sorrow had leached its way into the ground under the mango tree where in her mind, she had dug a deep hole and buried her beloved.

She drifted along like this in a chasm, being but not really being, floating and sinking in and out of life. Sometimes she would just hover at the edge, unsure of which way to go. Saras had taken to writing her letters; short ones just to coax Elaine to read them and, in them she told Elaine about her day, just a few lines of encouragement or even a silly story she might have heard in the market that morning. Elaine never replied to any of them. Until one day, cutting a sad and lonely picture, seated at the table; she was bent over writing without lifting her hand or head. She wrote, mixing her words with her tears.

What Saras found one morning was a thick bundle of partly smudged words. She took Elaine's letter and locked herself in her room. She read page after page of some coherent and some incomprehensible words that spelt out a mother's grief, pain and immense hurt. Saras added her own tears to Elaine's as she wept for her friend, for the life of a young man who so believed in the cause he had given his life to, for all Elaine's dreams for him and for Chin Nam's unspoken pain. She cried for Kah Hoe's last moments and for the torture she was sure he had endured.

When she saw Elaine later that morning, they clung to each other and they wept inconsolably. Their bodies wracked in tempo with their crying and when they were both finally spent of tears, everyone instinctively knew that the grieving at 912 had ended.

In the days that followed, the healing took its first tentative steps, groping about, trying not to fall over. Elaine was able to start talking about her deep seated anguish. She would look at her other children and touch them with less guilt and more tenderness. She would still go to the mango tree and hope to find a little glimpse of Kah Hoe there and in time to come, everyone believed that Kah Hoe did indeed visit his mother there.

She found one of his photographs which she gently placed in a silver frame by her bedside. Every night she touched his face and bade him sweet dreams.

44
KUALA LUMPUR
12TH DECEMBER 1944

In the animal kingdom, Rangaswamy might have been a meerkat as he always walked around the office with his back straight and his ears literally perked up, ready to receive any information that may have floated within his radar.

Today was no exception. He was sitting at his desk when he overheard two senior officers discussing 'some very important news' that had just been made available. Rangaswamy pretended to be buried in his work, head down, reading some documents but catching every whispered Japanese word that was spoken.

An informant had passed them detailed information about the whereabouts of the Anti-Japanese Army. "We have information on where the rogue guerrillas are hiding. There is going to be a meeting later to discuss the ambush of the enemy from their hiding spot. Chase them out like cockroaches and rats and give them poison to eat!"

Rangaswamy felt his blood run cold when he heard those words. Much had been said about the Japanese torture methods. If there was one thought that had tormented Rangaswamy, it was the fact that Kah Hoe would have suffered untold pain at the hands of these brutal people.

He battled with his conscience going to work every morning. Hate was not a strong enough word to describe his feelings for the Japanese, but he knew he had to persevere. He had spoken about his guilt to Chin Nam, who knew now more than ever that it was imperative for Rangaswamy to carry on as normally as he could.

"You must not give up now, Swamy! Kah Hoe would have died in vain. There is so much you can and are doing to help our cause. Those bastards trust you implicitly and you are one of the few privileged enough to have access to so much top-secret intelligence. You would be betraying us if you didn't continue your good work. So, don't be silly. Elaine and I understand your position and more importantly, we believe in you, my friend."

Chin Nam's words hadn't helped Rangaswamy assuage his guilt but it had made him determined to play them at their own game and win.

Rangaswamy walked into the meeting room where strategies were planned and discussed, under the pretext of looking for a 'missing letter'. The room was empty and he noticed an open map on the table. The black markings on the map indicated positions in Negeri Sembilan, Perak and Pahang. He tried to search the map for more details but he could sense that every extra second spent in the meeting room would only place him in grave danger. He looked up dejectedly, it was time to leave quickly. But there, on the blackboard in front of him, like an offering from God, was a list of locations written in Japanese. He quickly filed the information away in his mind and walked out with a sliver of a glimmer of hope and the weighty heaviness of information gleaned stealthily.

Rangaswamy couldn't contain his excitement. He had the urgent desire to leave his desk and run home to think. *This is an absolute godsend. I must get this news out! But how? The next courier doesn't come here till next month and that will be too late. Think!* He needed to pace and he could only do that at home so he had no choice but to watch the clock painfully crawl its way to 5pm.

Rangaswamy pedaled as fast as his skinny legs would allow him, frantic to get home. He kept repeating the names of the places to himself as he pedaled, thoughts keeping in rhythm with feet in a curious 'mind-foot' sequence. He decided that he would tell Chin Nam as this sort of information deserved at least an audience of two! They could both discuss the brevity of the news and make some decisions. *How am I going to get this information to those who need it in time?*

By the time he got home, he'd hatched several plans, each more unfeasible than the one before. Feeling exhausted, he went in search of Chin Nam.

They resembled two schoolboys sharing a deep and dark secret as they huddled in a corner of the living room, conspiring. They sat bent over a piece of paper and spoke in muffled voices. Elaine was the first to stumble upon them.

"What are you two up to? It looks like you have been caught with dynamite in your possession!" said Elaine.

The two men looked at each other, thinking how close to the truth she was.

"It's nothing," said Chin Nam, desperately trying to hide the piece of paper. "He's just showing me something that hasn't any real meaning or significance. Just something trivial." he tried to laugh off.

"You two look far too serious to be looking at something trivial and frivolous', said Elaine, her interest all piqued. "You can't keep Saras and me out of any information you might have," she added looking at them accusingly. "We have every right to know if it concerns the two of you and especially your safety," she said, wagging a finger at them.

It was Rangaswamy who relented and agreed with Elaine. He motioned for her to bend down and join their discussion.

"I happened to come across some vital information that will save the lives of the guerillas in the jungle. The Japanese have found out where they are hiding and are planning on ambushing them simultaneously," explained Rangaswamy.

"Are you absolutely certain?" asked Elaine, goosebumps rising up all over her body.

"I overheard two senior officials talking and I even saw the map in the meeting room marking out all the different areas. The fools had written the names of the places in Japanese on the blackboard, for all to see!' said Rangaswamy.

"But we have an even bigger problem," said Chin Nam. "We don't know how we are going to get this information out because the courier doesn't come for another month. The ambush is scheduled for three weeks time!" said Chin Nam. "This is our biggest dilemma."

"I'll go," said Elaine quietly and without any hesitation. "I could easily do it. You just need to brief me properly and give me exact locations and I can do it."

Rangaswamy and Chin Nam looked at her incredulously.

"Are you mad?" asked Chin Nam.

"I must agree with Chin Nam, Elaine. That is terribly naïve of you to think that we will allow you to do something as dangerous as this," added Rangaswamy.

"But listen, it's not like I am carrying anything on me. I can easily commit whatever information you give me to memory and it will all be in my head! It's not like I am carrying arms. I could easily make the journey to your closest contact point. I could say that I was going to visit a family member who is sick and dying. I do believe that I am your best bet."

"That's a ridiculous suggestion, Elaine," said Chin Nam.

"Listen. You can't go," she said to her husband. "You're in no condition and you, Swamy, can't not be at work. If you don't show up for one day, they'll come looking for you. So I'm the obvious choice and I insist on going. This is absolutely non-negotiable."

Elaine had such a resolute look that neither of them was willing to argue with her. They all knew why Elaine was so determined to take on this errand. It would be cathartic for her, an act she needed to carry out in Kah Hoe's memory and the two men could well understand her need to do this.

"All right, Elaine," said Rangaswamy. "I can see you have made up your mind and no amount of us trying to talk you out of it is going to work. But this is a dangerous mission, you must be very careful and wary of your surroundings, the people you may meet and those that will stop you along the way."

"Elaine," said Chin Nam tenderly, "you don't need to do this, you know. I can understand your reasons but there is a huge risk and you have four other children here. You don't need to put yourself in harm's way and be brave for the sake of Kah Hoe. He wouldn't have wanted you to do this."

"I am not trying to show off and prove that I am brave or stupid or whatever you may think. This is an important job that needs to be done and it needs to be done NOW. I am the right person for this job. That's all this is about. I promise you I'll be very careful and I'll be back here with you, safe and sound," assured Elaine as she squeezed his hand.

"Ok. The three states are Perak, Pahang and Negeri Sembilan," gushed Rangaswamy, as if he was calling the first three prize winners of a lottery. I have written them out. You need to memorise it."

Elaine picked up the piece of paper that read:

Perak
Confluence of Sungei Kinta and Sungei Perak.
Gunung Batu Puteh – 4000 ft above sea level; facing north east

Pahang
By Sungei Bentong – 26 miles south of Bentong town.
Midway between Sungei Sempan and Bukit Kubang Babi.

Negeri Sembilan
Town of Titi – 3 degrees North of the Equator.

That night Elaine reread and reread that piece of paper until the coordinates burned into her memory.

45
PERAK
18TH DECEMBER 1944

The dust and grime of the journey had given Elaine a new hairdo. She had made every effort to dress down for her journey without realizing that the trunk road she would be travelling on for three days would do the job so well. She wore an old sam foo, cut her hair short and carried only a green canvas knapsack with her food supplies and some clothes.

She had spent three days cycling, the whirring of the wheels keeping tempo with the poetry of coordinates she silently recited in her head. She was weary and her next stop would be Bidor where her cousin lived, she was looking forward to a cold changkul bath and a bed to sleep in. She had spent two nights roughing it out, spreading a mat out in the open under the night sky and she was craving the little luxury she had once taken for granted.

Her only companion on her arduous journey was Kah Hoe. She felt his presence and knew he was there with her, silently egging her on and giving her the invisible support she clung to. She was exhausted and unaccustomed to hardship and to look so dishevelled and unkempt was uncomfortable for her. Every evening, when she stopped to rest, she would patiently clean the dirt that had stuck under her fingernails. Fortunately for her, she didn't have a mirror or she would have done a double take at the vision staring back at her. But after the first day, she cared less about her outward appearance. Her mission had made her resolute and she understood that this calling was her destiny. Kah Hoe had seen to that.

Elaine dragged her mind back to the present. She had not seen her cousin Ah Yoong for three years and she was looking forward to the reunion. She had no idea if her family was still at the same house. Swamy had applied for a police permit that allowed her to travel from Kuala Lumpur to Bidor and she had rehearsed her story many times, in case she was stopped. Just as she was about to reach Bidor, she could see from a distance, a road-block set up by Japanese soldiers. Instinctively, her heart started racing and the palms of her hands became sweaty. She knew she had every right to be here as all her papers were in order, but the very sight of her son's tormentors made her stomach churn.

She slowed down and dismounted from her bicycle when one of the soldiers brusquely lifted his hand demanding her to stop. He spoke in Japanese asking her where she was going and why. Elaine explained in her pidgin Japanese, her story about her cousin who was unwell and whom she hadn't seen in three years. She peppered her story with half-truths that seemed completely plausible even to her. But the soldier persisted and grilled her with more questions, trying his best to unnerve her. Elaine stuck to her story and produced her police permit, making it difficult for the soldier to deny her entry into Bidor. So, much against his will, he allowed her to pass through.

Elaine would have done a celebratory jig if she could, but instead she had on the biggest smile. *We did it, Kah Hoe! You've brought me safely here. Now I need to find Ah Yoong's house and I need to pass this information on,* she thought. She cycled on through Bidor town with renewed energy and a sense of purpose.

She trusted her instinct to lead her to her cousin's house but when she finally found it she was disappointed to see a stranger come to the door.

"Ah, Ah Yoong ah," he said. "She move to the farm down the road lah."

She thanked him, got back on her bicycle and went in the direction of his pointing hand.

The house was a kampung house. It looked more like a makeshift hut with chickens running around and through the house. In the fading light of day, she made out a silhouette sitting on a chair in a corner and, with a sad realization, recognized Ah Yoong.

Ah Yoong wasn't expecting any visitors nor did she seem to be glad to see someone standing at her gate. All Elaine's visions of an ecstatic reunion quickly dissipated like a balloon expelling its trapped air. She waddled slowly to the gate, wondering who the intruder was and it was only when Elaine introduced herself that she had some recollection of this face from the past.

Once they had dispensed with the awkward introductions, the two women started to exchange selected chapters of their stories. Once they started, they found it hard to stop and their words of grief, pain and sorrow tripped over each other as they finally found their own voices. Ah Yoong's husband had been captured by the Japanese and was still missing, presumed dead. Her eldest daughter had been raped; she was now mute and immobile, just biding time for death to take her too. Elaine told her about Kah Hoe's death and Chin Nam's torture.

The war had stripped them both bare, stolen their children and husbands, and left them with an emptiness, a hollowness where sorrow and grief lay waiting. As they sat facing but not really seeing each other, that very same sorrow leaked out of their bodies to fill the empty space between them.

"The war kills us all a little at a time. Every day when I think of my Kah Hoe, I die a little," said Elaine, breaking the silence. "I try and tell myself that I have to be strong for my other children but it is very hard. When I have time on my hands, I always think of Kah Hoe and how much he must have suffered," she added.

Ah Yoong could only shake her head in agreement. Her words were too tired to be spoken. She sat there as mute as her daughter, shackled to this existence by complete and utter despair.

Elaine was reluctant to tell Ah Yoong of the real purpose of her visit, so she coined a plausible enough reason of visiting an old friend in Menglembu who was dying of cancer. Ah Yoong wasn't too concerned with the 'whys' and the 'hows' anyway. She was just a little relieved to have some company and a short respite from her drudgery. She begged Elaine to stay at least for a night. Elaine herself was more than happy to have a good bath and a mattress to rest on. The very thought of emptying pail after pail of cold, cold water over her body was something she had looked forward to for days.

Ah Yoong seemed to have found a reason to busy herself. She had a guest in her house and she felt the need to feed Elaine with what she had. She picked a few fresh eggs from the chickens she reared in her garden and she prepared an evening meal that was extravagant during these times of parsimony. Eventually, after Elaine had had her invigorating bath, they sat down to a feast of porridge with some sweet potato leaves from her vegetable patch, boiled eggs and salted fish.

Exhausted, she went straight to bed after helping Ah Yoong clean up. Elaine left a distraught Ah Yoong the next night as fresh tears were spent at the door. She had on the same set of clothes that had been washed and dried and smelled clean. She gave Ah Yoong a hug that said, *sister this is for your bravery, tenacity and mostly hope. Hope that the pain will eventually recede and for there to be more bright days than dark.* With that, Elaine mounted her bicycle and pedalled off into the night.

She got back on the same road she arrived on and continued her journey, not towards Menglembu but to Kampar. After a short while on the trunk road, Elaine turned off and kept to the side roads. This was the most crucial leg of her journey and she knew these roads were fringed with danger. Her police permit only allowed her entry to Bidor and if she was caught on this stretch she would not be able to explain her presence. Whatever her reasons may be, the fact was she had no valid papers for this segment of her journey and that was an offence. So, she kept away from the streetlights, wanting to attract the least possible attention.

The sound of her wheels whirring gave her some comfort as she tried to focus on the task at hand. She rehearsed the steps she had to take in her head. She needed to reach the safe house Swamy had told her about. What she had to do seemed simple enough; just tell anyone at the house that the 'Black Dove' had sent her and they would know immediately that it was a message from Swamy.

By the time Elaine got to Kampar, it was first light and she was feeling nervous and tired. The address to the shophouse was imprinted in her mind and she made her way there cautiously, afraid that she might stumble upon a road-block.

What she found when she arrived at her destination shocked and horrified her. All that was left in its place was a mangled heap of charred, twisted metal that had once been the gate to the shop house. She felt like screaming out loud and swearing. She wanted to pull her hair out in frustration. *How could this happen? Who would have done this?* she asked herself though she already knew the answer.

After composing herself, Elaine decided to go to the neighbours and try and uncover what had happened. She wasn't sure if anyone was home and after a few minutes of pounding on the aluminium gate, a thin figure poked his head out as if afraid of sunlight. He was unfriendly and looked at her suspiciously. It took her some time to convince the man that she meant him no harm and all she wanted to know was what had happened to the shop house next door.

When he finally seemed to trust her a little, he opened the gate to let her in. He wore nothing except a pair of stiff khaki shorts, his rake thin torso told her that he hadn't eaten a decent meal in weeks. In a quiet and monotonous voice, the man told her that the Japanese had come ten days ago because they had information that the owners of the bicycle repair shop were Communist sympathizers. They dragged the owner, his wife and two children into the street and called on the others around to come and watch. His lips began to tremble as he told Elaine how they had violently beheaded the husband and the two children before their eyes. The wife had screamed and screamed and yelled for them to stop but they turned on her and yelled obscenities. The soldiers shouted at all of us who were standing there that this is what they would do if they caught any traitors.

"We were all so petrified, we knew these people you know. We were neighbours for over twenty years and they came and hacked them like they were trees. How can people be so cruel?"

He was sobbing now, wiping his eyes with the back of his hand. "My wife still can't sleep at night. She is terrified to close her eyes. The scene keeps running through my head. They dragged the poor woman away. God knows if she is alive. For her sake, I hope they killed her too."

Elaine's shoulders slumped with the weight of this news. She uttered some empty words of consolation and rode to the nearest coffeeshop. She sat down to a bowl of pan mee and untangled her knotted thoughts. Turning back was not an option.

I haven't come this far to turn back. Where would I go if I needed to make contact? I can't possibly ask anyone for help. I wouldn't trust anyone nor would anyone trust me with the information even if they knew. Kah Hoe, what would you do if you were in my predicament?

Elaine stared out into space as she tried to recollect some of the conversations she had had with her son when he had come home. There were many snippets that came back to her and then like a light bulb, it dawned upon her.

Why didn't I think of that! Of course, it's the most obvious thing for me to do!

The realization liberated her and made her spirit soar. There was only one place to go to and that was Papan. She remembered Kah Hoe telling her about the doctor and his wife who were helping their cause, treating their wounded and providing them with medicines. Elaine had no idea where she would find them or how, but she knew that she had to try.

With this new plan craftily brewing in her head, she set off for Papan. She was exhausted, the trip was beginning to take its toll on her, both physically and mentally but she knew she had to see it through. The responsibility of the task winded her, taking her breath away. If she didn't get this message into the right hands, the human damage would be palpable and she would wear another layer of guilt for the rest of her life.

It would take Elaine the whole day to cycle to Papan and she had no idea what she would do or where she would go once she got there. She would take each step at a time and she tried hard not to focus on the absence of a police permit.

By the time Elaine rode in to Papan, it was dusk. She was bone tired and she stopped at the nearest coffee shop in search of food. She asked the owner for directions to the local doctor and was promptly told that Dr Kathigasu's house was only down the road. It took all of her effort to stop smiling at the lucky discovery.

Elaine walked up to the main door of 74 Main Street and knocked. Sybil herself opened the door and presumed this lady was there to see her husband. But what Elaine said to her made her stop short in her tracks.

"Are you Mrs Kathigasu? I need to speak to you privately, please," she whispered.

Sybil turned around and gave her a sharp look. "I think you need to leave now. Unless you are here to see my husband."

"Please don't misunderstand me or mistrust me. I had no intention to come out here to trouble you but the circumstances changed and I had no choice but to look for you to seek your assistance. I know you don't know who I am and there is no reason for you to trust me, but my son Kah Hoe told me about you and your assistant named Moru. We both had a good laugh back then at his name because we have very close Indian friends and we know what moru means," said Elaine.

She could see the look on Sybil's face softening, so she pushed on.

"The Japanese killed him and I have information that I need to pass to our boys in the jungle. I have just come from the safe house in Kampar or rather what is left of it. The Japanese razed it to the ground because they found it was used by the sympathizers. The Japanese are going to ambush them in the jungle and I need to let them know that their lives are in danger. They need to leave and find another safe hiding place. Can you please help me?" begged Elaine, clinging to her arm. "I don't know where else to go. I nearly turned back when I suddenly remembered that Kah Hoe had spoken so highly of you. You are my only hope."

Sybil looked at the sad and yet immensely spirited and strong woman standing across from her and knew instinctively that she was telling her the truth.

"I do remember your son. He struck a chord in me because he was so different from the others. He was well mannered and he spoke so well. I often wondered to myself how a privileged boy like him had got entangled in this dangerous life. Yes, I can help you get the message to the boys in the jungle. You are in luck. I am expecting Moru later tonight. You need a place to sleep and some hot food."

It was not a question, merely a statement of fact that Elaine could not refute.

Sybil squeezed her hand and wiped the tears that were rolling down Elaine's dust caked face.

"Let's find you some clothes and a clean towel, shall we?" she said, leading Elaine through the living room to the back of the house.

46

PERAK
20TH DECEMBER 1944

Elaine gratefully took up Sybil's offer of a hot meal and a bath but she declined to stay the night. She was feeling the strain of the journey and was desperately missing Chin Nam and the children. She wanted to leave for home as soon as she could.

She sat with Sybil at the kitchen table and the two women spoke between gaps of silence. Sybil told Elaine about the guerillas in the jungle and their stoic belief in their cause. She spoke well of Kah Hoe and she tried to ease Elaine's grief. Elaine in turn told her of what was happening in Kuala Lumpur, the betrayal by their friend and Chin Nam's torture.

"I would do anything to have one more day with my son, Sybil. I just want to hold him and tell him that I am so proud of him. This war has cast such a deep shadow on my life that there are days when I wonder if I'll make it. What really pains me is that he died alone and I don't even know where he's buried. I don't even know if he was given a burial," wept Elaine.

"Listen, Elaine, do you know where he died?" asked Sybil.

"Yes, he was captured and taken to Batu Gajah prison and killed there."

"If that's the case, I do know that those who die at the Batu Gajah prison are buried in the mass grave next to it. It is not marked, it's just an open field and it won't be very obvious," explained Sybil.

"Is that very far from here?" she asked.

"No, it's only five miles away, but... if you're thinking of going, you should know that it can be very dangerous. The prison is heavily guarded and they won't be pleased to see you loitering around," said Sybil. "Do you even have a police permit for Batu Gajah?"

"No, my police permit doesn't even allow me to be here! I can only travel as far as Bidor, so my being here is already an offence. I can't come this far and not visit his grave. I would never forgive myself. I will have to take the risk and live with the consequences. I don't think I have a choice," said Elaine quietly.

Sybil sighed, but she could understand Elaine's resolve.

"In that case, I would suggest you leave tonight and cycle through the night. Keep away from the main roads and try not to use your light. But once you have seen the prison and the grave, please, please leave immediately. You cannot imagine how dangerous it will be if you get caught."

Elaine nodded and gave Sybil a tight hug, leaving no space for words.

Elaine depended on the moonlight to guide her to the prison. Following Sybil's clear instructions, she arrived within an hour. The first thing that came into view was the guardhouse; the entire white block wrapped with barbed wire and looked menacingly on the outside world. Elaine could feel her hackles rise as she distractedly rubbed her arms to keep the chills at bay.

She kept her distance from the prison walls and quickly rode around to the burial ground. It was just where Sybil had said it would be. A large open field with no fencing and all she could make out in the moonlight were mounds of varying heights and sizes. She left her bicycle under a tree and walked towards the unmarked cemetery.

There was something ominous about this place. There were no frangipani trees to give the dead shade, so she imagined Kah

Hoe lying underneath in the scorching midday heat. She knew that Sybil had warned her that there would be no marked graves but she had naively hoped there would be some small markings that might indicate who was buried under the mound.

She walked from one mound to the next and soon she was running all over them hysterically calling out her son's name, hoping that he might give her a silent sign and lead her to his resting place. Somewhere in the middle of the field her body folded in half from guilt and regret. So lost was she in her grief that she didn't hear the sound of feet walking on dry grass until she felt a hand on her shoulder. She slowly turned around and stared into the face of a young Japanese soldier.

47

PENANG
3RD SEPTEMBER 1945

Colonel Suzuki sat in the lotus position deep in meditation. He was grateful for the quietude as he sat shrouded in peace and contemplative silence. The only sound was that of the waves, tirelessly crashing on the beach along Batu Ferringhi.

He came here once a week. It was his respite from the weighty worries and stress he carried on his shoulders. Here, he could discard them for a while, undress his mind of all the toxic thoughts and negative energy. Seated on the sand, he replenished his soul, washed it out, plumped it out with good thoughts and positive energy. He had mastered the art of cleansing his mind while chaos swirled her tumultuous dance around him.

Suzuki's lineage could be traced back to the gallant and fearless Samurai. He was born of a womb where virtues like honour, rectitude, courage, benevolence, respect, honesty and loyalty were a part of his being. He came into the world long after Emperor Meiji abolished the Samurai, but the code of Bushido coursed through his veins.

His father was larger than life. He believed and conducted his life by the Samurai Bushido code, where honour was next to godliness in his family. He was four when his father announced that the time had come for his son to learn the tenets of Zen Buddhism and the science of meditation. He was schooled in the ancient art of 'zazen', a form of meditation that made one focus on pushing his energy below his navel. In meditation, there was nothing to nurture other than the mind itself, while turning the eye inward in introspection.

Also true to his Samurai-heritage, he learned the martial art of Kendo or sword fencing. Just as this vision passed through his mind's eye, Colonel Suzuki smelled the sweaty bodies of boys and men in their armoured regalia. They looked menacing but were in fact innocuous. Like-minded boys of similar age engrossed and in love with an art that made his father beam with pride, for the young Suzuki was always at the top of his Kendo class.

This morning, a battle between opposing forces was brewing in Suzuki's head. All his years of excruciating training were being put to a test. The world as he knew it had collapsed around him. Only a month earlier, on the 6th August, the Allied Forces dropped an atom bomb on Hiroshima killing over a hundred thousand people with one singular move. On the 9th August, another atom bomb was dropped on Nagasaki. On the 15th August, Suzuki had to endure the shame of listening to his Emperor Hirohito urging his people to accept surrender. Suzuki now understood that there were layers to his shame; just when he thought his shame had reached its zenith, another layer was neatly piled on top, causing it to topple over. Yesterday had been the signing of Japan's formal surrender on board the USS Missouri in Tokyo Bay. The signatures on the document sealed the fate of Japan.

Today, British troops were returning to Penang and Suzuki knew that he would have to look shame directly in the face. He knew how to face adversity and hardship; it was something he had trained to do all his life. But no one had prepared him to stand up and face shame. It had never featured in his life. No one spoke the dirty word out loud, for fear that it might raise its shameless head and walk where only honour, bravery and courage were allowed. Suzuki's eyes were closed tight but the

241

tears found their way out into the open for all the world to see.

His life played itself out in his mind in silent technicolour. Moving pictures of people and places from his recent and distant past, vivid and in sequence. The faces of people he had forgotten popped up in his mind and his sense of smell was suddenly heightened. He could smell his past; the sweet aromas from his mother's kitchen, his mother's warm body, the foul waft of others… meshing together and confusing his thoughts.

His thoughts drifted back to his childhood. He saw his parents in their garden at home in Kyoto. Today, he knew the words to describe it. Those words were Structured and Manicured, two words he would borrow to describe the rest of his childhood, where everything grew in straight lines. The gravel path that led from one end of the garden to the other was a straight line of white. Trees grew in a certain way because they were forced to do so; just like he was. How ironic that his life was a parallel to the landscape of his home.

Structure dictated his childhood and his life. It was the one constant. He lived by it, he breathed it and if he could, he would die by it. He would like to organize his death just the same way he had organised his life, with precision and accuracy.

Of all the places of interest and worship he had visited, Kinkaku-ji stood out. He remembered it well. To him, it was everything the name implied – the Golden Pavilion Temple. He could see the gold leaf shimmer in the sun, gleaming and pure. He could see his younger self, strolling through the garden by the Mirror Pond and he felt nostalgic for his beautiful Kyoto.

His trips to Lake Biwa flooded his memory. It was his place of repose and sanctuary when he was confused, depressed or just disturbed. He could see it so clearly now. The pristine, still water that always soothed him, that always allowed him to think; that encouraged him to lose his negative thoughts. He would ride the canals to get there to spend his time in deep meditation.

It was always the virtue of honour that was paramount in the life of the young Suzuki. He remembered fondly the story his father told him of the forty-seven Ronin. He was always fascinated by their bravery and would often beg him to retell the same story over and over again. When he was older, they would travel to Tokyo to visit the burial site of the Ronin at Sengaku-ji, on the anniversary of their death. Today, as he meditated, he felt the presence of those brave and courageous warriors.

The path that Suzuki's life would take, seemed predestined. He always knew that he would be a soldier; it was his only calling and he had no desire to fight it. At the age of eighteen, he was conscripted into the Japanese army and because of his aptitude, was selected to be part of an elite group that would train in espionage. He was taught Malay, English and the art of photography. Suzuki was to be stationed in Malaya under the guise of a photographer and he was given a sum of money to set up his enterprise on Rodger Street in Kuala Lumpur.

His first impressions of Malaya were still as clear as day; the colourful sights, sounds and smells that were so different from his own experiences. His arrival in Malaya spelled the demise of Suzuki and the birth of Bob Nakamura. The affable, funny Bob who 'hated' the Japanese. He hadn't expected to assimilate with both the locals and the Europeans until he met Rangaswamy and Chin Nam.

He still remembered the day Swamy walked into his studio to have his picture taken. They had started a conversation and he had found the Indian man friendly and interesting without being too inquisitive. It was Swamy who had introduced him to Chin Nam and he soon found himself - despite Swamy's affiliation to the British and Chin Nam's vocal support for the China Relief Fund - warming up to them. Neither passed judgment on him because he was Japanese and had even embraced him and treated him like family; both accepting him for who he was or who they thought he was. That deception now caused him pain, guilt and deep shame, coagulating in a clot of remorse in his head.

When Japan entered the war, Suzuki had the unenviable task of rounding up pro-China supporters. He had struggled with his conscience whether to name Chin Nam and in the end, his country had come before his friend. He had rationalized that his loyalty was to the Emperor of Japan and that all his training had been put to test when he himself had gone to arrest Chin Nam.

He had beaten him brutally, not because of his friend's political leanings, but to exorcise himself of his affection for the man. It had amazed him, bewildered him and finally angered him that he could allow feelings for another human being to interfere with his duty to his Emperor and country.

Every blow that he landed on Chin Nam was, in a bizarre and twisted way, catharsis for Suzuki. It convinced him that he was doing it for the greater good of Japan. And yet, when he came so close to snuffing out Chin Nam's life, he had backed down. The man who had inflicted bruises in various shades of purple could not bear to see the bright red of fresh blood staining his hands. Suzuki then unceremoniously dumped his friend's pulp of a body outside 912 Batu Road.

Finally, he succumbed to shame. It rained on him heavily; drenching him and soaking into his skin, making him shudder and shiver. Shame, the unkind and unwelcome visitor to a Japanese soldier. It stripped him of self-respect, self-confidence and most importantly, honour. It had left him feeling deep, deep remorse for the loss of Japan's colonial ambitions and on a personal level, at his betrayal of two men he had come to call 'friends'. Sitting on the beach, waiting for the British soldiers to march into Penang, he realized that his greatest regret was his betrayal of Rangaswamy and Chin Nam.

Now in this hour of truth, Colonel Suzuki sat bathed in daylight as the sun shone brightly on his shame. Suzuki closed his eyes tight but its black silhouette danced in front of his pupils. He tried to clear his mind, but he couldn't push away the images of his parents and his two friends. He sent a silent apology to all four of them.

There was no way out; there would be no escape and there would be no turning back. With a sense of foreboding at his imminent capture, he knew there was only one honourable thing to do, the sound of the steely blade as it drew from its sheath, magnified. Without blinking, he plunged the blade into the left side of his abdomen and dragged it in a jagged fashion across to his right and then upwards towards his sternum, releasing his spirit. All the while, Colonel Suzuki's mouth moved without making any sound, a soliloquy of his death poem. *Duty is heavier than a mountain. Death - lighter than a feather.*

Blood sprung out of him, merging with the milky white foam of the waves, instantly changing its colour. He fell forward into the blood-tinted water, the sea lapping at his gaping wound as a devoted dog would his master.

48
A VISIT FROM THE PAST
KUALA LUMPUR, 2010

The young man sat patiently waiting to be shown into Geeta's office. He had called two days ago and made an appointment to see her 'about a personal matter.' He sat up straight with his back to the door and ran his hand over a thin brown envelope that sat on his lap. He was jolted out of his reverie when a young lady in traditional dress asked him to follow her.

Geeta was sitting at her desk when her secretary gently knocked on the door, informing her of a visitor. She entered the conference room and introduced herself to the well-groomed man standing in front of her. She asked him to take a seat and as soon as she had sat down, he started to speak.

"I am not here for legal advice," he said. "I have come here on a very personal matter, about something you may not even be aware of," he said with a nervous smile.

Geeta raised her eyebrows as she straightened her back instinctively. *What on earth can this be about?*

She kept silent, allowing the young man to continue, "I have come a long way because I made a promise to a very old man. I have with me something you need to watch. Do you have a DVD player in your office?" Geeta was now completely baffled by his request.

"I don't understand what you're trying to tell me. Is this DVD going to make it all clear to me? Can't you just tell me what it's about?" asked Geeta, trying to keep her irritation under control.

"It's a long story and I think the intention is for you to watch the DVD. This will tell you everything you need to know."

With her curiosity completely piqued, she played the DVD on her laptop.

Geeta watched a frail, old man talk into the camera. He spoke slowly but coherently in good English. She was puzzled when he began explaining that his message was to the families of Rangaswamy and Tan Chin Nam.

My God, this goes all the way back to Tata! Who is this and what is he about to tell me? Do I really want to know? It sounds like a dark insidious secret...

The old man continued, "I doubt you will know me. My name is Yoeishi Suzuki. But your families knew me as Bob Nakamura. I am a Japanese man who was in your country during the Second World War. I was actually a soldier with the Japanese army but I came to Malaya as a spy. My job was to pose as a photographer and I therefore set up a small photo studio in Kuala Lumpur. Two of my regulars were gentlemen by the names of Rangaswamy and Tan Chin Nam. When I say gentlemen, I mean they were exactly that. They were honest men with high standards of integrity. I am here to tell you a story of three friends and how they were betrayed by one.

"I knew Rangaswamy first. He came to my studio with his family to have their family portrait taken. He was the kindest man I knew. He never had a bad word to say to me about the Japanese. He treated me only with respect despite the fact that I was far younger. Our early friendship started in that studio and in time we nurtured it and we watched it grow. He brought his good friend Chin Nam to my studio so that his family too, could have their portraits taken. Soon the three of us became close friends. Rangaswamy used to invite me to his house on 912 Batu Road to share meals with his family. I clearly remember his lovely wife Saraswathi and the delicious food that she used to cook! They made me feel like a part of their family, that was the kind of man Rangaswamy was.

"Chin Nam too, used to drop by my studio and spend time with me, talking about politics and the war. He was more vocal about his political leanings than Rangaswamy was. But he too used to say, "Not all Japanese are bad. Look at our Bob!" I can never forget Elaine's culinary skills, her Nyonya food was simply the best.

"What did I do? How did I repay their kindness? I betrayed them and I have spent the rest of my life living with that regret. You see, I knew that Chin Nam was supporting the cause in China and I passed the authorities his name and address. At that time I did battle with my conscience but I thought that loyalty to country was above all else, even friendship. How wrong I was. I went to pick him up and it was these very hands that beat him up. I have come to realize that I used the hands that God gave me to do evil things, not good. I beat him so badly but I couldn't bring myself to kill him. I dumped him on the street and with that act, I destroyed not just one man, but his family and their lives.

"My friends finally knew me for what I really was, a spy. They couldn't believe it. Could a 'friend' do this? Would a friend behave like this? I was not worthy of their friendship. I had no appreciation of it, so how could I comprehend the depth and scope of it? If you, a family member of Rangaswamy or Chin Nam is watching this, then you would have met my grandson, Yoshii."

Geeta instinctively turned to look at the man he was talking about. She involuntarily nodded her head in agreement, as if answering the man on the DVD. Her head was reeling from all the information but she couldn't stop. She continued listening to his raspy voice.

"Yoshii knows the whole story. My childhood was a strict one. I was trained from a very young age in Japanese martial arts and I was taught that honour and valour were important, but what I didn't understand then, was something as precious and priceless as friendship. I sacrificed real people with good hearts

248

for intangibles like the Emperor and country. What good did that do me in the end?

"Since the war ended, I have lived a tortured life. When Japan surrendered, I knew that I understood the colours of shame. I suffered the shame of my country losing the war and more than that, I suffered the shame of betraying my friends. That shame has lived with me all my life. It has followed me like a black shadow, always haunting me like a ghost.

"As the British troops were marching into Penang, I sat alone on the beach willing it to be the final moment of my miserable life. My memories flooded back and the ones I cherished dearly were the happy times I had with Chin Nam and Rangaswamy. I tried to commit hara-kiri. It was not a brave act on my part. I was a coward, looking for a quick exit from the pain and suffering I had brought upon myself. I thought I would die that morning but here is the irony! I was found by British troops who took me to a hospital and saved my life.

"I was so badly cut up that I spent a few months in the hospital. When I finally recovered I was sent back to Japan. This is what war does; it makes sane people insane and insane people sane. I would have preferred to die. I am now 95 years old and I feel like a dead man amongst the living. God has cursed me with a long but wretched life, a life full of regrets and internal sorrow. I have become a burden to my children and grandchildren. But I can't rest until I tell you the truth.

"I made Yoshii promise me that he would come to you and tell you my story. I pray for death to take me everyday. But now I pray that I will live to hear from Yoshii that both your families will forgive me. I have no fear of what the afterlife has for me. I have had to deal with demons in this life. Nothing could be more tragic than that. I am twisted and bitter. I seek solace. I seek forgiveness from the children and the grandchildren of two great men. Two men whom I hope I will see in the hereafter so that I may fall at their feet and seek their pardon. But I need to make a start here, in this life. So, I ask you, no, I beg you, please forgive me."

With that, the screen went blank and all there was, was the

quiet sound of two grown people sniffling. Geeta had no idea where the tissue had appeared from, but she was wiping her wet face with it. Yoshii seemed to be equally moved. The air in the room was charged with emotions and it was Geeta who finally broke the silence.

"I never knew my grandfather's story. I was not fortunate like you," she said gently. "Your grandfather sounds like a man wracked by guilt and pain but he needs to understand that he did what he did in a time when reason and rhyme often fled from the psyche of the sane. Yoshii, I am sure that if my grandfather were alive today he would have wept tears of forgiveness. He would have understood the travesty of a war and the frailties of a man consumed by a passion for what he truly believed was the right thing to do. I think you need to contact your grandfather and tell him that Rangaswamy's family is well and that they forgive him. Please promise him that I will show this to Tan Chin Nam's family."

Yoshii stood up and bowed deeply. His face was wet with tears too.

49
TENSION BUILDS
KUALA LUMPUR, 2010

Geeta had spoken to her father about Yoshii's visit and shared the DVD with him. It took some serious convincing on her part to persuade him to come along with her. She decided that it was necessary for them to do this together and deep down she hoped that this would be a good ice-breaker to get both friends back on the road of friendship.

So, after much arguing and persuasion, Ramesh agreed to pay Kah Sing a visit. He told Geeta he wanted it to be as official as possible so a visit to his home was out of the question. Geeta had made an appointment for 6.30pm at Uncle Kah Sing's office and they were there, right on time.

She had forgotten the familiar feeling of Uncle Kah Sing's office. There were a few staff who acknowledged her and even smiled at her awkwardly. Kah Sing was in his room sitting at his desk when his secretary showed Ramesh and Geeta in. He stood immediately and walked around to greet them. He had a big smile for Geeta and he hugged her warmly. He put his hand out to shake Ramesh's hand; Ramesh hesitated a moment before taking Kah Sing's hand in his and he could feel his daughter's hard gaze on him.

"Please come and sit down. Geeta, it's lovely to see you! How have you been? You are looking well. What have you been up to?" The affection he felt for Geeta was obvious and Ramesh sat next to her, back ramrod straight, feeling rather uncomfortable at all this familiarity. He interjected their conversation by clearing his throat loudly, to remind Geeta of the real reason they were there. Kah Sing understood from their terse looks that they were not here to bury the hatchet and move on, that was obvious from Ramesh's stand-offish body language.

Geeta took a deep breath and began, "Uncle Kah Sing, the reason my father and I are here is because of a visit from a Japanese man by the name of Yoshii. His grandfather knew both your father and my grandfather. He used to be known as Bob Nakamura."

She saw the dark clouds of recognition pass over Kah Sing's face and she realized that this wasn't going to go down well, but she persisted.

"Yoshii visited me in the office last week with a DVD of his grandfather's confession. Bob Nakamura is in his nineties now and is basically asking the both of you to forgive him."

At first, there was complete silence which misled Geeta into believing that Uncle Kah Sing was contemplating coming to terms with the past. How very wrong she was.

"You have got to be joking!" bellowed Kah Sing, cracking open the apparent calm. "How dare that bastard send his grandson here to do his dirty work? Does he think just because he is an old man and that so many years have passed that we have forgotten the pain? I will never forgive him. How can we?" he asked Geeta, pointing at Ramesh and himself.

"But Uncle…" Geeta began. Kah Sing put up a hand and continued.

"We lived through the torture. We know what our fathers and families went through. That bastard tortured my father and they killed my brother and he has the audacity to ask us for forgiveness! Huh! I will burn in hell before I do that and my brother and father will turn in their graves. Never, Geeta! You can tell that grandson of his that this is not going to happen. Period! I refuse to watch the DVD. You can chuck it back in his face. Tell him to get back on the plane and never to return to Malaysia. At least not while I am alive!" he shouted.

The room fell silent for a time. Geeta could hear her heart pounding in her ears. *Shit! I've really offended Uncle Kah Sing, what now? Think!*

"Listen, Kah Sing," spoke Ramesh for the first time, "maybe you shouldn't be so hasty. Why don't you watch the DVD? I did and I can tell you he is a broken old man with a lot of regret."

"Ramesh, I can't believe you are sitting here and preaching to me about forgiveness! You, who won't allow my son and your daughter to get married, sitting here and sanctimoniously telling me that I should forgive that bugger for all the atrocities he so graciously bestowed upon us! Look who's talking about prejudices!" said Kah Sing sarcastically.

"Listen, I'm not asking you to forgive. All I'm saying is perhaps you ought to listen to what he has to say and then make a decision. The issue between our children doesn't come up here at all," said Ramesh.

Before Kah Sing could answer, there was a soft knock on the door and in walked Ken. Right behind him was a tall, leggy and stunning Eurasian girl with shoulder length hair. Geeta could feel her heart jump out and land in her mouth. She involuntarily caught her breath and adjusted her clothes without being too obvious in front of her father.

He looks gorgeous! But who is she? When did he come back? Damn! This is an unexpected surprise. I should have touched up my lipstick...

"Hi Uncle Ramesh, Geeta," he said politely while nodding his head. "This is Sandra," he said introducing the woman standing next to him.

"Ken, you have come at the right time," said Kah Sing. "Something's come up and I think you should listen in and let us have your views."

Ken looked at Sandra and she took her cue to leave. He saw

her out and came back in to join the tense conversation.

"When did you get back?" asked Geeta, feeling a little slighted.

"Oh, it's been nearly two months. You know that Dad's been asking me to come join him so I thought it was time to come home to roost." He gave her a knowing look and the hint of a smile. "You're looking well," said Ken graciously. "Obviously legal practice agrees with you."

"Well, it has been interesting as I have had some exciting cases to work on," said Geeta, trying very hard to keep her voice calm.

Geeta felt so self-conscious with her father sitting next to her as she tried to put some imaginary space between them. Their attention was brought back to the present when Kah Sing explained the reason for their visit.

"I think Uncle Ramesh is right, I don't think there's any harm in watching the DVD and seeing what he has to say. If Uncle Ramesh and G... I mean Geeta feel that he sounds like he has repented and has come to realize the mistakes of his past, then there's no harm in letting go and trying to move on, Pa," said Ken.

"You may say that Ken, because you didn't live through the war. The Japanese were cruel to us and he in particular was supposed to be a friend to my father but he betrayed him. How can you ask me to forget?" added Kah Sing.

"Pa, not all Japanese are cruel and that was the war. People did things that weren't rational and remember the story you told me about Poh Poh? How a Japanese soldier had found her in the cemetery near the Batu Gajah prison looking for Uncle Kah Hoe's grave? How he had hidden her, given her food and a police permit to be there? He saved her life, remember? So there were good people during the war, even if they were the enemy," Ken said gently. "It's time to let go, Pa. It doesn't do anyone any good to have prejudices and to be myopic. It's a different world today. You don't want to be consumed by hate after all these years and you don't want your grandchildren to inherit your hate either," said Ken.

As Ken spoke, Ramesh spent most of the time looking out

the window, not making a sound. Geeta sat quietly, playing with her nails. She found it so hard to be in the same room as him and not reach out and touch him. She wondered if the woman he had walked in with was his girlfriend; she knew she would be unreasonable to feel upset but she was. The whole episode ruffled her feathers. Her thoughts turned inwards. *How different things might have been if I was not Brahmin. Here is the one man I love within my reach but beyond my grasp. How unfair life can be. I wonder what he must be feeling. But by the looks of that woman, he can't be that put out. The look she gave me, hmmph! Maybe she knows who I am.*

Her muddled head could barely make out the droning voices just outside her consciousness. With a jolt she sat up and realised that her father was announcing to all in the room, that it was time for them to leave.

"Geeta, may I have the DVD please?" Ken asked, putting his hand out. She looked at him with such sadness that she was certain he noticed; she made sure she brushed her hand against his as she did. She thought she could feel the electricity, but when she looked up at him, he seemed to be somewhere else.

Ramesh stood up and Geeta followed suit; with quiet goodbyes bravely spoken by all four, father and daughter stepped out. Daughter with a heart that felt as heavy as lead and father with his head bent, deep in thought.

50
THE MANDAPAM
KUALA LUMPUR, 2010

The navy blue thermos was hard at work, keeping the pashumpal coffee hot after ten years of unscrew-pour-close. In fact, all that was left of its original bright gold lettering was 'hermo'.

The maid in charge of making and pouring coffee in the ladies' dressing room was busy topping up Telawi Mami's styrofoam cup, when Puchong Mami walked in ready to take charge. Her trademark hanky was tucked into the right side of her sari which meant she was ready for business. For the uninitiated, Puchong Mami's business was organizing and overseeing all things Brahmin; from the poonal ceremony, to Nischaithambul and kalyanams, and in the end, death and funerals. She covered it all. So in the know was she, that it was often whispered that "Puchong Mami knows who's going to marry and who's going to die even before they do!" She appeared at places like Rumpelstiltskin and just like her folktale counterpart, she could magically get things done.

A temporary silence, like a magic spell, fell on the ladies in the dressing room when she walked in. Her shrewd eyes took in the entire scene with one perfunctory scan. She wasted no time

256

in moving people and things around so that Geeta was eventually seated in the middle, surrounded by a melee of Brahmin women desperate to play a part in dressing the bride.

In no time at all, Puchong Mami had the prerequisite jewellery for the bride all laid out on the wobbly folding table beside her. Geeta sat on a dining chair in her sari blouse and pavadai. She had in her hand her favourite home-brewed, decoction coffee.

Sowmya occupied the same spot Geeta had at her wedding and couldn't help smiling at her. Geeta was well on her way to becoming a bride. Her defiant hair pulled into a compliant plait with little white jasmine flowers.

Geeta stamped her own brand on her wedding. She shot down any suggestion of overdrawn eyebrows, pasty orange foundation and exaggerated kohl-drawn eyes that came packaged in 'bespoke Indian bridal service.'

The nine-yard sari in red or mustard was quickly dispensed with. In its place, a beautiful sky blue and silver one. A regular sari with no extra yardage to fuss with. While she won the sari and make up rounds, she lost the jewellery round. There was no compromise with the gold bangles, diamond earrings and gold chains.

When Geeta finally stood in front of the mirror to consider the whole effect, they appeared to be a surplus of traditional Iyer customs. *I promised myself that I would never become a victim and here I am, nearly every inch a Brahmin bride, what I swore I would never be. Have I learned my lesson to never say never?*

Parvathi stood slightly behind, looking at her daughter's reflection. She too, deep in her own thoughts. They both looked at each other in the mirror. *She is strong this mother of mine,* thought Geeta. *The silent one in front but behind closed doors, her thoughts are loud and vocal. Anyone who can leave her family behind to marry a strange man and live in a strange country is neither meek nor weak. She holds and binds this family together. She doesn't give in easily and neither does she give up without a fight.*

Parvathi and Geeta stood there, one, an embodiment of

tradition and customs of her Brahmin heritage, in a maroon red nine-yard sari with her mukuthi and metti and the other, a beacon for the younger generation of Brahmin girls in Malaysia who may be afraid to speak out. Both looked defiant, both looked like they had won and yet both knew that the younger was just like the older, without the subtle ways of the village but with the brash and bold ways of the urban jungle. They each acknowledged the other with a smile that said, "I recognize the person you are and I respect you".

The mandapam was heaving with relatives and friends. Athais, Athimbairs, Mamas, Mamis, Chitappas, Chittis, Periappas and Perriammmas were all present as were cousins, nieces, nephews and friends. Geeta's brothers were both back; Suresh for good with his wife and two kids, while Ravi was home from Houston, specially for the wedding. As was true with all weddings, it was a time to celebrate life and all its precious moments. Many nights were spent in some relative's house with a spread of good food and conversation. Raman, Ramesh and Krishna were a riot when it came to regaling the family with their old stories and the three brothers were well known for their wicked sense of humour, especially when delivering jokes in Tamil.

Parvathi, Padma and the Brahmin Mamis had been busy with the wedding preparations. They had to oversee the making of all the traditional sweets - ladoos and mysore pak to be given away to all who came to the mandapam. Geeta had given them strict instructions on the kind of wrapping she wanted and had put Sowmya in charge. "I want the sweets wrapped in glass paper first and then in candy-coloured tissue." She had put Karen in charge of all the flower arrangements both at the mandapam and the Red Flame, where the high tea reception was to be held. She wanted white jasmines, white roses and white lilies. Parvathi's full lips became a thin long line when she heard that the flowers would be white. She bit her tongue and swallowed her words. *White is the colour of widows! Foolish idiot, as if she doesn't know that! Why start married life with bad shahanam like this,* she thought privately.

Geeta had sat with her team of friends getting all the arrangements down pat. She had conducted it like a military operation, assigning each friend to a specific task. "I hope we'll all still be friends at the end of this!" she laughed. Her wedding cake was a dark triple chocolate fudge cake with snow-white icing. The cake was outlined with a black grosgrain ribbon with white specks; exactly what she wanted it to look like, straight out of Martha Stewart's wedding magazine.

Now, she stood in front of the mirror in the bare dressing room of the Scott Road Kalyana Mandapam. Suresh's two toddlers were dressed in their turquoise and orange pattu pavadais with jasmine flowers pinned into their hair. Sowmya and Karen were there with her too, ready to open the door and walk out to face the beaming smiles of the guests.

Geeta sent up a silent prayer. *Ambal walk with me. Bless us with a happy married life and keep us in your grace.*

She took a deep breath and hugged her mother, Sowmya and Karen and walked out the door.

51
KUALA LUMPUR
17TH OCTOBER 1976

He was the first of the stalwarts to fall and the rest were there to bid him goodbye. The fat priest had arrived early and they sat around the fire chanting prayers for the soul while pouring little drops of ghee into the greedy fire. Ramesh sat behind his father and copied the priest's movements. Saraswathi sat just behind her first born, her head drooped to one side in a combination of grief and to get a better angle of her beloved husband. The rest of the family sat around her, lending her support and plying her with tissue.

She was oblivious of the crowd that had built up all around them and filled up the living space of 912 Batu Road. She had shed so many tears that she didn't think there was room for anymore in her swollen puffy eyes. Saraswathi recognized those closest to her; her children of course, Chin Nam and Elaine; both red and swollen-eyed; Kah Sing and his wife, Mui Leng. She noticed Tochi who was in a wheelchair and his children, Satnam and Surinder seated behind him. The rest were a blurry sea of faces. She looked at Rangaswamy and miraculously she found fresh tears forming again.

His heart attack had come without warning. He had had his usual check up two months earlier and had been given a clean bill of health. The shocking news of his death had spread like wildfire through the Brahmin community; and in true community spirit, they had come out in full force to lend the grieving family a hand.

His family had only one request, for Chin Nam to deliver the eulogy. He gave his friend a sending off that was befitting of a man like Rangaswamy. They were friends who had been young, middle aged and grown old together, they had shared experiences and had been on journeys no one could replicate or understand. They shared a brotherhood that had stood the test of time.

"He was not just about his work. Yes, he was Director of Education right up until his retirement, but that you all know. The reason I am standing here, is to give you a glimpse or perhaps even a little insight into the life of one of the most extraordinary men I know." Chin Nam scanned the crowd looking for other familiar faces and he spotted Tochi.

"This man was of a different calibre. Tochi and I remember the time long before some of you were even a glint in your parents' eye when we were caught up in the drama of war. Rangaswamy was a teacher then and he was seconded to work for the Japanese as their translator. This man," he emphasised, pointing at his friend, "embraced the opportunity to work for the enemy so that he could help those with whom he empathized. Instead of protecting himself and his family, he put himself in harm's way by surreptitiously providing the resistance with information he was privy to.

"Rangaswamy was a true patriot; an unsung hero who loved his adopted country without having to declare it from rooftops. He took my family and me in during the war when we had to hide and he fed and housed us without any fuss. We would spend so many nights discussing our different belief systems and our perception of the war and there were many issues that we didn't always agree on, but we heartily agreed to disagree!"

Chin Nam stood quiet for a moment before resuming, "I find it hard to accept that your mission here is over. I shall miss you my dear, dear friend and truth be told, you take a part of me with you as I bid you farewell. Sleep tender and we will meet on the other side, I promise."

There wasn't a dry eye in the house. Saraswathi watched on without really registering anything that was happening around her. She wondered what her life was going to be like, especially as she was now a Hindu widow. She would have to take off her thali and not wear her kumkumam pottu anymore. But those were only the physical changes. Who would she make coffee for? Or cook for? Or talk to? Or fight and argue with? How could and how would anyone understand that she had lost a part of her soul? She too, had died with him.

She felt Ramesh and Raman gently lift her up from the floor as they made way for Rangaswamy to be carried out of his home, feet first. She would have to stay with the women in the house while the men led him on his final journey. Elaine appeared at her side, sobbing and the two women wailed as Swamy left them behind.

Tochi watched quietly in his wheelchair as the tears escaped his eyes and he hoped his body would not rack with grief. His stroke had taken away his spoken words so he sent Rangaswamy a silent prayer. *Bon Voyage my friend, the 'Black Dove'. How many lives did you save with your heroic contribution? What a debt the younger generation owes you and yet, how many know of your bravery? To think of the journey we have been on and how incredible that we have lived long enough to remember them with those who shared those adventures with us. Gurchan, wherever you are, I salute you too, for your bravery and belief in what we did. I was the better swimmer, as you will grudgingly accept! How can I ever forget our unforgivable sin of cutting our hair and escaping to Burma! Who here apart from us stalwarts can put their hands up and say 'I have been on a journey that would rival Sinbad!' If I had my life to re-live, I would not edit a single scene and I know neither would you and Gurchan.*

52
THE LAST LETTER
BALI, 2010

18th November 1935

My dear Saraswathi,

I am writing to you with the deepest regret and a heart that feels as heavy as lead. My entire homecoming was destroyed because what I thought would be a joyous celebration of parents and an only son turned out to be one of my darkest days.

Appa has passed on, Saraswathi. It pains me to write these words to you but that is the truth. I reached Kuthur after spending two days in Madras and I knew something was wrong when the postmaster saw me at the train station and paid me his condolences. When I asked him why, he was surprised and shocked that I had not heard the news as it had happened three weeks ago.

Appa had suffered a stroke that was fatal while I was on the ship. How cruel is Ambal that she couldn't wait for a son to return? What could have been her plan? Have I not been her faithful servant? Was I not a filial son that she had to curse me like this?

When I saw Amma, I could not contain my grief. For the second time in my adult life I hugged my mother and we wept for the lost years, her source of strength and husband. She looks so small and frail, Saraswathi.

I have decided that there is only one thing to do. I am bringing Amma home with me. I cannot imagine how she lived here on her own the last three weeks before I arrived. My conscience will not allow me to leave her behind here. The children will be good for her and she will be good for them too.

I have booked our passage for the 21 December. That will give me sufficient time to sort out everything at this end and it will give Amma enough time to say her goodbyes.

My best wishes to the kuttis. Tell them Patti will be there soon to tell them wonderful stories about Rama, Sita, Krishna and Hanuman! That should excite them!

Warm regards,
Rangaswamy

She had wrapped it carefully and carried it with her in her suitcase to Bali where she was on honeymoon. *My last letter,* thought Geeta with a heavy heart; the final letter bore the weight of the death of her great-grandfather. This letter had been at the bottom of the pile of letters given to her by Krishna Chittappa and it was different from all the rest. This was written by her Tata to her Patti and it was drenched in sorrow. Geeta felt that if she were to wring the letter, ancient trapped tears might seep out of the sepia.

She had added her own tears to it and she was grateful she was alone in the Villa. This was her special umbilical cord to her past. The landscape of her ancestors' home had changed little but one brave man had taken that big step to transform his life and that of the rest of this Iyer generation forever.

The everyday stories that Patti used to tell me about the people who touched her life would transport me back to a place and time that seemed so real to me. What a storyteller Patti was! Will I remember to tell my own children? I must. They cannot die with me. These letters will outlive us all and provide the next generation with their footprints in the world.

53
WHITE LILIES II
PENANG, 2011

Some of the houses on the street had been given a facelift, a fresh coat of paint and even waxy shiny new plants. The houses sat on a busy street that was perfect for traffic watching as cars, buses and lorries fought for space with the rickshaws, bicycles, motorbikes and pedestrians.

These pre-war townhouses were built in the Peranakan fashion; the houses were narrow and long, with beautifully designed tiles on the floor and floral-embossed tiles on the walls in front of the house. Windows with quaint wooden shutters that could be opened and closed to either keep out the sun or prying eyes, whichever was more intrusive.

88 Sri Bahari Road looked like a spanking new house. From the outside, passersby would know that painstaking hours of love and dedication had been poured into the restoration of this home. The owner had given it much thought and had lent it a contemporary feel without losing its old charm. It had sent tongues wagging when the work first started. People couldn't understand why anyone would "throw good money after bad", but once ready, they would stop and stare in amazement at the transformation; not that the exterior looked drastically different,

but so much attention had been paid to the fretwork and metal work that it drew gasps of appreciation from passersby.

Inside, the original tiles had survived and the years had lent these a patina that all the polishing in the world could not replicate. The living and dining areas shared one large space and boasted a timeless mix of Danish and Malayan colonial furniture from the 50s and 60s.

Surinder sat contemplatively on her favourite Papa Bear chair. This was her second favourite time of day, when the day was slowly bowing out, making way for its night time counterpart. She sat cradling a slightly chilled glass of her favourite Chianti and her mind wandered, contemplating her story when these words came to her softly and gently.

Solitude

The quiet time of dawn, when the sky is slowly waking up; the sun kissing my eyes awake, when the birds realise it is time for their voices to fight that of the traffic; that is my favourite time.

I am solitude itself; I unwrap my soul and bury my physical self within. And I wrap myself, as if in a blanket – well worn, soft and mostly comforting. Thoughts, sentiments, ideas – pre conceived or otherwise play hide and seek games with the intellect. Sweet words spoken, bad thoughts thought out, lurk in the corners.

I am a beautiful person or am I a soul? I can overcome pettiness and anger. The world is mine, even if for a few moments. I can hold it tenderly in the palms of my hands or I can squeeze it and watch it pulsate. Thanks and gratitude are offered to the Universe for the blessings.

And then, my world starts rising, like hot steam from the black tar road; hissing its way up and around me, thick liquid mundanity. Morning sounds – shower on shower off. Music on and on. Cupboard doors open, clothes picked. Hair combed, reflections observed.

The doors open and we tumble out, racing to face the world, to grab it by its horns or to be squashed under its belly.

Either way, we take it.

She heard a loud knock on her door, drawing her thoughts back to the present. She looked up, completely puzzled and totally irritated at being distracted from herself. She picked up her glass of wine as if it were a weapon and walked to the door. Standing behind it was a well-dressed man with all the required lines that age added to one's face. He held a bunch of white lilies in his right hand. The look on Surinder's face said it all.

"Lovely to see you. Please come in."

EPILOGUE
FINAL THOUGHTS
OSAKA, 2015

Of all the seasons, autumn is the prettiest. The deep burnt colour of falling leaves in varying shades of maroon, red and copper makes the ground look like a bed of tea leaves, thought Geeta. The air was chilly and crisp enough to take a bite out of. The silence of her surroundings gave her thoughts a more audible voice.

What a beautiful place this is. Imagine waking up to this everyday! I could spend a large part of my day just strolling through these grounds and I would probably discover some new species of bird or flora everyday. That would be cool.

Geeta was walking through the garden that was a part of Bob Nakamura's house. It seemed endless and she wondered at the cost of mowing the lawn. Yoshii had told her that she would reach a small Buddhist temple at the bottom of the garden right beside a little stream that ran through the property.

She finally caught a glimpse of the temple through the gap in the trees, framed like a picture. It took Geeta's breath away; she stopped and admired its beauty. She walked towards it with a sense of reverence, marvelling at the peace and tranquillity. She stood at the edge first, taking her time before walking over the threshold. Right in the middle of the temple stood a wall with three small tablets. The one in the centre had a beautiful blue and white urn with an inscription in Japanese and a date under it. What caught Geeta's attention were the two tablets with pictures of her grandfather and Ken's grandfather with Japanese and English inscriptions below them that read:

Rangaswamy Iyer   Tan Chin Nam
17 October 1976   20 September 1982

Geeta felt a pang deep inside of her and she turned her face away. *Obviously, despite all his wealth, Bob must have been an unhappy man, caught up in the misery of his past. How sad to live a life full of guilt and regret. Still… he did try to make amends in the only way he knew how.* Geeta shivered as the cold air and her thoughts gave her goosebumps.

And yet… I am deeply indebted to this man who unwittingly did me the biggest favour! If not for you, Bob Nakamura, I would not have married Ken. How ironic that I am forever in your debt and in the end, you showed my father what a prejudiced life he was leading. How true the law of karma is and I am so glad that you lived long enough to know that you were forgiven by both families. It would have been an absolute tragedy if you had died before receiving the absolution you so wanted. I hope your soul is at peace and I pray that the souls of both grandfathers are at peace too.

Geeta looked at the pictures of the two men whose lives were so intrinsically connected and yet so culturally different. *Isn't it amazing how circumstances bring people together? These two men came as migrants to a strange land and they worked and slogged to give themselves and us a better life. Tata had never seen a Chinese man until he came to Malaya and would he have ever thought that one day his best friend would be Chinese and that he would share his home with him? For all his strict upbringing as a Brahmin, Tata understood that race and religion were never meant to divide man. How astute he was and so forward thinking for his time,* thought Geeta fondly of her grandfather.

I still remember the stories Patti told me about how her mother would never eat if a non-Brahmin walked past her while she was sitting down to lunch; and how all the servants had to leave the dining room when the family was ready to sit down to lunch! How awful it must have been then.

Kollu Patti was so strict she would not allow anyone to touch her after she'd had a bath and before she said her prayers. If any of her children even brushed past her, she would take another bath as she felt she was unclean! Even then, as a child, I thought this was so unfair to the others and when I asked Patti, all she said was, "It was the way it was in the graamam. We were all brought up not to share our yechal with anyone else. It was hygienic, Geeta. We all had our own thatus and lottas and no one used one that belonged to another."

Mind you, even in our home it was a little like that. Appa had his own silver plate and we all had ours and while we never ate from Appa or Amma's plate, we kids used to share each other's plates. There, it was already starting to break down before our very eyes in our home! And here I am today, married to a Chinese man, it almost makes me laugh!

Oh Patti! I promise you the children will be vegetarians and I promise you I will play the suprabatham at least once a week and I promise you that I will yennai theche them once a week! You will be proud of me, I sing Giridharalal and Krishna Ne Begene and I, too, say adi kozhambe yaanai kutti poolle as they finish their paal! So you see, I do remember our customs, but only the ones I respect. I don't want to lose these valuable customs, I do love our food and some of our carnatic music. Patti, I can't promise you I'll make them learn Bharata Natyam though. I hated it and I don't want to force them!

To think that Ramesh Iyer actually relented and allowed his daughter to marry a Chinese man! Who would have thought that Appa would have ended up with a Chinese son-in-law. Patti, you should have seen the arguments Appa and Uncle Kah Sing had; there were some nasty things said, but thankfully in the end, Appa realized that my happiness meant more than the entire Brahmin community. I am so proud of your son, once he had accepted that

I would marry Ken, he stood by me. Isn't it strange Patti, you and Tata opened your hearts and home to Tan Chin Nam all those years ago and now the wheel has come full circle.

The loud laughter brought Geeta sharply back to the present; she looked up from her thoughts and caught Ken and Yoshii horsing around with Lekha and Tara on the grass.

ACKNOWLEDGEMENTS

This book has had several births – breached, delayed and overdue. It started off as a chapter handwritten on auspicious turmeric coloured letter paper, a birthday gift to the husband. That somewhat lame excuse of a gift grew larger than the envelope it came in.

An idea was born in the husband's head, and I became a reluctant writer. We spent many hours talking, arguing and debating the idea of a book. Its storyline, its time frame, its breadth and span. And it continued to grow larger than that wretched envelope.

The husband helped me with the research and soon words filled pages and a story started to unfold – a past, a present and a super past.

What you have in your hands today took 15 years of plucking up the courage, to finally 'do something with the damn manuscript.'

My love and gratitude to my very first storyteller of *One Eye, Two Eyes and Three Eyes* – my mother, Beng Choo. To my sister Kala – the best there ever will be. My children – Nikhil and Maya who are waiting for the audio book, my cousins – Swa, Ambi, Gopal and Swami, nieces and nephews and family and friends whom I am privileged and blessed to call mine.

A special thank you to Veena, Nimmi, Shan and Theresa for reading it in the raw and giving it the thumbs up. Thank you, Jackie Bear, for the many hours spent editing and dotting the i's and crossing the t's and Madhavi Murali for reading the chapters on the mandapam and working through the complexities of a Brahmin wedding. If there are any mistakes, these are mine. To Roz Chua, my publisher, thank you for having faith in this book and agreeing to take it on and for ever so gently nudging me from time to time!

Finally, the husband, Ranjit for quite soppily being the wind beneath my wings and the shade under which I sit.

SELECT BIBLIOGRAPHY

AKASHI YOJI & YOSHIMURA MAKO eds., New Perspectives on the Japanese Occupation in Malaya and Singapore, 1941 – 1945, NUS Press, Singapore, 2008.

BARBER, ANDREW, Kuala Lumpur at War 1939 – 1945, Karamoja, Kuala Lumpur, 2012.

BARBER, NOEL, Sinister Twilight The Fall of Singapore, Cassel, London, 2007.

BAN KAH CHOON & YAP HONG KUAN, Rehearsal for War, Horizon Books, Singapore, 2002.

CHEAH BOON KHENG, Red Star over Malaya, 3rd Ed, Singapore University Press, Singapore, 2003.

CHIN KEE ONN, Malaya Upside Down, 3rd Ed, Federal Publications, Kuala Lumpur, 1976.

DORAISAMY, JOHN, Victoria Institution, the First Century, 1893 – 1993, VI Centenary Celebrations Committee, Malaysia, 1993.

FARREL, BRIAN P., The Defence and Fall of Singapore 1940 – 1942, Tempus Publishing, Gloucestershire, 2005.

FOONG CHOON HAN ed., Price Of Peace – True Accounts of the Japanese occupation, translated by Clara Show, 3rd Edition, Asiapac Books, Singapore, 1997.

GULLICK, J.M, A history of Kuala Lumpur 1857 – 1939, The Malaysian Branch of the Royal Asiatic Society, Malaysia, 2000.

HOLDER, R.W., The Flight for Malaya, Military Paperbacks, Editions Didier Millet, Kuala Lumpur, 2007.

LAWLOR, ERIC, Murder on the Verandah, Flamingo, London, 2000.

LEE GEOK BOI, The Syonan Years: Singapore under Japanese Rule 1942 – 1945, National Archives of Singapore and Epigram, Singapore, 2005.

LIM PUI HEAN, P. & DIANA WONG eds., War & Memory in Malaysia & Singapore, Institute of Southeast Asian Studies, Singapore, 2000.

LOW NGIONG ING, When Singapore was Syonan – To, 2nd Ed, Times Editions – Marshall Cavendish, 2004.

MIRAFLOR, NORMA & WARD, IAN, Faces of Courage, Incorporating:
- No Dram of Mercy by Kathigasu, Sybil
- The Papan Guerrillas and Mrs K by Chin Peng
- Exploring the Legend by Miraflor, Norma & Ward, Ian, Media Masters, Singapore, 2006.

MODDER, RALPH, The Singapore Chinese Massacre, Horizon Books, Singapore/Kuala Lumpur, 2004.

MORRISON, IAN, Malaya Postscript, Faber & Faber London, 1945.

OOI KEAT GIN, St Xavier's Institution 1852 – 1992, a pictorial history, Malaysia, 1992.

SINGH, GURCHAN, Singa The Lion of Malaya, Quality Press, London, 1949.

SMITH, COLIN, Singapore Burning, Viking, London, 2005.

TAN CHONG TEE, Force 136 English Edition, 3rd Ed, Asiapac books, Singapore, 2007.

THOMPSON, PETER, The Battle for Singapore, Portrait, London, 2005.

ABOUT THE PUBLISHER

Clarity Publishing focuses on high-quality, fiction and non-fiction titles that bring together great stories with outstanding design, photography and artwork. Our editorial policy is driven by investing in and promoting Malaysian talent to a wider audience.

Visit our website at www.clarity8.com

AWARD-WINNING FICTION
FROM CLARITY PUBLISHING

Twenty-something author and minor media influencer Stasys Šaltoka – or Stanley Colder to his adoring IG followers – has hit an existential wall. Abandoning his clichéd and stifling New York city life, he buys a one-way ticket to Southeast Asia in search of life-changing experiences.

A chance meeting with an enigmatic Russian leads Stasys to a documentary project – the murder of a mysterious Mongolian model that implicates a prime minister and his jewel-hoarding wife. Unravelling the truth takes Stasys deeper through the murky swamp of extreme corruption, death, Islamophobia and media manipulation.

Will he ever figure out the meaning of life or find a decent espresso?

WINNER PENANG MONTHLY BOOK PRIZE 2018

EUROPEAN UNION
PRIZE FOR LITERATURE

SHORTLISTED FOR THE EU PRIZE FOR LITERATURE 2019